Satan Sanderson

By Hallie Erminie Rives

CHAPTER I AS A MAN SOWS

"To my son Hugh, in return for the care and sorrow he has caused me all the days of his life, for his dissolute career and his desertion, I do give and bequeath the sum of one thousand dollars and the memory of his misspent youth."

It was very quiet in the wide, richly furnished library. The May night was still, but a faint suspiration, heavy with the fragrance of jasmin flowers, stirred the Venetian blind before the open window and rustled the moon-silvered leaves of the aspens outside. As the incisive professional pronouncement of the judge cut through the lamp-lighted silence, the grim, furrowed face with its sunken eyes and gray military mustaches on the pillow of the wheel-chair set more grimly; a girl seated in the damask shadow of the fire-screen caught her breath; and from across the polished table the Reverend Henry Sanderson turned his handsome, clean-shaven face and looked at the old man.

A peevish misogynist the neighborhood labeled the latter, with the parish chapel for hobby, and for thorn-in-the-flesh this only son Hugh, a black sheep whose open breaches of decorum the town had borne as best it might, till the tradition of his forebears took him off to an eastern university. A reckless life there and three wastrel years abroad, had sent him back to resume his peccadilloes on a larger scale, to quarrel bitterly with his father, and to leave his home in anger. In what rough business of life was Hugh now chewing the cud of his folly? Harry Sanderson was wondering.

"Wait," came the querulous voice from the chair. "Write in 'graceless' before the word 'desertion'."

"For his dissolute career and his—graceless—desertion," repeated the lawyer, the parchment crackling under his pen.

The stubborn antagonism that was a part of David Stires' nature flared under the bushy eyebrows. "As a man sows!" he said, a kind of bitter jocularity in the tone. "That should be the text, if this sermon of mine needed any, Sanderson! It won't have as large an audience as your discourses draw, but it will be remembered by one of its hearers, at least."

Judge Conwell glanced curiously at Harry Sanderson as he blotted the emendation. He knew the liking

of the cross-grained and taciturn old invalid—St. James' richest parishioner—for this young man of twenty-five who had come to the parish only two months before, fresh from his theological studies, to fill a place temporarily vacant—and had stayed by sheer force of personality. He wondered if, aside from natural magnetic qualities, this liking had not been due first of all to the curious resemblance between the young minister and the absent son whom David Stires was disinheriting. For, as far as mold of feature went, the young minister and the ne'er-do-well might have been twin brothers; yet a totally different manner and coloring made this likeness rather suggestive than striking.

No one, perhaps, had ever interested the community more than had Harry Sanderson. He had entered upon his duties with the marks of youth, good looks, self-possession and an ample income thick upon him, and had brought with him a peculiar charm of manner and an apparent incapacity for doing things in a hackneyed way. Convention sat lightly upon Harry Sanderson. He recognized few precedents, either in the new methods and millinery with which he had invested the service, or in his personal habits. Instead of attending the meeting of St. Andrew's Guild, after the constant custom of his predecessor, he was apt to be found

playing his violin (a passion with him) in the smart study that adjoined the Gothic chapel where he shepherded his fashionable flock, or tramping across the country with a briar pipe in his mouth and his brown spaniel "Rummy" nosing at his heels. His athletic frame and clean-chiselled features made him a rare figure for the reading-desk, as his violin practice, the cut of his golf-flannels, the immaculate elegance of his motor-car— even the white carnation he affected in his buttonhole—made him for the younger men a goodly pattern of the cloth; and it had speedily grown to be the fashion to hear the brilliant young minister, to memorize his classical aphorisms or to look up his latest quotation from Keats or Walter Pater. So that Harry Sanderson, whose innovations had at first disturbed and ruffled the sensibilities of those who would have preferred a fogy, in the end had drifted, apparently without special effort, into a far wider popularity than that which bowed to the whim of the old invalid in the white house in the aspens.

Something of all this was in the lawyer's mind as he paused—a perfunctory pause—before he continued:

"... *I do give and bequeath the sum of one thousand dollars, and the memory of his misspent youth.*"

Harry Sanderson's eyes had wandered from the chair to the slim figure of the girl who sat by the screen. This was Jessica Holme, the orphaned daughter of a friend of the old man's early years, who had recently come to the house in the aspens to fill the void left by Hugh's departure. Harry could see the contour of throat and wrists, the wild-rose mesh of the skin against the Romney-blue gown, the plenteous red-bronze hair uncoiled and falling in a single braid, and the shadowy pathos of her eyes. Clear hazel eyes they were, wide and full, but there was in them no depth of expression—for Jessica Holme was blind. As the crisp deliberate accent pointed the judicial period, as with a subterranean echo of irrefutable condemnation, Harry saw her under lip indrawn, her hands clasp tightly, then unclasp in her lap. Pliant, graceful hands, he thought, which even blindness could not make maladroit. In the chapel porch stood the figure of an angel which she had modelled solely by the wonderful touch in the finger-tips.

"Go on," rasped the old man.

"The residue of my estate, real and personal, I do give and bequeath to my ward, Jessica Holme, to be and become—"

He broke off suddenly, for the girl was kneeling by the chair, groping for the restless hand that wandered

on the afghan, and crying in a strained, agitated voice: "No ... no ... you must not! Please, please! I never could bear it!"

"Why not?" The old man's irritant query was belligerent. "Why not? What is there for you to bear, I'd like to know!"

"He is your son!"

"In the eyes of the law, yes. But not otherwise!" His voice rose. "What has he done to deserve anything from me? What has he had all his life but kindness? And how has he repaid it? By being a waster and a prodigal. By setting me in contempt, and finally by forsaking me in my old age for his own paths of ribaldry."

The girl shook her head. "You don't know where he is now, or what he is doing. Oh, he was wild and reckless, I have no doubt. But when he quarrelled and left you, wasn't it perhaps because he was too quick-tempered? And if he hasn't come back, isn't it perhaps because he is too proud? Why, he wouldn't be your son if he weren't proud! No matter how sorry he might be, it would make no difference then. I could give him the money you had given me, but I couldn't change the fact. You, his own father, would have disowned him, disinherited him, taken away his birthright!"

"And richly he'd deserve it!" he snapped, his bent

fingers plucking angrily at the wool of the afghan. "He doesn't want a father or a home. He wants his own way and a freedom that is license! I know him. You don't; you never saw him."

"I never saw you either," she said, a little sadly.

"Come," he answered a shade more gently. "I didn't mean your eyes, my dear! I mean that you never met him in your life. He had shaken off the dust of his feet against this house before you came to brighten it, Jessica. I've not forgiven him seven times; I've forgiven him seventy times seven. But he doesn't want forgiveness. To him I am only 'the old man' who refused to 'put up' longer for his fopperies and extravagances! When he left this house six months ago, he declared he would never enter it again. Very well—let him stay away! He shan't come back when I am in my grave, to play ducks and drakes with the money he misuses! And I've fixed it so that you won't be able to give it away either, Jessica. Give me the pen," he said to the judge, "and, Sanderson, will you ring? We shall need the butler to witness with you."

As Harry Sanderson rose to his feet the girl, still kneeling, turned half about with a hopeless gesture. "Oh, won't you help me?" she said. She spoke more to herself, it seemed, than to either of the men who waited.

Harry's face was in the shadow. The lawyer with careful deliberation was putting a new pen into the holder.

"Sanderson," said the old man with bitter fierceness, lifting his hand, "I dare say you think I am hard; but I tell you there has never been a day since Hugh was born when I wouldn't have laid down my life for him! You are so like! When I look at you, I seem to see him as he might have been but for his own wayward choice! If he were only as like you in other things as he is in feature! You are nearly the same age; you went to the same college, I believe; you have had the same advantages and the same temptations. Yet you, an orphan, come out a divinity student, and Hugh—my son!—comes out a roisterer with gambling debts, a member of the 'fast set,' one of a dissolute fraternity known as 'The Saints,' whose very existence, no doubt, was a shame to the institution!"

Harry Sanderson turned slowly to the light. A strange panorama in that moment had flashed through his brain—kaleidoscopic pictures of an earlier reckless era when he had not been known as the "Reverend Henry Sanderson." An odd, sensitive flush burned his forehead. The hand he had outstretched to the bell-cord dropped to his side, and he said, with painful steadiness:

"I think I ought to say that I was the founder, and at the time you speak of, the Abbot of The Saints."

The pen rattled against the mahogany, as the man of law leaned back to regard the speaker with a stare of surprise whetted with a keen edge of satiric amusement. The old man sat silent, and the girl crouched by the chair with parted lips. The look in Harry's face was not now that of the decorative young churchman of the Sabbath surplice. It held a keen electric sense of the sharp contrasts of life, touched with a wakeful pain of conscience.

"I was in the same year with Hugh," Harry went on. "We sowed our wild oats together—a tidy crop, I fancy, for us both. That page of my life is pasted down. I speak of it now because it would be cowardly not to. I have not seen Hugh since college closed four years ago. But then I was all you have called him—a waster and a prodigal. And I was more; for while others followed, I led. At college I was known as 'Satan Sanderson'."

He stopped. The old man cleared his throat, but did not speak. He was looking at Harry fixedly. In the pause the girl found his gnarled hand and laid her cheek against it. Harry leaned an elbow upon the mantelpiece as he continued, in a low voice:

"Colleges are not moral strait-jackets. Men have

there to cast about, try themselves and find their bearings. They are in hand-touch with temptation, and out of earshot of the warnings of experience. The mental and moral machine lacks a governor. Slips of the cog then may or may not count seriously to character in the end. They sometimes signify only a phase. They may be mere idiosyncrasy. I have thought that it stood in this case," he added with the glimmer of a smile, "with Satan Sanderson; he seems to me from this focus to be quite another individual from the present rector of St. James."

"It is only the Hugh of the present that I am dealing with," interposed the old man. For David Stires was just and he was feeling a grim respect for Harry's honesty.

Harry acknowledged the brusque kindliness of the tone with a little motion of the hand. As he spoke he had been feeling his way through a maze of contradictory impulses. For a moment he had been back in that old irresponsible time; the Hugh he had known then had sprung to his mind's eye—an imitative idler, with a certain grace and brilliancy of manner that made him hail-fellow-well-met, but withal shallow, foppish and incorrigible, a cheap and shabby imitator of the outward manner, not the inner graces, of good-fellowship. Yet Hugh had been one of his own "fast set"; they had called him "Satan's shadow," a tribute to the actual resemblance as well as to the palpable imitation he affected. Harry shivered a little. The situation seemed, in antic irony, to be reversing itself. It was as if not alone Hugh, but he, Harry Sanderson, in the person of that past of his, was now brought to bar for judgment in that room. For the instant he forgot how utterly characterless Hugh had shown himself of old, how devoid of all desire for rehabilitation his present reputation in the town argued him. At that moment it seemed as if in saving Hugh from this condemnation, he was pleading for himself as he had been—for the further chance which he, but for circumstances, perhaps, had needed, too. His mind, working swiftly, told him that no appeal to mere sentiment would suffice—he must touch another note. As he paused, his eyes wandered to an oil portrait on the wall, and suddenly he saw his way.

"You," he said, "have lived a life of just and balanced action. It is bred in the bone. You hate all loose conduct, and rightly. You hate it most in Hugh for the simple reason that he is your son. The very relation makes it more impossible to countenance. He should be like you—of temperate and prudent habit.

But did you and he start on equal terms? Your grandfather was a Standish; your ancestry was undiluted Puritan. Did Hugh have all your fund of resistance?"

The old man's gaze for the first time left Harry's face. It lifted for an instant to the portrait at which Harry had glanced—a picture of Hugh's dark gipsy-like mother, painted in the month of her marriage, and the year of her death—and in that instant the stern lines about the mouth relaxed a little. Harry had laid his finger on the deepest cord of feeling in the old man's gruff nature. The glow that had smoldered in the cavernous eyes faded and a troubled cloud came to belie their former wrath.

"'As a man sows,' you say, and you deny him another seeding and it may be a better harvest. You shut the door;—and if you shut it, it may not swing open again! With me it was the turning of a long lane. Hugh perhaps has not turned—yet." A breath of that past life had swept anew over Harry, the old shuddering recoil again had rushed upon him. It gave his voice a curious energy as he ended: "And I have seen how far a man may go and yet—come back!"

There was a pause. The judge had an inspiration. He folded the parchment, and rose.

"Perhaps it would be as well," he said in a

matter-of-fact way, "if the signing be left open for the present. Last testaments, whatever their provisions, are more or less serious matters, and in your case,"—he nodded toward the occupant of the chair—"there is not the element of necessitous haste. Of course," he added tentatively, "I am at your service at any time."

He rose as he spoke, and laid the document on the table.

For a moment David Stires sat in silence. Then he said, with a glint of the old ironic fire: "You should have been a special pleader, Sanderson. There's no client too bad for them to make out a case for! Well ... well ... we won't sign to-night. I will read it over again when I am more equal to it."

His visitors made their adieux, and as the door closed upon them, the girl came to the wheel-chair and wistfully drew the parchment from his hands.

"You're a good girl, Jessica," he said, "too good to a rascal you've never known. But there—go to your room, child. I can ring for Blake when I want anything."

For long the old man sat alone, musing in his chair, his eyes on the painted portrait on the wall. The image there was just as young and fair and joyous as though yesterday she had stood in bridal white beside him,

instead of so long ago—so long ago! His lips moved. "In return for the care and sorrow," he muttered, "all the days of his life!"

At length he sighed and took up a magazine. He was thinking of Harry Sanderson.

"How like!" he said aloud. "So Sanderson sowed his wild oats, too!... When he stood there, with the light on his face—when he talked—I—I could almost have thought it was Hugh!"

CHAPTER II DOCTOR MOREAU

Harry Sanderson and the judge parted at the gate, and Harry walked slowly home in the moonlight.

The youthful follies that he had resurrected when he had called himself his old nickname of "Satan Sanderson" he had left so far behind him, had buried so deep, that the ironic turn of circumstance that had dragged them into view, sorry skeletons, seemed intrusive and malicious. Not that he was desirous of sailing under false colors; he had brought into his new career more than a *soupçon* of the old indifference to popular estimation, the old propensity to go his own way and to care very little what others thought of him. The sting was a nearer one; it was his own present of fair example and good repute that recoiled with a fastidious sense of abasement from the recollection.

As he stood in the library, his hand on the mantelpiece, he had been painfully conscious of detail. He remembered vividly the half amused smile of the lawyer, the silent, listening attitude of the girl crouched

by the wheel-chair. He had seen Jessica Holme scarcely a half-dozen times, then only at service, or driving behind the Stires bays. That moment when she had thrown herself beside the old man's chair to plead for the son she had never seen—an instant revelation wrought by the strenuous agitation of the moment—had been illuminative; it had given him a lightning-like glimpse into the unplummeted deeps of womanly unselfishness and sympathy. He flushed suddenly. He had not realized that she was so beautiful.

What a tragedy to be blind, for a woman with temperament, talent and heart! To be sightless to the beauty of such a perfect night, with that silver bridge of stars, those far hills rising like purple tulips—an alluring night for those who saw! The picture she had made, kneeling with the lamplight rosying in her hair, hung before him. The flower-scent with which the room had been full was in his nostrils, and verses flashed into his mind:

Under his thought the lines repeated themselves in a mystical monotone.

He had saved an old college-mate from possible disinheritance and the grind of poverty, for David Stires' health was precarious. He thought of this with a tinge of satisfaction. The least of that peculiar clan, one who had held his place, not by likable qualities but by a versatile talent for entertainment, Hugh Stires yet deserved thus much. Harry Sanderson had never shirked an obligation. "As a man sows"—the old man's words recurred to him. Did any man reap what he sowed, after all? Was he, the "Satan Sanderson" that was, getting his deserts?

"If there is a Providence that parcels out our earthly rewards and penalties," he said to himself, "it has missed me! If there is any virtue in example, I ought to be the black sheep. Hugh never influenced anybody; he was a natural camp-follower. I was in the van. All I said was a sneer, all I did a challenge to respectability. Yet here I am, a shepherd of the faithful, a brother of Aaron!"

Harry stepped more briskly along the gas-lighted square, nodding now and then to an acquaintance, and bowing on a crossing to a carriage that bowled by with the wife of the Very Reverend, the Bishop of the Diocese. As he passed a darkened entrance, a door with a small barred window in its upper panel opened, and a

man came into the street—a man light and fair with watery blue eyes and a drooping, blond mustache. He lifted his silk hat with a faded, Chesterfieldian grace as he came down the steps with outstretched hand.

"My dear Sanderson!" he said effusively. "In the interest of sweetness and light, where did you stumble on your new chauffeur? His style is the admiration of the town. Next to having your gift of eloquence, I can think of nothing so splendid as possessing such a *tonneau*! The city is in your debt; you have shown it that even a cleric can be 'fast' without reproach!"

Harry Sanderson saw the weak features and ingratiating smile, the clayey, dry-lined skin and restless eyes, but he did not seem to see the extended hand. He did not smile at the badinage as he replied evenly:

"My chauffeur, Doctor, is a Finn; and his style is his own. I see, however, that I must decrease his speed-limit."

Doctor Moreau stood a moment looking after him, his womanish hands clenching and his cynical glance full of an evil light.

"The university prig!" he said under his breath. "Doesn't he take himself for the whole thing, with his money and his buttonhole bouquet, and his smug self-righteousness! He thinks I'm hardly fit to speak to since I've had to quit the hospital! I'd like to take him down a peg!"

He watched the alert, ministerial figure till it rounded the corner. He looked up and down the street, hesitating; then, shrugging his shoulders, he turned and reëntered the door with the narrow barred window.

CHAPTER III THE COMING OF A PRODIGAL

The later night was very still and the moon, lifting like a paper lantern over the aspen tops, silvered all the landscape. In its placid radiance the white house loomed in a ghostly pallor. The windows of one side were blank, but behind the library shade the bulbous lamp still drowsed like a monster glow-worm. From the shadowy side of the building stretched a narrow L, its front covered by a rose-trellis, whose pale blossoms in the soft night air mingled their delicate fragrance with that of the jasmin.

Save for the one bright pane, there seemed now no life or movement in the house. But outside, in the moonlight, a lurching, shabbily-clothed figure moved, making his uncertain way with the deliberation of composed inebriety. The sash of the window was raised a few inches and he nodded sagely at the yellow shade.

"Gay old silver-top!" he hiccoughed; "see you in the morning!"

He capsized against an althea bush and shook his

head with owlish gravity as he disentangled himself. Then he staggered serenely to the rose-trellis, and, choosing its angle with an assurance that betrayed ancient practice, climbed to the upper window, shot its bolt with a knife, and let himself in. He painstakingly closed both windows and inner blinds, before he turned on an electric light.

In the room in which he now stood he had stored his boyish treasures and shirked his maturer tasks. It should have had deeper human associations, too, for once, before the house had been enlarged to its present proportions, that chamber had been his mother's. The *Maréchal Niel* rose that clambered to the window-sill had been planted by her hand. In that room he had been born. And in it had occurred that sharp, corrosive quarrel with his father on the night he had flung himself from the house vowing never to return.

As Hugh Stires stood looking about him, it seemed for an instant to his clouded senses that the past six months of wandering and unsavory adventure were a dream. There was his bed, with its clean linen sheets and soft pillows. How he would like to lie down just as he was and sleep a full round of the clock! Last night he had slept—where had he slept? He had forgotten for the moment. He looked longingly at the spotless

coverlid. No; some one might appear, and it would not do to be seen in his present condition. It was scarcely ten. Time enough for that afterward.

He drew out the drawer of a chiffonier, opened a closet and gloated over the order and plenty of their contents. He made difficult selection from these, and, steadying his progress by wall and chair, opened the door of an adjoining bath-room. It contained a circular bath with a needle shower. Without removing his clothing, he climbed into this, balancing himself with an effort, found and turned the cold faucet, and let the icy water, chilled from artesian depths, trickle over him in a hundred stinging needle-points.

It was a very different figure that reëntered the larger room a half-hour later, from the slinking mud-lark that had climbed the rose-trellis. The old Hugh lay, a heap of soiled and sodden garments; the new stood forth shaven, fragrant with fresh linen and clean and fit apparel. The maudlin had vanished, the gaze was unvexed and bright, the whole man seemed to have settled into himself, to have grown trim, nonchalant, debonair. He held up his hand, palm outward, between the electric globe and his eye—there was not a tremor of nerve or muscle. He smiled. No headache, no fever, no

uncertain feet or trembling hands or swollen tongue, after more than a week of deep potations. He could still "sober-up" as he used to do (with Blake the butler to help him) when it had been a mere matter of an evening's tipsiness! And how fine it felt to be decently clad again!

He crossed to a cheval-glass. The dark handsome face that looked out at him was clean-cut and aristocratic, perfect save for one blemish—a pale line that slanted across the right brow, a birth-mark, resembling a scar. All his life this mark had been an eyesore to its owner. It had a trick of turning an evil red under the stress of anger or emotion.

On the features, young and vigorous as they were, subtle lines of self-indulgence had already set themselves, and beneath their expression, cavalier and caressing, lay the unmistakable stigmata of inherited weakness. But these the gazer did not see. He regarded himself with egotistic complacency. Here he was, just as sound as ever. He had had his fling, and taught "the Governor" that he could get along well enough without any paternal help if he chose. Needs must when the devil drives, but his father should never guess the coarse and desperate expediences that had sickened him of his bargain, or the stringent calculation of his return. He

was no milksop, either, to come sneaking to him with his hat in his hand. When he saw him now, he would be dressed as the gentleman he was!

He attentively surveyed the room. It was clean and dusted—evidently it had been carefully tended. He might have stepped out of it yesterday. There in a corner was his banjo. On the edge of a silver tray was a half-consumed cigar. It crumbled between his fingers. He had been smoking that cigar when his father had entered the room on that last night. There, too, was the deck of cards he had angrily flung on to the table when he left. Not a thing had been disturbed—yes, one thing. His portrait, that had hung over his bed, was not in its place. A momentary sense of trepidation rushed through him. Could his father really have meant all he had said in his rage? Did he really mean to disown him?

For an instant he faced the hall door with clenched hands. Somewhere in the house, unconscious of his presence, was that ward of whose coming he had learned. Moreau was a good friend to have warned him! Was she part of a plan of reprisal—her presence there a tentative threat to him? Could his father mean to adopt her? Might that great house, those grounds, the bulk of his wealth, go to her, and he, the son, be left in

the cold? He shivered. Perhaps he had stayed away too long!

As he turned again, he heard a sound in the hall. He listened. A light step was approaching—the swish of a gown. With a sudden impulse he stepped into the embrasure of the window, as the figure of a girl paused at the door. He felt his face flush; she had thrown a crimson kimono over her white night-gown, and the apparition seemed to part the dusk of the doorway like the red breast of a robin. She held in her hands a bunch of the pale *Maréchal Niel* roses, and his eye caught the long rebellious sweep of her bronze hair, and the rosy tint of bare feet through the worsted meshes of her night-slippers.

To his wonder the sight of the lighted room seemed to cause her no surprise. For an instant she stood still as though listening, then entered and placed the roses in a vase on a reading-stand by the bedside.

Hugh gasped. To reach the stand the girl had passed the spot where he stood, but she had taken no note of him. Her gaze had gone by him as if he had been empty air. Then he realized the truth; Jessica Holme was blind! Moreau's letter had given him no inkling of that. So this was the girl with whom his father now threatened him! Was she counting on his not coming

back, waiting for the windfall? She was blind—but she was beautiful! Suppose he were to turn the tables on the old man, not only climb back into his good graces through her, but even—

The thin line on his brow sprang suddenly scarlet. What a supple, graceful arm she had! How adroit her fingers as they arranged the rose-stems! Was he already wholly blackened in her opinion? What did she think of him? Why did she bring those flowers to that empty room? Could it have been she who had kept it clean and fresh and unaltered against his return? A confident, daring look grew in his eyes; he wished she could see him in that purple tie and velvet smoking-jacket! What an opportunity for a romantic self-justification! Should he speak? Suppose it should frighten her?

Chance answered him. His respiration had conveyed to her the knowledge of a presence in the room. He heard her draw a quick breath. "Some one is here!" she whispered.

He started forward. "Wait! wait!" he said in a loud whisper, as she sprang back. But the voice seemed to startle her the more, and before he could reach her side she was gone. He heard her flying steps descend the stair, and the opening and closing of a door.

The sudden flight jarred Hugh's pleasurable sense of

novelty. He thrust his hands deep into his pockets. Now he was in for it! She would alarm the house, rouse the servants—he should have a staring, domestic audience for the imminent reconciliation his sobered sense told him was so necessary. Why could he not slip back into the old rut, he thought sullenly, without such a boring, perfunctory ceremony? He had intended to postpone this, if possible, until a night's sleep had fortified him. But now the sooner the ordeal was over, the better! Shrugging his shoulders, he went quickly down the stair to the library.

He had known exactly what he should see there—the vivid girl with the hue of fright in her cheeks, the shaded lamp, the wheel-chair, and the feeble old man with his furrowed face and gray mustaches. What he himself should say he had not had time to reflect.

The figure in the chair looked up as the door opened. "Hugh!" he cried, and half lifted himself from his seat. Then he settled back, and the sunken, indomitable eyes fastened themselves on his son's face.

Hugh was melodramatic—cheaply so. He saw the girl start at the name, saw her hands catch at the kimono to draw its folds over the bare white throat, saw the rich color that flooded her brow. He saw himself suddenly the moving hero of the stagery, the

tractive force of the situation. Real tears came to his eyes—tears of insincere feeling, due partly to the cheap whisky he had drunk that day, whose outward consequences he had so drastically banished, and partly to sheer nervous excitation.

"Father!" he said, and came and caught the gaunt hand that shook against the chair.

Then the deeps of the old man's heart were suddenly broken up. "My son!" he cried, and threw his arms about him. "Hugh—my boy, my boy!"

Jessica waited to hear no more. Thrilling with gladness, and flushing with the sudden recollection of her bare throat and feet, she slipped away to her room to creep into bed and lie wide-eyed and thinking.

What did he look like? Of his face she had never seen even a counterfeit presentment. Through what adventures had he passed? Now that he had come home, forgiving and forgiven, would he stay? He had been in his room when she entered it with the roses—must have guessed, if he had not already known, that she was blind. Would he guess that she had cared for that room, had placed fresh flowers there often and often?

Since she had come to the house in the aspens Jessica had found the imagined figure of Hugh a dominant
—the very mystery of his whereabouts—had taken strong hold of her imagination. Of the quarrel which had preceded Hugh's departure, she had made her own version. That he should have come back on this very night, when the disinheritance she had dreaded had been so nearly consummated, seemed now to have an especial and an appealing significance.

Presently she rose, slipped on the red kimono, and, taking a key from the pocket of her gown, stole from the room. She ascended a stairway and unlocked the door of a wide, bare attic where the moonlight poured through a skylight in the roof upon an unfinished statue. In this statue she had begun to fashion, in the imagined figure of Hugh, her conception of the Prodigal Son; not the battered and husk-filled wayfarer of the parable, but a figure of character and pathos, erring through youthful pride and spirit. The unfinished clay no eyes had seen, for those walls bounded her especial domain.

Carefully, one by one, she unwound the wet cloths that swathed the figure. In the streaming radiance of the night, the clay looked white as snow and she a crimson ghost. She passed her fingers lightly over the features. Was the real Hugh's face like that? One day, perhaps, her own eyes would tell her, and she would finish it. Then she might show it to him, but not now.

She replaced the coverings, relocked the door, and went softly down to her bed.

When Hugh went shamefacedly up the stair from the library, the artificial glow that had tingled to his finger-tips had faded. The poise of mind, the certitude of all the faculties of eye and hand that his icy bath had given him, were yielding. The penalties he had dislodged were returning reinforced. He was rapidly becoming drunk.

He groped his way to his room, turned out the light, threw himself fully dressed upon the bed, and slept the deep sleep of deferred intoxication.

CHAPTER IV THE LANE THAT HAD NO TURNING

On a June day a month later, Harry Sanderson sat in his study, looking out of the window across the dim summer haze of heat, negligently smoking. On the distant hill overlooking the town was the cemetery, flanked by fields of growing corn where sulky, round-shouldered crows quarrelled and pilfered. He could see the long white marl road, bending in a broad curve between clover-stippled meadows, to skirt the willow-green bluff above the river. There, miles away, on the high bank, he could distinguish the railroad bridge, a long black skeleton spanning "the hole," a deep, fish-haunted pool, the deepest spot in the river for fifty miles. From the nearer, elm-shaded streets came the muffled clack of trade and the discordant treble of a huckster, somewhere a trolley-bell was buzzing angrily, and the impudent scream of a blue jay sheared across the monotone. Harry's gaze went past the streets—past the open square, with its chapel spire lifting from a beryl sea of foliage—to a white colonial porch, peering from between aspens that quivered in the tremulous sunlight.

The dog on the rug rose, stretching, and came to thrust an eager insinuating muzzle into its master's lap. Rummy whined, the stubby tail wagged, but his master paid no heed, and with dejected ears, he slunk out into the sunshine. Harry was looking, with brows gathered to a frown, at the far-away porch. The look was full of a troubled question, a vague misgiving, an interrogative anxiety. He was thinking of a night when he had saved the son of that house from the calamity of disinheritance—to what end?

For since that moonlighted evening of the will-making Harry had learned that the long lane had had no true turning for Hugh. He had sifted him through and through. At college he had put him down for a weakling—unballasted, misdemeanant. Now he knew him for what he really was—a moral mollusk, a scamp in embryo, a decadent, realizing an ugly propensity to a deplorable *finale*. A consistent career of loose living had carried Hugh far since those college days when he had been dubbed "Satan's Shadow." While to Harry Sanderson the eccentric and agnostical had then been, as it were, the mask through which his temperament looked at life, to Hugh it had spelled shipwreck. Harry Sanderson had done broadly as he pleased. He had entertained whom he listed; had gone "slumming"; had once boxed to a finish, for a wager, a local pugilist whose acquaintance he affected, known as "Gentleman Jim." He had been both the hardest hitter and the hardest drinker in his class, yet withal its most brilliant student. Native character had enabled him to persist, as the exasperating function of success which dissipation declined to eliminate. But the same natural gravitation which in spite of all aberration had given Harry Sanderson classical honors, had brought Hugh Stires to the imminent brink of expulsion. And since that time, without the character which belonged to Harry as a possession, Hugh had continued to drift aimlessly on down the broad lax way of profligacy.

The conditions he found upon his return, however, had opened Hugh's eyes to the perilous strait in which he stood. He was a materialist, and the taste he had had of deprivation had sickened him. In the first revulsion, when the contrast between recent famine and present plenty was strong upon him, he had been at anxious pains to make himself secure with his father—and with Jessica Holme. Harry's mental sight—keen as the hunter's sight on the rifle-barrel—was sharpened by his knowledge of the old Hugh, an intuitive knowledge gained in a significant formative period. He saw more clearly than the townfolk who, in a general way, had

known Hugh Stires all their lives. Week by week Harry had seen him regain lost ground in his father's esteem; day by day he had seen him making studious appeal to all that was romantic in Jessica, climbing to the favor of each on the ladder of the other's regard. Hugh was naturally a *poseur*, with a keen sense of effect. He could be brilliant at will, could play a little on piano, banjo and violin, could sing a little, and had himself well in hand. And feeling the unconscious cord of romance vibrate to his touch, he had played upon it with no unskilful fingers.

Jessica was comparatively free from that coquetry by means of which a woman's instinct experiments in emotion. Although she had been artist enough before the cloistered years of her blindness to know that she was comely, she had never employed that beauty in the ordinary blandishments of girlish fascination. But steadily and unconsciously she had turned in her darkness more and more to the bright and tender air with which Hugh clothed all their intercourse. Her blindness had been of too short duration to have developed that fine sense-perception with which nature seeks to supplement the darkened vision. The ineradicable marks which ill-governed living had set in Hugh's face—the self-indulgence and egotism—she could not see. She mistook impulse for instinct. She read him by the untrustworthy light of a colorful imagination. She deemed him high-spirited and debonair, a Prince Charming, whose prideful rebellion had been atoned for by a touching and manly surrender.

All this Harry had watched with a painful sense of impotence, and this feeling was upon him to-day as he stared out from the study toward the white porch, glistening in the sun.

At length, with a little gesture expressive at once of helplessness and puzzle, he turned from the window, took his violin and began to play. He began a barcarole, but the music wandered away, through insensible variations, into a moving minor, a composition of his own.

It broke off suddenly at a dog's fierce snarl from the yard, and the rattle of a thrown pebble. Immediately a knock came at the door, and a man entered.

"Don't stop," said the new-comer. "I've dropped in for only a minute! That's an ill-tempered little brute of yours! If I were you, I'd get rid of him."

Harry Sanderson laid the violin carefully in its case and shut the lid before he answered. "Rummy is impulsive," he said dryly. "How is your father to-day, Hugh?"

The other tapped the toe of his shining patent-leather with his cane as he said with a look of ill-humor:

"About as well as usual. He's planning now to put me in business, and expects me to become a staid pillar of society—'like Sanderson,' as he says forty times a week. How do you do it, Harry? There isn't an old lady in town who thinks her parlor carpet half good enough for you to walk on! You're only a month older than I am, yet you can wind the whole vestry, and the bishop to boot, around your finger!"

"I wasn't aware of the idolatry." Harry laughed a little—a distant laugh. "You are observant, Hugh."

"Oh, anybody can see it. I'd like to know how you do it. It was always so with you, even at college. You could do pretty much as you liked, and yet be popular, too. Why, there was never a jamboree complete without you and your violin at the head of the table."

"That is a long time ago," said Harry.

"More than four years. Four years and a month to-morrow, since that last evening of college. Yet I imagine it will be longer before we forget it! I think of it still, sometimes, in the night—" Hugh went on more slowly,— "that last dinner of The Saints, and poor Archie singing with that wobbly smilax wreath over one eye and the claret spilled down his shirt-front—

then the sudden silence like a wet blanket! I can see him yet, when his head dropped. He seemed to shrivel right

up in his chair. How horrible to die like that! I didn't touch a drink for a month afterward!" He shivered slightly, and walked to the window.

Harry did not speak. The words had torn the network of the past as sheet-lightning tears the summer dusk; had called up a ghost that he had labored hard to lay—a memory-specter of a select coterie whose wild days and nights had once revolved about him as its central sun. The sharp tragedy of that long-ago evening had been the awakening. The swift, appalling catastrophe had crashed into his career at the pivotal moment. It had shocked him from his orbit and set him to the right-about-face. And the moral *bouleversement* had carried him, in abrupt recoil, into the ministry.

An odd confusion blurred his vision. Perhaps to cover this, he crossed the room to a small private safe which stood open in the corner, in which he kept his tithes and his charities. When Hugh, shrugging his shoulders as if to dismiss the unwelcome picture he had painted, turned again, Harry was putting into it some papers from his pocket. Hugh saw the action; his eyes fastened on the safe avidly.

"I say," he said after a moment's pause, as Harry made to shut its door, "can you loan me another fifty?

I'm flat on my uppers again, and the old man has been tight as nails with me since I came back. I'm sure to be able to return it with the rest, in a week or two."

Harry stretched his hand again toward the safe—then drew it back with compressed lips. He had met Hugh with persistent courtesy, and the other had found him sufficiently obliging with loans. Of late, however, his nerves had been on edge. The patent calculation of Hugh's course had sickened, and his flippant cynicism had jarred and disconcerted him. A growing sense of security, too, had made Hugh less circumspect. More than once during the past month Harry had seen him issue from the shadowed door whose upper panel held the little barred window—the door at which Doctor Moreau had entrance, though decent doors were closed in his face.

Hugh's lowered gaze saw the arrested movement and his cheek flushed.

"Oh, if it's inconvenient, I won't trouble you for the accommodation," he said. "I dare say I can raise it."

The attempt at nonchalance cost him a palpable effort. Comparatively small as the amount was, he needed it. He was in sore straits. By hook or crook he must stave off an evil day whose approach he knew not how to meet.

"It isn't that it is inconvenient, Hugh," said Harry. "It's that I can't approve your manner of living lately, and—I don't know where the fifty is going."

The mark on Hugh's brow reddened. "I wasn't aware that I was expected to render you an accounting," he said sulkily, "if I do borrow a dollar or two now and then! What if I play cards, and drink a little when I'm dry? I've got to have a bit of amusement once in a while between prayers. You liked it yourself well enough, before you discovered a sudden talent for preaching!"

"Some men hide their talents under a napkin," said Harry. "You drown yours—in a bottle. You have been steadily going downhill. You are deceiving your father—and others—with a pretended reform which isn't skin-deep! You have made them believe you are living straight, when you are carousing; that you keep respectable company, when you have taken up with a besotted and discredited gambler!"

"I suppose you mean Doctor Moreau," returned Hugh. "There are plenty of people in town who are worse than he is."

"He is a quack—dropped from the hospital staff for addiction to drugs, and expelled from his club for cheating at cards."

"He's down and out," said Hugh sullenly, "and any cur can bite him. He never cheated me, and I find him better company than your sanctimonious, psalm-singing sort. I'm not going to give him the cold shoulder because everybody else does. I never went back on a friend yet. I'm not that sort!"

A steely look had come to Harry Sanderson's eyes; he was thinking of the house in the aspens. While he talked, shooting pictures had been flashing through his mind. Now, at the boast of this eager protester of loyalty, this recreant who "never went back on a friend," his face set like a flint.

"You never had a friend, Hugh," he said steadily. "You never really loved anybody or anything but yourself. You are utterly selfish. You are deliberately lying, every hour you live, to those who love you. You are playing a part—for your own ends! You were only a good imitation of a good fellow at college. You are a poor imitation of a man of honor now."

Hugh rose to his feet, as he answered hotly: "And what are you, I'd like to know? Just because I take my pleasure as I please, while you choose to make a stained-glass cherub of yourself, is no reason why I'm not just as good as you! I knew you well enough before you set up for such a pattern. You didn't go in much

then for a theological diet. Pshaw!" he went on, snapping his fingers toward the well-stocked book-shelves. "I wonder how much of all that you really believe!"

Harry passed the insolence of the remark. He flecked a bit of dust from his sleeve before he answered, smiling a little disdainfully:

"And how much do *you* believe, Hugh?"

"I believe in running my own affairs, and letting other people run theirs! I don't believe in talking cant, and posing as a little-tin-god-on-wheels! If I lived in a glass-house, I'd be precious careful not to throw stones!"

Harry Sanderson was staring at him curiously now—a stare of singular inquiry. This shallow witness of his youthful misconduct, then, judged him by himself; deemed him a mere masquerader in the domino of decorous life, carrying the reckless and vicious humors of his nonage into the wider issues of living, and clothing an arrant hypocrisy under the habit of one of God's ministers!

The elastic weight of air in the study seemed suddenly grown suffocating. He reached and flung open the chapel door, and stood looking across the choir, through the mellow light of the duskily tinted nave, solemn as with the hush of past prayer. On this

interior had been lavished the special love of the invalid, who had given of his riches that this place for the comfort of souls might be. It was an expanse of dim colors and dark woodwork. At its eastern end was the high altar, with tall flowers in stately gilt vases on either side, and a brass lectern glimmered near-by. In the western wall was set a great rose-window of rich stained glass—a picture of the eternal tragedy of Calvary. As Harry stood gazing into the mellow light, Hugh paced moodily up and down behind him. Suddenly he caught Harry's arm and pointed.

Harry turned and looked.

Above the mantel was set a mirror, and from where they stood, this reflected Hugh's face. It startled Harry, for some trick of the atmosphere, or the sunlight falling through the painted glass, lightening the sallow face and leaving the hair in deeper shade—as a cunning painter by a single line will alter a whole physiognomy—had for the instant wiped out all superficial unresemblance and left a weird likeness. As Hugh's mocking countenance looked from the oval frame, Harry had a queer sensation as if he were looking at his own face, with some indefinable smear of attaint upon it—the trail of evil. As he drew away from the other's touch, his eye followed the bar of

amber light to the rose-window in the chapel; it was falling through the face of the unrepentant thief.

The movement broke the spell. When he looked again the eerie impression of identity was gone.

Hugh had felt the recoil. "Not complimented, eh?" he said with a half-sneer. "Too bad the prodigal should resemble Satan Sanderson, the fashionable parish rector who waves his arms so gracefully in the pulpit, and preaches such nice little sermons! You didn't mind it so much in the old days! Pardon me," he added with malice, "I forgot. It's the 'Reverend Henry' at present, of course! I imagine your friends don't call you 'Satan' now."

"No," returned Harry quietly. "They don't call me 'Satan' now!"

He went back to the safe.

The movement set Hugh instantly to regretting his hasty tongue. If he had only assumed penitence, instead of flying into a passion, he might have had the money he wanted just as well as not!

"There's no sense in us two quarrelling," he said hastily. "We've been friends a long time. I'm sure I didn't intend to when I came in. I suppose you're right about some things, and probably dropping Moreau wouldn't hurt me any. I'm sorry I said all I did.

Only—the money seemed such a little thing, and I—I needed it."

Harry stood an instant with his hand on the knob, then instead of closing the door, he drew out a little drawer. He lifted a packet of crisp yellow-backs and slowly counted out one hundred dollars. "I'm trying to believe you mean what you say, Hugh," he said.

Hugh's fingers closed eagerly over the crackling notes. "Now that's white of you, after everything I said! You're a good fellow, Harry, after all, and I'll always say so. I wish Old Gooseberry was half as decent in a money way. He seems to think fifty dollars a week is plenty till I marry and settle down. He talks of retiring then, and I suppose he'll come down handsomely, and give me a chance to look my debts in the face." He pocketed the money with an air of relief and picked up his hat and cane.

Just then from the dusty street came the sound of carriage-wheels and the click of the gate-latch.

"It's Bishop Ludlow," he said, glancing through the window. "He's coming in. I think I'll slip out the side way. Thanks for the loan and—I'll think over what you've said!"

Avoiding the bishop, Hugh stepped toward the gate. The money was in his pocket. Well, one of these days

he would not have to grovel for a paltry fifty dollars! He would be his own master, and could afford to let Harry Sanderson and everybody else think what they liked.

"So I'm playing a part, am I!" he said to himself. "Why should your Holiness trouble yourself over it, if I am! Not because you're so careful of the Governor's feelings; not by a long shot! It's because you choose to think Jessica Holme is too good for me! That's where the shoe pinches! Perhaps you'd like to play at that game yourself, eh?"

He walked jauntily up the street—toward the door with the little barred window.

"The old man is fond of her. He thinks I mean to settle down and let the moss grow over my ears, and he'll do the proper thing. It'll be a good way to put my head above water and keep it there. It must be soon, though!" A smile came to his face, a pretentious, boastful smile, and his shining patent-leathers stepped more confidently. "She's the finest-looking girl in this town, even without her eyes. She may get back her sight sometime. But even if she doesn't, blindness in a wife might not be such a bad thing, after all!"

CHAPTER V THE BISHOP SPEAKS

Inside the study, meanwhile, the bishop was greeting Harry Sanderson. He had officiated at his ordination and liked him. His eyes took in the simple order of the room, lingering with a light tinge of disapproval upon the violin case in the corner, and with a deeper shade of question upon the jewel on the other's finger—a pigeon-blood ruby in a setting curiously twisted of the two initial letters of his name.

There came to his mind for an instant a whisper of early prodigalities and wildnesses which he had heard. For the lawyer who had listened to Harry Sanderson's recital on the night of the making of the will had not considered it a professional disclosure. He had thought it a "good story," and had told it at his club, whence it had percolated at leisure through the heavier strata of town-talk. The tale, however, had seemed rather to increase than to discourage popular interest in Harry Sanderson. The bishop knew that those whose approval had been withheld were in the hopeless minority, and that even these could not have denied that he possessed

desirable qualities—a manner by turns sparkling and grave, picturesqueness in the pulpit, and the unteachable tone of blood—and had infused new life into a generally sleepy parish. He had dismissed the whisper with a smile, but oddly enough it recurred to him now at sight of the ruby ring.

"I looked in to tell you a bit of news," said the bishop. "I've just come from David Stires—he has a letter from Van Lennap, the great eye-surgeon of Vienna. He disagrees with the rest of them—thinks Jessica's case may not be hopeless."

The cloud that Hugh's call had left on Harry's countenance lifted.

"Thank God!" he said. "Will she go to him?"

The bishop looked at him curiously, for the exclamation seemed to hold more than a conventional relief.

"He is to be in America next month. He will come here then to examine, and perhaps to operate. An exceptional girl," went on the bishop, "with a remarkable talent! The angel in the chapel porch, I suppose you know, is her modelling, though that isn't just masculine enough in feature to suit me. The Scriptures are silent on the subject of woman-angels in Heaven; though, mind you, I don't say they're not common on earth!" The bishop chuckled mildly at his own epigram.

"Poor child!" he continued more soberly. "It will be a terrible thing for her if this last hope fails her, too! Especially now, when she and Hugh are to make a match of it."

Harry's face was turned away, or the bishop would have seen it suddenly startled. "To make a match of it!" To hide the flush he felt staining his cheek, Harry bent to close the safe. A something that had darkled in some obscure depth of his being, whose existence he had not guessed, was throbbing now to a painful resentment. Jessica was to marry Hugh!

"A handsome fellow—Hugh!" said the bishop. "He seems to have returned with a new heart—a brand plucked from the burning. You had the same *alma mater*, I think you told me. Your influence has done the boy good, Sanderson!" He laid his hand kindly on the other's shoulder. "The fact that you were in college together makes him look up to you—as the whole parish does," he added.

Harry was setting the combination, and did not answer. But through the turmoil in his brain a satiric voice kept repeating:

"No, they don't call me 'Satan' now!"

CHAPTER VI WHAT CAME OF A WEDDING

The white house in the aspens was in gala attire. Flowers—great banks of bloom—were massed in the hall, along the stairway and in the window-seats, and wreaths of delicate fern trembled on the prim-hung chandeliers. Over all breathed the sweet fragrance of jasmin. Musicians sat behind a screen of palms in a corridor, and a long scarlet carpet strip ran down the front steps to the driveway, up which passed bravely dressed folk, arriving in carriages and on foot, to witness the completion of a much-booted romance.

For a fortnight this afternoon's event had been the chat of the town, for David Stires, who to-day retired from active business, was its magnate, the owner of its finest single estate and of its most important bank. From his scapegrace boyhood Hugh Stires had made himself the subject of uncomfortable discussion. His sudden disappearance after the rumored quarrel with his father, and the advent of Jessica Holme, had furnished the community sufficient material for gossip. The

wedding had capped this gossip with an appropriate climax. Tongues had wagged over its pros and cons—for Hugh's past had induced a wholesome skepticism of his future. But the carping were willing to let bygones be bygones, and the wiseacres, to whose experience marriage stood as a sedative for the harum-scarum, augured well.

There was an additional element of romance, too, in the situation; for Jessica, who had never yet seen her lover, would see her husband. The great surgeon on whose prognostication she had built so much, had arrived and had operated. He was not alone an eminent consultant in diagnosis, but an operator of masterly precision, whose daring of scalpel had made him well-nigh a last resort in the delicate adventurings of eye surgery. The experiment had been completely successful, and Jessica's hope of vision had become a sure and certain promise.

To see once again! To walk free and careless! To mold the plastic clay into the shapes that thronged her brain! To finish the statue which she had never yet shown to any one, in the great sky-lighted attic! To see flowers, and the sunset, the new green of the trees in spring, and the sparkle of the snow in winter, and people's faces!—to see Hugh! That had been at the

core of her thought when it reeled dizzily back from the merciful oblivion of the anesthetic, to touch the strange gauze wrappings on her eyes—the tight bandage that must stay for so long, while nature plied her silent medicaments of healing.

Meanwhile the accepted lover had become the importunate one. The operation over, there had remained many days before the bandages could be removed—before Jessica could be given her first glimpse of the world for nearly three years. Hugh had urged against delay. If he had stringent reasons of his own, he was silent concerning them. And Jessica, steeped in the delicious wonder of new and inchoate sensations, had yielded.

So it had come about that the wedding was to be on this hot August afternoon, although it would be yet some time before the eye-bandages might be laid aside, save in a darkened room. In her girlish, passionate ideality, Jessica had offered a sacrifice to her sentiment. She had promised herself that the first form her new sight should behold should be, not her lover, but her husband! The idea pleased her sense of romance. So, hugging the fancy, she had denied herself. She was to see Hugh for the first time in a shaded room, after the glare and nervous excitement of the ceremony.

Gossip had heard and had seized upon this tidbit with relish. The blind marriage—a bride with hoodwinked eyes, who had never seen the man she was to marry—the moment's imperfect vision of him, a poor dole for memory to carry into the honeymoon—these ingredients had given the occasion a titillating sense of the extraordinary and romantic, and sharpened the buzz of the waiting guests, as they whiled away the irksome minutes.

It was a sweltering afternoon, and in the wide east parlor, limp handkerchiefs and energetic fans fought vainly against the intolerable heat. There, as the clock struck six, a hundred pairs of eyes galloped between two centers of interest: the door at which the bride would enter, and the raised platform at the other end of the room where, prayer-book in hand, in his wide robes and flowing sleeves, Harry Sanderson had just taken his stand. Perhaps more looked at Harry than at the door.

He seemed his usual magnetic self as he stood there, backed by the flowers, his waving brown hair unsmoothed, the ruby-ring glowing dull-red against the dark leather of the book he held. Few felt it much a matter of regret that the humdrum and less personable Bishop of the Diocese should be away at convocation, since the young rector furnished the final esthetic touch to a perfectly appointed function. But Harry Sanderson was far from feeling the grave, alien, figure he appeared. In the past weeks he had waged a silent warfare with himself, bitterer because repressed. The strange new thing that had sprung up in him he had trampled mercilessly under. From the thought that he loved the promised wife of another, a quick, fastidious sense in him recoiled abashed. This painful struggle had been sharpened by his sense of Hugh's utter worthlessness. To that rustling assemblage, the man who was to make those solemn promises was David Stires' son, who had had his fling, turned over his new leaf becomingly, and was now offering substantial hostages to good repute. To him, Harry Sanderson, he was a *flâneur*, a marginless gambler in the futures of his father's favor and a woman's heart. He had shrunk from the ceremony, but circumstances had constrained him. There had been choice only between an evasion—to which he would not stoop—and a flat refusal, the result of which would have been a footless scandal—ugly town-talk—a sneer at himself and his motives—a quietus, possibly, to his whole career.

So now he stood to face a task which was doubly painful, but which he would go through with to the bitter end!

Only a moment Harry stood waiting; then the palm-screened musicians began the march, and Hugh took his place, animated and assured, looking the flushed and

expectant bridegroom. At the same instant the chattering and hubbub ceased; Jessica, on the arm of the old man, erect but walking feebly with his cane, was advancing down the roped lane.

She was in simple white, the point-lace on the frock an heirloom. Her bronze hair was drawn low, hiding much of the disfiguring bandage, under which her lips were parted in a half-smile, human, intimate and eager, full of the hope and intoxication of living.

Harry's eyes dropped to the opened book, though he knew the office by heart. He spoke the time-worn adjuration with clear enunciation, with almost perfunctory distinctness. He did not look at Hugh.

"If any man can show just cause why they may not lawfully be joined together, let him speak, or else hereafter for ever hold his peace." In the pause—the slightest pause—that turned the page, he felt an insane prompting to tear off his robes, to proclaim to this roomful of heated, gaping, fan-fluttering humanity, that he himself, a minister of the gospel, the celebrant of the rite, knew "just cause"!

The choking impulse passed. The periods rolled on—the long white glove was slipped from the hand, the ring put on the finger, and the pair, whom God and Harry Sanderson had joined together, were kneeling on

the white satin prie-dieu with bowed heads under the final invocation. As they knelt, choir voices rose:

Then, while the music lingered, the hush of the room broke in a confused murmur; the white ribbon-wound ropes were let down, and a voluble wave of congratulators swept over the spot. In a moment more Harry found himself laying off his robes in the next room.

With a sigh of relief, he stepped through the wide French window into the garden, fresh with the scent of growing things and the humid odors of the soil. The twitter and bustle he had left came painfully out to him, and a whiff of evening coolness breathed through the oppressive air. The strain over, he longed for the solitude of his study. But David Stires had asked him to remain for a final word, since bride and groom were to leave on an early evening train; the old man was to accompany them a part of the journey, and "the Stires place" was to be closed for an indefinite period. Harry found a bench and sat down, where camelias dropped like blood.

What would Jessica suffer in the inevitable awakening, when the tinted petals of her dreams were shattered

and strewn? For the first time he looked down through his sore sense of outrage and protest to deeps in himself—as a diver peers through a water-glass to the depths of a river troubled and opaque, dimly descrying vague shapes of ill. Poetry, passion and dreams had been his also, but he had dreamed too late!

It was not long before the sound of gay voices and of carriage-wheels came around the corner of the house, for the reception was to be curtailed. There had been neither bridesmaids nor groomsmen, and there was no skylarking on the cards; the guests, who on lesser occasions would have lingered to throw rice and old shoes, departed from the house in the aspens with primness and dignity.

One by one he heard the carriages roll down the graveled driveway. A bicycle careened across the lawn from a side-gate, carrying a bank messenger—the last shaft of commerce before old David Stires washed his tenacious mind of business. A few moments later the messenger reappeared and rode away whistling. A last chime of voices talking together—Harry could distinguish Hugh's voice now—and at length quiet told him the last of the guests were gone. Thinking that he would now see his old friends for a last farewell, he rose and went slowly back through the French window.

The east room was empty, save for servants who were gathering some of the cut flowers for themselves. He stood aimlessly for a few moments looking about him. A white carnation lay at the foot of the dais, fallen from Jessica's shower-bouquet. He picked this up, abstractedly smelled its perfume, and drew the stem through his buttonhole. Then, passing into the next room, he found his robes leisurely and laid them by—he had now only to embellish the sham with his best wishes!

All at once he heard voices in the library. He opened the door and entered.

Harry Sanderson stopped stock-still. In the room sat old David Stires in his wheel-chair opposite his son. He was deadly pale, and his fierce eyes blazed like fire in tinder. And what a Hugh! Not the indolently gay prodigal Harry had known in the past, nor the flushed bridegroom of a half-hour ago! It was a cringing, a hang-dog Hugh now; with a slinking dread in the face—a trembling of the hands—a tense expectation in the posture. The thin line across his brow was a livid pallor. His eyes lifted to Harry's for an instant, then returned in a kind of fascination to a slip of paper on the desk, on which his father's forefinger rested, like a nail transfixing an animate infamy.

"Sanderson," said the old man in a low, hoarse, unnatural voice, "come in and shut the door. God forgive us—we have married Jessica to a common thief! Hugh—my son, my only child, whom I have forgiven beyond all reckoning—has forged my name to a draft for five thousand dollars!"

CHAPTER VII OUT OF THE DARK

For a moment there was dead silence in the room. In the hall the tall clock struck ponderously, and a porch blind slammed beneath a caretaker's hand. Harry's breath caught in his throat, and the old man's eye again impaled his hapless son.

Hugh threw up his head with an attempt at jauntiness, but with furtive apprehension in every muscle—for he could not solve the look he saw on his father's face—and said:

"You act as if it were a cool million! I'm no worse than a lot who have better luck than I. Suppose I did draw the five thousand?—you were going to give me ten for a wedding present. I had to have the money then, and you wouldn't have given it to me. You know that as well as I do. Besides, I was going to take it up myself and you would never have been the wiser. He promised to hold it—it's a low trick for him to round on me like this. I'll pay him off for it sometime! I don't see that it's anybody else's business but

ours, anyway," he continued, with a surly glance at Harry.

Harry had been staring at him, but with a vision turned curiously backward—a vision that seemed to see Hugh standing at a carpeted dais in a flower-hung room, while his own voice said out of a lurid shadow: "*Wilt thou have this man to be thy wedded husband....*"

"Stay, Sanderson," said the old man; then turning to Hugh: "Who advanced you money on this and promised to 'hold it'?"

"Doctor Moreau."

"He profited by it?"

"He got his margin," said Hugh sullenly.

"How much margin did he get?"

"A thousand."

"Where is the rest?" David Stires' voice was like a whip of steel.

Hugh hesitated a moment. He had still a few hundreds in pocket, but he did not mention them.

"I used most of it. I—had a few debts."

"Debts of honor, I presume!"

Hugh's sensibility quivered at the fierce, grating irony of the inquiry.

"If you'd been more decent with spending-money," he said with a flare of the old effrontery, "I'd have been all right! Ever since I came home you've kept me strapped. I was ashamed to stick up any more of my friends. And of course I couldn't borrow from Jessica."

"Ashamed!" exclaimed the old man with harsh sternness. "You are without the decency of shame! If you were capable of feeling it, you would not mention her name now!"

Hugh thought he saw a glimmer through the storm-cloud. Jessica was his anchor to windward. What hurt him, would hurt her. He would pull through!

"Well," he said, "it's done, and there's no good making such a row about it. She's my wife and she'll stand by me, if nobody else does!"

No one had ever seen such a look on David Stires' face as came to it now—a sudden blaze of fury and righteous scorn, that burned it like a brand.

"You impudent blackguard! You drag my name in the gutter and then try to trade on my self-respect and Jessica's affection. You thought you would take it up yourself—and I would be none the wiser! And if I did find it out, you counted on my love for the poor deluded girl you have married, to make me condone your criminality—to perjure myself—to admit the signature and shield you from the consequences. You imagine because you are my son, that you can do this thing and all still

go on as before! Do you suppose I don't consider Jessica? Do you think because you have fooled and cheated her—and me—and married her, that I will give her now to a caught thief—a common jailbird?"

Hugh started. A sickly pallor came to his sallow cheek. That salient chin, that mouth close-gripped—those words, vengeful, vindictive, the utterance of a wrath so mighty in the feeble frame as to seem almost uncouth—smote him with a mastering terror.

A jailbird! That was what his father called *him*! Did he mean to give him up, then? To have him arrested—tried—put in prison? When he had canvassed the risks of discovery, he had imagined a scene, bitter anger— perhaps even disinheritance. His marriage to Jessica, he had reckoned, would cover that extremity. But he had never thought of something worse. Now, for the first time, he saw himself in the grip of that impersonal thing known as the law—handcuffs on his wrists, riding through the streets in the "Black-Maria"—standing at the dock an outcast, gazed at with contempt by all the town—at length sitting in a cell somewhere, no more pleasures or gaming, or fine linen, but dressed in convict's dress, loose, ill-shapen, hanging on him like bags, with broad black-and-white stripes. He had been through the penetentiary once. He remembered the

sullen, stolid faces, the rough, hobnailed shoes, the cropped heads! His mind turned from the picture with fear and loathing.

In the thoughts that were darting through Hugh's mind, there was none now of regret or of pity for Jessica. His fear was the fear of the trapped spoiler, who discerns capture and its consequent penalties in the patrolling bull's-eye flashed upon him. He studied his father with hunted, calculating eyes, as the old man turned to Harry Sanderson.

"Sanderson," said David Stires, once more in his even, deadly voice, "Jessica is waiting in the room above this. She will not understand the delay. Will you go to her? Make some excuse—any you can think of—till I come."

Harry nodded and left the room, shutting the door carefully behind him, carrying with him the cowering helpless look with which Hugh saw himself left alone with his implacable judge. What to say to her? How to say it?

As he passed the hall, the haste of demolition had already begun. Florists' assistants were carrying the plants from the east room, and through the open door a man was rolling up the red carpet. The cluttered emptiness struck him with a sense of fateful symbolism—as though it shadowed forth the shattering of

Jessica's ordered dream of happiness. He mounted the stair as if a pack swung from his shoulders. He paused a moment at the door, then knocked, turned the knob, and entered.

There, in the middle of the blue-hung room, in her wedding-dress, with her bandaged eyes, and her bridal bouquet on the table, stood Jessica. Twilight was near, but even so, all the shutters were drawn save one, through which a last glow of refracted sunlight sifted to fall upon his face. Her hands were clasped before her, he could hear her breathing—the full hurried respiration of expectancy.

Then, while his hand closed the door behind him, a thing unexpected, anomalous, happened—a thing that took him as utterly by surprise as if the solid floor had yawned before him. Slim fingers tore away the broad encircling bandage. She started forward. Her arms were flung about his neck.

"Hugh!... Hugh!" she cried. "My husband!"

The paleness was stricken suddenly from Harry's face. An odd, dazed color—a flush of mortification, of self-reproach, flooded it from chin to brow. Despite himself, he had felt his lips molding to an answering kiss beneath her own. He drew a gasping breath, his hand nervously caught the bandage, replaced it over

the eyes, and tied it tightly, putting down her protesting hands.

"Oh, Hugh," she pleaded, "not for a moment—not when I am so happy! Your face is what I dreamed it must be! Why did you make me wait so long? And I can see, Hugh! I can really see! Let it stay off, just for one little moment more!"

He held her hands by force. "Jessica—wait!" he said in a broken whisper. "You must not take it off again—not now!"

An incredible confusion enveloped him—his tongue cleaved to the roof of his mouth. Not only had the painful *contretemps* nonplussed and dismayed him; not only had it heightened and horrified the realization of what she must presently be told. It had laid a careless hand upon his own secret, touching it with an almost vulgar mockery. It had overthrown in an instant the barricades he had been piling. The pressure of those lips on his had sent coursing to the furthest recesses of his nature a great wave which dikes nor locks might ever again forbid.

Her look, leaping to his face, had not noted the ministerial dress, nor in the ecstasy of the moment did she catch the agitation in his voice; or if she did, she attributed it to a feeling like her own. She was laughing

happily, while he stood, trembling slightly, holding himself with an effort.

"What a dear goose you are!" she said. "The light didn't hurt them— indeed, indeed! Only to think, Hugh! Your wife will have her sight! Do go and tell your father! He will be waiting to know!"

Harry made some incoherent reply. He was desperately anxious to get away—his thought was a snarl of tatters, threaded by one lucid purpose: to spare her coming self-abasement this sardonic humiliation. He did not think of a time in the future, when her error must naturally disclose itself. The tangle spelled *Now*. Not to tell her—not to let her know!

He almost ran from the room and down the stair.

CHAPTER VIII "AM I MY BROTHER'S KEEPER?"

At the foot of the landing he paused, drawing a deep breath as if to lift a weight of air. He needed to get his bearings—to win back a measure of calmness.

As he stood there, Hugh came from the library. His head was down and he went furtively and slinkingly, as though dreading even a casual regard. He snatched his hat from the rack, passed out of the house, and was swallowed up in the dusk. David Stires had followed his son into the hall. He answered the gloomy question in Harry's eyes:

"He is gone," he said, "and I hope to Heaven I may never see his face again!" Then, slowly and feebly, he ascended the stair.

The library windows were shadowed by shrubbery, and the sunset splintered against the wall in a broad stripe, like cloth of crimson silk. Harry leaned his hot forehead against the chill marble of the mantelpiece and gazed frowningly at the dark Korean desk—an antique gift of his own to David Stires—where the slip

of paper still lay that had spelled such ruin and shame. From the rear of the house came the pert, tittering laugh of a maid bantering an expressman, and the heavy, rattling thump of rolled trunks. There was something ghastly in the incomprehension of all the house save the four chief actors of the melodrama. The travesty was over, the curtain rung down to clapping of hands, the scene-shifters clearing away—and behind all, in the wings, unseen by any spectator, the last act of a living tragedy was rushing to completion.

Ten, fifteen minutes passed, and old David Stires reëntered the room, went feebly to his wheel-chair, and sat down. He sat a moment in silence, looking at a portrait of Jessica—a painting by Altsheler that hung above the mantel—in a light fleecy gown, with one white rose in the bronze hair. When he spoke the body's infirmity had become all at once pitifully apparent. The fiery wrath seemed suddenly to have burned itself out, leaving only dead ashes behind. His eyes had shrunk away into almost empty sockets. The authority had faded from his face. He was all at once a feeble, gentle-looking, ill, old man, with white mustaches and uncertain hands, dressed in ceremonial broadcloth.

"I have told her," he said presently, in a broken voice. "You are kind, Sanderson, very kind. God help us!"

"What has God to do with it?" fell a voice behind them. Harry faced about. It was Jessica, as he had first seen her in the upper room, with the bandage across her eyes.

"What has God to do with it?" she repeated, in a hard tone. "Perhaps Mr. Sanderson can tell us. It is in his line!"

"Please—" said Harry.

He could not have told what he would have asked, though the accent was almost one of entreaty. The harsh satire touched his sacred calling; coming from her lips it affronted at once his religious instinct and his awakened love. It was all he said, for he stopped suddenly at sight of her face, pain-frosted, white as the folded cloth.

"Oh," she said, turning toward the voice, "I remember what you said that night, right here in this very room—that you sowed your wild oats at college with Hugh—that they were 'a tidy crop'! You were strong, and he was weak. You led, and he followed. You were 'Satan Sanderson,' Abbot of The Saints, the set in which he learned gambling. Why, it was in your rooms that he played his first game of poker—he told me so himself! And now he has gone to be an outcast, and you stand in the pulpit in a cassock, you, the 'Reverend Henry

Sanderson'! You helped to make him what he has become! Can you undo it?"

Harry was looking at her with a stricken countenance. He had no answer ready. The wave of confusion that had submerged him when he had restored the bandage to her eyes had again welled over him. He stood shocked and confounded. His hand fumbled at his lapel, and the white carnation, crushed by his fingers, dropped at his feet.

"I am not excusing Hugh now," she went on wildly. "He has gone beyond excuse or forgiveness. He is as dead to me as though I had never known him, though the word you spoke an hour ago made me his wife. I shall have that to remember all my life—that, and the one moment I had waited for so long, for my first sight of his face, and my bride's kiss! I must carry it with me always. I can never wipe that face from my brain, or the sting of that kiss from my lips—the kiss of a forger—of my husband!"

The old man groaned. "I didn't know he had seen her!" he said helplessly. "Jessica, Hugh's sin is not Sanderson's fault!"

In her bitter words was an injustice as passionate as her pain, but for her life she could not help it. She was a woman wrenched and torn, tortured beyond control, numb with anguish. Every quivering tendril of feeling was a live protest, every voice of her soul was crying out against the fact. In those dreadful minutes when her mind took in the full extent of her calamity, Hugh's past intimacy and present grim contrast with Harry Sanderson had mercilessly thrust themselves upon her, and her agony had seared the swift antithesis on her brain.

To Harry Sanderson, however, her words fell with a wholly disproportionate violence. It had never occurred to him that he himself had been individually and actively the cause of Hugh's downfall. The accusation pierced through the armor of self-esteem that he had linked and riveted with habit. The same pain of mind that had spurred him, on that long-ago night, to the admission she had heard, had started to new life a bared, a scathed, a rekindling sin.

"It is all true," he said. It was the inveterate voice of conscience that spoke. "I have been deceiving myself. I was my brother's keeper! I see it now."

She did not catch the deep compunction in the judicial utterance. In her agony the very composure and restraint cut more deeply than silence. She stood an instant quivering, then turned, and feeling blindly for the door, swept from their sight.

White and breathless, Jessica climbed the stair. In her room, she took a key from a drawer and ran swiftly to the attic-studio. She unlocked the door with hurried fingers, tore the wrappings from the tall white figure of the Prodigal Son, and found a heavy mallet. She lifted this with all her strength, and showered blow upon blow on the hard clay, her face and hair and shimmering train powdered with the white dust, till the statue lay on the floor, a heap of tumbled fragments.

Fateful and passionate as the scene in the library had been, her going left a pall of silence in the room. Harry Sanderson looked at David Stires with pale intentness.

"Yet I would have given my life," he said in a low voice, "to save her this!"

Something in the tone caught the old man. He glanced up.

"I never guessed!" he said slowly. "I never guessed that you loved her, too."

But Harry had not heard. He did not even know that he had spoken aloud.

David Stires turned his wheel-chair to the Korean desk, touching the bell as he did so. He took up the draft and put it into his pocket. He pressed a spring, a panel dropped, and disclosed a hidden drawer, from

which he took a crackling parchment. It was the will against whose signing Harry had pleaded months before in that same room. The butler entered.

"Witness my signature, Blake," he said, and wrote his name on the last page. "Mr. Sanderson will sign with you."

An hour later the fast express that bore Jessica and David Stires was shrieking across the long skeleton railroad bridge, a dotted trail of fire against the deepening night. The sound crossed the still miles. It called to Harry Sanderson, where he sat in his study with the evening paper before him. It called his eyes from a paragraph he was reading through a painful mist—a paragraph under heavy leads, on its front page:

This city has seldom seen so brilliant a gathering as that witnessed, late this afternoon, at the residence of the groom, the marriage of Mr. Hugh Stires and Miss Jessica Holme, both of this place.

The ceremony was performed by the Reverend Henry Sanderson, rector of St. James.

The groom is the son of one of our leading citizens, and the beauty and talent of the bride have long made her noted. The happy couple, accompanied by the groom's father, left on an early train, carrying with them the congratulations and good wishes of the entire community.

A full account of the wedding will be given in to-morrow morning's issue.

CHAPTER IX AFTER A YEAR

Night had fallen. The busy racket of wheeled traffic was still, the pavements were garish with electric light, windows were open, and crowds jostled to and fro on the cool pavements. But Harry Sanderson, as he walked slowly back from a long ramble in knickerbockers and norfolk jacket over the hills, was not thinking of the sights and sounds of the pleasant evening. He had tramped miles since sundown, and had returned as he set out, gloomy, unrequited, a follower of a baffled quest. Even the dog at his heels seemed to partake of his master's mood; he padded along soberly, forging ahead now and again to look up inquiringly at the preoccupied face.

Set back from the street in a wide estate of trees and shrubbery, stood a great white-porched house that gloomed darkly from amid its aspens. Not a light had twinkled from it for nearly a year. The little city had wondered at first, then by degrees had grown indifferent. The secret of that prolonged honeymoon, that dearth and absence, Harry Sanderson and the bishop alone

could have told. For the bishop knew of Hugh's criminal act; he was named executor of the will that lay in the Korean chest, and him David Stires had written the truth. His heart had gone out with pity for Jessica, and understanding. The secret he locked in his own breast, as did Harry Sanderson, each thinking the other ignorant of it.

Since that wedding-day no shred of news had come to either. Harry had wished for none. To think of Jessica was a recurrent pang, and yet the very combination of the safe in his study he had formed of the letters of her name! In each memory of her he felt the fresh assault of a new and tireless foe—the love which he must deny.

Until their meeting his moral existence had been strangely without struggle. When at a single blow he had cut away, root and branch, from his old life, he had left behind him its vices and temptations. That life had been, as he himself had dimly realized at the time, a phase, not a quality, of his development. It had known no profound emotions. The first deep feeling of his experience had come with that college catastrophe which had brought the abrupt change to all his habits of living. He did not know that the impulse which then drew him to the Church was the gravitational force of an

austere ancestry, itself an inheritance from a long line of sectarian progenitors—an Archbishop of Canterbury among them—reaching from

Colony times, when King George had sent the first Sanderson, a virile, sport-loving churchman, to the tobacco emoluments of the Old Dominion. He did not know that in the reaction the pendulum of his nature was swinging back along an old groove in obeisance to the subtle call of blood.

In his new life, problems were already solved for him. He had only to drift with the current of tradition, whereon was smooth sailing. And so he had drifted till that evening when "Satan Sanderson," dead and done and buried, had risen in his grave-clothes to mock him in the person of Hugh. Each hour since then had sensitized him, had put him through exercises of self-control. And then, with that kiss of Jessica's, had come the sudden illumination that had made him curse the work of his hands—that had shown him what had dawned for him, too late!

Outcast and criminal as he was, castaway, who had stolen a bank's money and a woman's love, Hugh was still her husband. Hugh's wife— what could she be to him? And this fevered conflict was shot through with yet another pang; for the waking smart of compunction which had risen at Jessica's bitter cry, "You helped to

make him what he has become!" would not down. That cry had shown him, in one clarifying instant, the follies and delinquencies of his early career reduplicated as through the facets of a crystal, and in the polarized light of conscience, Hugh—loafer, gambler and thief—stood as the type and sign of an enduring accusation.

But if the recollection of that wedding-day and its aftermath stalked always with him—if that kiss had seemed to cling again and again to his lips as he sat in the quiet of his study—no one guessed. He seldom played his violin now, but he had shown no outward sign. As time went on, he had become no less brilliant, though more inscrutable; no less popular, save perhaps to the parish heresy-hunter for whom he had never cared a straw. But beneath the surface a great change had come to Harry Sanderson.

To-night, as he wended his way past the house in the aspens, through the clatter and commotion of the evening, there was a kind of glaze over his whole face—a shell of melancholy.

Judge Conwell drove by in his dog-cart, with the superintendent of the long, low hospital. The man of briefs looked keenly at the handsome face on the pavement. "Seems the worse for wear," he remarked sententiously.

The surgeon nodded wisely. "That's the trouble with most of you professional people," he said; "you think too much!" The judge clucked to his mare and drove on at a smart trot.

The friendly, critical eye clove to the fact; it discerned the mental state of which gloom, depression and insomnia were but the physical reagents. Harry had lately felt disquieting symptoms of strain—irritable weakness, fitful repose, a sense of vague, mysterious messages in a strange language never before heard. He had found that the long walks no longer brought the old reaction—that even the swift rush of his motor-car, as it bore him through the dusk of an evening, gave him of late only a momentary relief. To-morrow began his summer vacation, and he had planned a month's pedestrian outing through the wide ranch valleys and the further ranges, and this should set him up again.

Now, however, as he walked along, he was bitterly absorbed in thoughts other than his own needs. He passed more than one acquaintance with a stare of non-recognition. One of these was the bishop, who turned an instant to look after him. The bishop had seen that look frequently of late, and had wondered if it betokened physical illness or mental unquiet. More than once he had remembered with a sigh the old whisper of Harry

Sanderson's early wildness. But he knew youth and its lapses, and he liked and respected him. Only two days before, on the second anniversary of Harry's ordination, he had given him for his silken watch-guard a little gold cross engraved with his name, and containing the date. The bishop had seen his gift sparkling against Harry's waistcoat as he passed. He walked on with a puzzled frown.

The bishop was pursy and prosy, conventional and somewhat stereotyped in ideas, but he was full of the milk of human kindness. Now he promised himself that when the hour's errand on which he was hastening was done, he would stop at the study and if he found Harry in, would have a quiet chat with him. Perhaps he could put his finger on the trouble.

At a crossing, the sight of a knot of people on the opposite side of the street awoke Harry from his abstraction. They had gathered around a peripatetic street preacher, who was holding forth in a shrill voice. Beside him, on a short pole, hung a dripping gasoline flare, and the hissing flame lit his bare head, his thin features, his long hair, and his bony hands moving in vehement gestures. A small melodeon on four wheels stood beside him, and on its front was painted in glaring white letters:

From over the way Harry gazed at the tall, stooping figure, pitilessly betrayed by the thin alpaca coat, at the ascetic face burned a brick-red from exposure to wind and sun, at the flashing eyes, the impassioned earnestness. He paused at the curb and listened curiously, for Hallelujah Jones with his evangelism mingled a spice of the rancor of the socialist. In his thinking, the rich and the wicked were mingled inextricably in the great chastisement. He was preaching now from his favorite text: *Woe to them that are at ease in Zion.*

Harry smiled grimly. He had always been "at ease in Zion." He wore sumptuous clothes—the ruby in his ring would bring what this plodding exhorter would call a fortune. At this moment, Hede, his dapper Finn chauffeur, was polishing the motor-car for him to take his cool evening spin. That very afternoon he had put into the little safe in the chapel study two thousand dollars in gold, which he had drawn, a part for his charities and quarterly payments and a part to take with

him for the exigencies of his trip. The street evangelist over there, preaching paradise and perdition to the grinning yokels, often needed a square meal, and was lucky if he always knew where he would sleep. Yet did the Reverend Henry Sanderson, after all, get more out of life than Hallelujah Jones?

The thread of his thought broke. The bareheaded figure had ended his harangue. The eternal fires were banked for a time, while, seated on a camp-stool at his crazy melodeon, he proceeded to transport his audience to the heavenly meads of the New Jerusalem. He began a "gospel song" that everybody knew:

The voice was weather-cracked, and the canvas bellows of the instrument coughed and wheezed, but the music was infectious, and half from overflowing spirits, and

half from the mere swing of the melody, the crowd chanted the refrain:

Two, three verses of the old-fashioned hymn he sang, and after each verse more of the bystanders—some in real earnestness, some in impious hilarity—shouted in the chorus:

Harry walked on in a brown study, the refrain ringing through his brain. There came to him the memory of Hugh's old sneer as he looked at his book-shelves—whereon Nietzsche and Pascal sat cheek by jowl with *Theron Ware* and *Robert Elsmere*—"I wonder how much of all that you really believe!" How much *did* he really believe? "I used to read Thomas à Kempis then," he said to himself, "and Jonathan Edwards; now I read Rénan and the *Origins of Christian Mythology*!"

At the chapel-gate lounged his chauffeur, awaiting orders.

"Bring the car round, Hede," said Harry, "and I shan't need you after that to-night. I'll drive her myself. You can meet me at the garage."

Hede, the dapper, good-looking Scandinavian, touched his glossy straw hat respectfully. It was a piece of luck that his master had not planned a motor trip instead of a tour afoot. For a month, after to-night, his time was his own. His quarter's wages were in his pocket, and he slapped the wad with satisfaction as he sauntered off to the bowling-alley.

The study was pitch-dark, and Rummy halted on the threshold with a low, ominous growl as Harry fumbled for the electric switch. As he found and pressed it and the place flooded with light, he saw a figure there—the figure of a man who had been sitting alone—beside the empty hearth, who rose, shrinking back from the sudden brilliancy.

It was Hugh Stires.

CHAPTER X THE GAME

Harry Sanderson stared at the apparition with a strange feeling, like rising from the dead. There flashed into his mind the reflection he had seen once in the mirror above the mantel—the face on which fell the amber ray from the chapel window, shining through the figure of the unrepentant thief—the face that had seemed so like his own!

The likeness, however, was not so startling now. The aristocratic features were ravaged like a nicked blade. Dissipation, exposure, shame and unbridled passion had each set its separate seal upon the handsome countenance. Hugh's clothes were shabby-genteel and the old slinking grace of wearing them was gone. A thin beard covered his chin, and his shifty look, as he turned it first on Harry and then nervously over his shoulder, had in it a hunted dread, a dogging terror, constant and indefinable. From bad to worse had been a swift descent for Hugh Stires.

The wave of feeling ebbed. Harry drew the window-curtains, swung a shade before the light, and motioned to the chair.

"Sit down," he said.

Hugh looked his old friend in the face a moment, then his unsteady glance fell to the white carnation in his lapel as he said: "I suppose you wonder why I have come here."

Harry did not answer the implied question. His scrutiny was deliberate, critical and inquiring. "What have you been doing the last year?" he asked.

"A little of everything," replied Hugh. "I ran a bucket-shop with Moreau in Sacramento for a while. Then I went over in the mining country. I took up a claim at Smoky Mountain—that's worth something, or may be sometime."

"Why did you leave it?"

Hugh touched his parched lips with his tongue—again that nervous, sidelong look, that fearful glance over his shoulder.

"I had no money to work it. I had to live. Besides, I'm tired of the whole thing."

The backward glance, the look of dread, were tangible tokens. Harry translated them:

"You are not telling the truth," he said shortly. "What have you *done*?"

Hugh flinched, but he made sullen answer: "Nothing. What should I have done?"

"That is what I am now inquiring of myself," said Harry. "Your face is a book for any one to read. I see things written on it, Hugh—things that tell a story of wrong-doing. You are afraid."

Hugh shivered under the regard. Did his face really tell so much?

"I don't care to be seen in town," he said. "You wouldn't either, probably, under the circumstances." His gaze dropped to his frayed coat-sleeve. In his craven fear of something that he dared not name even to himself, and in his wretched need, he remembered a night once before, when he had sidled into town drunken and soiled—to a luxurious room, a refreshing bath, clean linen and a welcome. Abject drops of self-pity started in his eyes.

"You're the only one in the world I dared come to," he said miserably. "I've walked ten miles to-day, for I haven't a red cent in my pocket. Nor even decent clothes," he ended.

"That can be partly remedied," said Harry after a pause. He took a dark coat from its hook and tossed it to him. "Put that on," he said. "You needn't return it."

Hugh caught the garment. In another moment he
had exchanged it for the one he wore, and was emptying the old coat's pockets.

"Don't sneak!" said Harry with sudden contempt. "Don't you suppose I know a deck of cards when I see it?"

The thin scar on Hugh's brow reddened. He thrust into his pocket the pasteboards he had made an instinctive move to conceal and buttoned the coat around him. It fitted sufficiently. His eyes avoided the well-set figure standing in white negligée shirt, norfolk jacket and leather belt. As they had been wont to do in the comfortable past, they fixed themselves on the little safe.

"Look here, Harry," he began, "you were a good fellow in the old days. I'm sorry I never paid you the money I borrowed. I would have, but for—what happened. But you won't go back on me now, will you? I want to get out of the country and begin over again somewhere. Will you loan me the money to do it?"

Hugh was eager and voluble now. The man to whom he appealed was his forlorn hope. He had come with no intention of throwing himself upon his father's mercy. He had wished to see anybody in the world but him. In his urgent need, he had had a wild thought of appealing to Jessica, or at worst to get speech with Blake, the old butler who many a time of old had hidden his backslidings from the parental eye. But he had found the white house in the aspens closed and desolate, the servants gone. Harry Sanderson was his last resort.

"If you will, I'll never forget it, Harry!" he cried. "Never, the longest day I live! I'll use every dollar of it just as I say! I will, on my honor!"

But the sight of the poker deck had been steel to Harry's soul. It had touched an excoriated spot that in the past months had grown as sensitive as an exposed nerve. The pictured squares were the ironic badge of Hugh's incorrigibility. They had ruined him, and the ruin had broken his father's heart, and wrecked the life of Jessica Holme. And out of this havoc a popular rector named Harry Sanderson had emerged pitifully the worse.

"Honor!" he said. "Have you enough to swear by? You are what you are because you are a bad egg! You were born a gentleman, but you choose to be a rogue. Do you know the meaning of the word honor, or right, or justice? Have you a single purpose of mind which isn't crooked?"

"You're just like the rest, then," Hugh retorted. "Just because I did that one thing, you'll give me no more chance. Yet the first thing I did with that money was to square myself. I paid every debt of honor I had.

That's why I'm in the hole now. But I get no credit for it, even from you. I wish you could put yourself in my place!"

Harry had been looking steadily at the sallow face with its hoof-print of the satyr, not seeing it, but hearing his own voice say to Jessica: "I was my brother's keeper! I see it now." And out of the distance, it seemed, his voice answered:

"Put myself in your place! I wish I could! I wish to God I could!"

The exclamation was involuntary, automatic, the cumulative expression of every throe of conscience Harry had endured since then, the voice of that remorse that had cried insistently for reparation, dinning in his ears the fateful question that God asked of Cain! Suddenly a whirl of rage seized him, unmeasured, savage, malicious. He had despised Hugh, now he hated him; hated him because he was Jessica's husband, and more than all, because he was the symbol of his own self-abasement. A daredevil side of the old Satan Sanderson that he had chained and barred, rose up and took him by the throat. He struck the oak wainscoting with his fist, feeling a red mist grow before his eyes.

"So you paid every 'debt of honor' you had, eh? You acknowledge a gamester's honor, but not the obligation

of right action between man and man! Very well! Give me that pack of cards. You want money—here it is!"

He swiftly turned the clicking combination of the safe, wrenched open the door and took out two heavy canvas bags. He snapped the cord from the neck of one of these and a ringing stream of double-eagles swept jingling on the table. He dipped his hand in the yellow pile. A thought mad as the hoofs of runaway horses was careening through his brain. He felt an odd lightness of mind, a tense tingling of every nerve and muscle.

"Here is two thousand dollars!—yours, if you win it! For you shall play for it, you gambler who pays his debts of 'honor' and no other! You shall play fair and straight, if you never play again!"

Hugh gazed at Harry in a startled way. This was not the ministerial Harry Sanderson he had known—this *gauche* figure, with the white infuriate face, the sparkling eyes and the strange, veiled look. This reminded him of the reckless spirit of his college days, that he had patterned after and had stood in awe of. Only he had never seen him look so then. Could Harry be in earnest? Hugh glanced from him to the pile of coin and back again. His fingers itched.

"How can I play," he said, "when you know very well I haven't a *sou markee*?"

Harry stuffed the gold back into the bag. He snatched the cards from Hugh's hand and a box of waxen envelope wafers from his desk. There was a strange light in his eye, a tremor in his fingers.

"It is I who play with money!" he said. "My gold against your counters! Each of those hundred red disks represents a day of your life—a day, do you understand?—a red day of your sin! A day of yours against a double-eagle! What you win you keep. But for every counter I win, you shall pay me one straight, white day, a clean day, lived for decency and for the right!"

He was the old Satan Sanderson now, with the blood bubbling in his veins—the Satan Sanderson who could "talk like Bob Ingersoll or an angel," as the college saying was—the cool, daring, enigmatical Abbot of The Saints, primed for any audacity. It was the old character again, but curiously changed. The new overlaid it. Under the spur of some driving impulse the will was travelling along a disused and preposterous channel to a paramount end.

Hugh's eyes were fastened on the gold in Harry's fingers. Two thousand dollars! If luck came his way he could go far on that—far enough to escape the nameless terror that pursued him in every shadow. Money

against red wafers? Why, it was plenty if he won, and if he lost he had staked nothing. What a fool Harry was!

Harry saw the shrewd, calculating look that came to his eyes. He caught his wrist.

"Not here!" he said hoarsely. He flung open the chapel door and pushed him inside. He seized one of the altar candles, lit it with a match and stuck it upright in its own wax on the small communion table that stood just inside the altar-rail, with the cards, the red wafers and the bags of coin. He dragged two chairs forward.

"Now," he said in a strained voice, "put up your hand—your right hand—and swear before this altar, on the gambler's honor you boast of, win or lose, to abide by this game!"

Hugh shrank. He was superstitious. The calculating look had fled. He glanced half fearfully about him—at Harry's white face—at the high altar with its vases of August lilies—at the great rose-window, now a mass of white, opaque blotches on which the three black crosses stood out with weird distinctness—at the lurking, unlighted shadows in the corners. He looked longingly at the gold, shining yellow in the candle-light. It fascinated him.

He lifted his hand. It was trembling.

"I swear I will!" he said. "I'll stand by the cards, Harry, and for every day you win, I'll walk a chalk line—so help me God!"

Harry Sanderson sat down. He emptied one of the bags at his elbow, and pushed the box of wafers across the table. He shuffled the cards swiftly and cut.

"Your deal!" he said.

CHAPTER XI HALLELUJAH JONES TAKES A HAND

Hallelujah Jones had finished his labor for the night. The crowd had grown restive, and finally melted away, and, his audience gone, he folded the camp-stool, turned off the gasoline flare, shut down the lid of his melodeon, and trundled it up the street. A goodly number of coppers had rattled into his worn hat, and to the workman belonged his wage. There was a little settlement on the river, a handful of miles away, and the trudge under the stars would be cool and pleasant. If he grew tired, there was his blanket strapped atop the melodeon, and the open night was dry and balmy.

As he pushed up the street he came to a great motor-car standing at the curb under the maples. There was no one in it, but somewhere in its interior a muffled whirring throb beat evenly like a double, metallic heart. He stopped and regarded it inquisitively; a rich man's property, to be sure!

He looked up—it was at the gate of the chapel. No doubt it belonged to the fashionable rector who had been pointed out to him on the street the day before.

He remembered the young, handsome face, the stylish broadcloth. He thought he would have liked to lean over the Reverend Henry Sanderson's shoulder and lay his finger on a text: *How hardly shall a rich man enter into the kingdom of Heaven*. Yet it was a beautiful edifice that wealth had built there for Christ! He saw dimly the stone angel standing in the porch, and, leaving his melodeon on the pavement, entered the gate to examine it.

He noticed now a dim flicker that lit one corner of the great rose-window. Moving softly over the cropped grass, he approached, tilted one of the hinged panels, and peered in. Two men were there, behind the altar-railing, seated at the communion table.

Hallelujah Jones started back. There on the table was a bag of coin, cards and counters. They were playing—he heard the fall of the cards on the hard wood, saw the gleam of a gold-piece, the smear of melted wax marring the polished oak. The reddish glow of the candle was reflected on the players' faces. Well he knew the devil's tools: had he not sung and exhorted in Black Hill mining camps and prayed in frontier faro "joints"? They were gambling! At God's holy altar, and on Christ's table! Who would dare such a profanation?

He craned his neck. Suddenly he gave a smothered cry. The player facing him he recognized—it was the rector himself! He bent forward, gazing with a tense and horrified curiosity.

In that hazard within the altar-rail strange forces were contending, whose meaning he could not fathom. Between the two men who played, not a word had been spoken save those demanded by the exigencies of the game. Harry had seemed to act almost automatically, but his mind was working clearly, his hand was firm and cool as the blossom on his coat; he made his play with that old steely nonchalance with which, once upon a time, he had staked—and lost—so often. But in his brain a thousand spindles were whirring, a maze of refractory images was rushing past him into an eddying phantasmagoria. A kind of exaltation possessed him. He was putting his past into the dice-box to redeem a soul in pawn, fighting the devil with his own fire, gambling for God!

Five times, ten times, the cards had changed hands, and with every deal he lost. The gold disks had slipped steadily across the table. But Harry had seemed to be looking beyond the ebb and flow of the jettons and the pale face opposite him that gloated over its yellow pile. Though that pile grew larger and larger, Harry's face

had never changed. Hugh's was the shaking hand when he discarded, the convulsed features when he scanned his draw, the desperate anxiety when for a moment fortune seemed to waver. He had never in his life had such luck! He swept his winnings into his pockets with a discordant laugh as he noted that, of the contents of the opened bag, Harry had but one double-eagle remaining.

Harry paused an instant. He snapped the little gold cross he wore from its silken tether and set it upright by him on the table.

His hand won, and the next, and the next. Hugh hoarded his gold: he staked the red wafers—each one a day! He had won almost a thousand dollars, but the second bag had not yet been opened, and the vampire intoxication was running molten-hot in his veins. The untouched bag drew him as the magnet mountain drew the adventurous Sindbad—he could have snatched it in his eagerness.

But the luck had changed; his red counters diminished, melted; he would soon have to draw on his real winnings. Cold beads of sweat broke on his forehead.

Neither had heard the creak of the rose-window as the hinged panel drew back. Neither saw the face pressed against the aperture. Neither guessed the wild and terrible thoughts that were raging through the mind of the solitary watcher as he peered and peered.

This minister! This corrupt, ungodly shepherd! He could be neither hanged nor put in jail, yet he committed a crime for which hell itself scarce held adequate penalty and punishment! The street preacher's eyes dilated, the hand that held the panel trembled, spots of unhealthy white sprang into his burning cheeks. The flaring candles—the table with its carven legend, *This Do In Remembrance of Me*—the little gold cross, set there, it seemed to him, in a satanic derision! It was the evil the Apostle Paul wrestled against, of "wicked spirits in high places." It was sacrilege! It was blasphemy! It was the Arch-Fiend laughing, making a mock of God's own altar with the guilty pleasures of the pit—a very sacrament of the damned!

Scarce knowing what he did, he closed the panel softly and ran across the chapel lawn. On the pavement outside he met a man approaching. It was the bishop, on his way to his contemplated chat with Harry Sanderson. The excited evangelist did not know the man, but his eye caught the ministerial dress, the plain, sturdy piety of the face. In his zeal he saw an instrument to his hand. He grasped the bishop's arm.

"Quick! Quick!" he gasped. "There's devil's work

doing in there! Come and see!" He fairly pulled him inside the gate.

The puzzled bishop saw the intense excitement of the other's demeanor. He saw the faint glow in the corner of the rose-window. Were there thieves after the altar-plate?

He shook off the eager hand that was drawing him toward the window. "Not there—come this way!" he said, and hurried toward the porch. He tried the chapel door—it was fast. He had a key to this in his pocket. He inserted it with caution, opened the door noiselessly and went in, the street preacher at his heels.

What the bishop saw was photographed instantaneously on his mind in fiery, indelible colors. It ate into his soul like hot iron into quivering flesh, searing itself upon his memory. It was destined to haunt his sleep for many months afterward, a phantom of regret and shame. He was, in his way, a man of the world, travelled, sophisticated, acquainted with sin in unexpected forms and places. But this sight, in all its coarse suggestion of license, in its harrowing implication of hidden vice and hypocrisy, was damning and appalling. The evangelist of the pave had been horrified, shocked to word and action; the bishop was frozen, inarticulate, impaled. For any evil in Hugh Stires he was prepared—since the forgery. But Hugh's companion now was the man whom he himself had ordained and anointed, by the laying on of hands, with the chrism of his holy ministry.

It was sin, then, that had set the look he had marvelled at in Harry Sanderson's face—sin, flaunting, mocking and terrible! He whom the church had ordained to shepherd its little ones, to comfort its afflicted, to give in marriage and to bless, to hold before the world the white and stainless banner—a renegade, polluting the sanctuary! A priest apostate, surprised in a hideous revel, gambling, as the Roman soldiers gambled for the seamless garment, at the foot of the cross! An irrepressible exclamation burst from his lips.

With the sound both men at the table started to their feet. Hugh, with a single glance behind him, uttering a wild laugh, leaped the railing, dashed through the study, and vanished into the night; Harry, as though suddenly turned to stone, stood staring at the accusatory figure, with the eager form of the evangelist behind it. It was as if the horror on the stern, set face of the bishop mirrored itself instantaneously upon his countenance, his imagination opening in a shocked, awed way to the concentrated light of feeling, so that he stood bewildered in the paralysis of a like dismay.

To the bishop it seemed the attitude of guilt detected.

What was Harry Sanderson thinking, as, under that speechless regard, he mechanically gathered the scattered cards and lifted the little cross and the unopened bag of double-eagles from the table? Where was the odd excitement, the strange exaltation that had possessed him? The spindles in his brain had stilled, and an algid calm had succeeded, as abrupt as the quiet, deadly assurance with which his mind now saw the pit into which his own feet had led him. The paradoxical impulse that had bred this sinister topsyturvydom had fallen away. The same judicial Harry Sanderson who had said to Jessica, "I was my brother's keeper," arraigned and judged himself, and pronounced the sentence on the bishop's face conclusive, irrefutable, without the power of explanation or appeal.

He blew out the candle, replaced it carefully in its altar bracket, made shift to wipe the wax from the table, and slowly, half blindly, and without a word, went into the study.

The bishop came forward, drew the key from the inside of the study door, closed it and locked it from the chapel side. Harry did not turn, but he was acutely conscious of every sound. He heard the door shut sharply, the harsh grate of the key in the lock, and the sound came to him like the last sentence—the realization of a soul on whom the gate of the good closes for ever.

In the dark silence of the chapel Hallelujah Jones smote his thin hands together approvingly, as he followed the bishop to the outer door. There the older man laid his hand on his shoulder.

"*Let him that thinketh he standeth,*" he said, "*take heed lest he fall*! Let not this knowledge be spread abroad that it make the unrighteous to blaspheme. When you pray for your own soul to-night, pray for the soul of that man from whom God's face is turned away!"

Something in the churchless evangelist bowed to the voice of ecclesiastical authority. He went without a word.

In the study Harry Sanderson stood for a moment with the cards and the bag of double-eagles in his hand. In his soft shirt and disordered hair, with his preternaturally bright eyes, the white blossom on his lapel, and the brilliant light upon his face, he might have been that satin-sleeved colonial ancestor of his, in dissolute maturity, coming from an unclerical bout at Loo, two hundred years ago.

Finally he put the cards and the canvas bag
methodically into the safe and closed it. Then he knelt by his desk and said, clearly and aloud—to that cold inner symbol of consciousness in his soul:

"O God, I do not know if Thou art, as has been said, a seer of the good that is in the bad, and of the bad that is in the good, and a lover of them both. But I know that I am in a final extremity. I can no longer do my labor consistently before the world and before Thee. If I am delivered, it must be by some way of Thine own that I can not conceive, for I can not help myself. Amen."

He rose to his feet, mechanically put on a coat that was lying on a chair—Hugh's coat, but he did not notice this—and bareheaded passed out to the street. The motor-car stood there. He took his place in the forward seat, and threw on the power.

Barking joyously, Rummy, the brown spaniel, tore out of the gate, but his master did not stop. The little creature pursued the moving car, made a frantic leap to gain his seat, but missed, and the huge armored wheel struck and hurled him to the gutter.

Harry did not hear the sharp yelp of pain; his hand was on the lever, pushing it over, over, to its last notch, and the great mechanism, responding with a leap, sped away, faster and faster, through the night.

CHAPTER XII THE FALL OF THE CURTAIN

Harry Sanderson was acting in a kind of fevered dream. His head and hands were bare, his face white and immobile, and his eyes stared straight before him with the persistent fixity of the sleep-walker's. They did not see a bowed, plodding figure pushing a rickety, wheeled melodeon, who scurried from before the hurtling weight that had all but run him down. Nor could they see far behind in the eddying dust a little dog, moaning, limping piteously on three legs, with tongue lolling and shaggy coat caked with mud—following the hopeless, bird-like flight.

One mile, two miles, three miles. The streets were far behind now. The country road spun before him, a dusty white ribbon, along which the dry battered corn rattled as if in a surge of torrid wind. The great motor-car was reeling off the distance like a maddened thing, swooping through the haloed dark, the throttle out, the lever pushed to its utmost limit of speed, rocking drunkenly, every inch of tested steel ringing and throbbing. Yet Harry's fingers had no tremor, no hesitancy, no lack of cunning. His heart was beating measuredly.

He kept the road by a kind of instinct as rudimentary as that which points the homing carrier-pigeon. He seemed to be moving in a mental world created by some significant clairvoyancy, in which the purpose operated without recourse to the spring of reason. The light of neurasthenia burned behind his eyelids; he felt at once a consuming flame within, a paralyzing frost without. The light autumn mist drenched him like a fine, sifting rain; the wheel-flung dust adhered like yellow mud, and above the clatter of the exhaust the still air shrieked past like a shrewd wind.

Five miles, through the dark, under the breathless, expectant stars. The car was on the broad curve now, where the road bent to the bluff above the river to pass the skeleton railroad bridge. But Harry knew neither place nor time. He was conscious only of motion—swift, swallow-like, irresistible—this, and the racing pictures in his brain, stencilled on the blur of night that closed around him. These pictures came and went; the last revel of The Saints when he was Satan Sanderson—Hugh sneering at his calling—Jessica facing him with unbandaged eyes—Hallelujah Jones, preaching on the street corner. The figure of the street evangelist recurred again and again with a singular persistency. It grew more tangible! It threatened him!

Something in Harry's brain seemed to snap. A tiny shutter, like that of a camera, fell down. His hands dropped from the steering-wheel, and, swaying in his seat, he began to sing, in a voice made high and uneven by the speed of the car:

He sang but the three lines. For suddenly the car left the road—the inflated tires rebounded from the steel ridge of the railroad track—the forward axle caught an iron signal post—and the great motor-car, its shattered lamp jingling like a gong, its pistons thrusting in midair, reared on two wheels, hurling its occupant out like a pebble thrown from a sling, half-turned, and, leaving a trail of sparks like the tail of a rocket behind it, plunged heavily over the rim of the bluff into the river.

A moment later the deep black waters of "the hole" had closed above the mass of sentient steel. The swift current had smoothed away every trace of the strange monster it had engulfed, and there, by the side of the track, huddled against the broken signal post, his clothing plastered with mud and grime, motionless, and with a nasty cut on the temple, lay Harry Sanderson.

CHAPTER XIII THE CLOSED DOOR

A long saturating peace, a deep and drenching darkness, had folded Harry Sanderson. Dully at first, at length more insistently and sharply, a rhythmic pulsing sound began to annoy the quietude. K-track, k-track, k-track—it grew louder; it grew more momentous and material; it irritated the calm that had wrapped the animate universe. Shreds of confusing impression had begun to arrange themselves on a void of nothingness, blurred inchoate images to struggle through a delicious sensation of indifference and repose. Outlines were filling, contours growing distinct; the brain was beginning to resume its interrupted function. As though from an immeasurable distance he heard a low continuous roar, and now and again, through the roar, nearer voices.

Harry awoke. His mind awoke, but his eyes did not open at once, for the gentle swaying that cradled him was pleasant and the muffled clack and hum soothed him like opium. He was as serenely comfortable as a stevedore who dozes out of the long stupefaction of exhaustion to the realization that the day is a holiday.

His blood was coursing like quicksilver. He felt a buoyancy, a volatile pleasure, a sense of complete emancipation from all that clogged and cloyed—the sensuous delight of the full pulse and the perfect bodily mechanism.

He opened his eyes.

It was daylight. He was lying on dusty boards that rattled and vibrated beneath him—the floor of an empty freight car in motion. The sliding door was part-way open, and through it was borne the moist air of a river bay and the purring wash of the tide. A small brown dog, an abject, muddied and shivering morsel, was snuggled close to his side. It whined, as if with joy to see his eyes opened, and its stubby tail beat the floor.

Harry turned his head. Two men in dingy garments were seated on the floor a little distance away, thumbing a decrepit pack of cards over an empty box. He could see both side-faces, one weather-beaten and good-humored, the other crafty—knights of the road.

The sudden movement had sent a momentary twinge to his temple; he put up his hand—it touched a coarse handkerchief that had been bound tightly about it. The corner hung down—it was soiled and stiff with blood. What was he doing there? Where was he? *Who was he?*

It came to him with a start that he actually for the moment did not know who he was—that he had ridiculously slipped the leash of his identity. He smiled at his predicament. He would lie quietly for a few moments and it would come: of course it would come!

Yet it did not come, though he lay many moments, the fingers of his mind fumbling for the latch of the closed door. He had waked perfectly well—all save the slight cut on his temple, and that was clearly superficial, a mere scratch. Not a trouble or anxiety marred his soul; his mind was as clear and light as a lark's. Body and brain together felt as if they had never had a serious ache in the world. But all that had preceded his awakening was gone from him as completely as though it had had no existence. His mind, so far as memory of incident was concerned, was wiped clean, as a wet sponge wipes off a slate. Yet he felt no trouble or anxiety. That part of his brain which had vibrated to these emotions was, as it were, under a curious anesthesia. Goaded and overkeyed into a state of hypertension, it had retaliated with insensibility. All that had vexed and hurt was gone into the limbo with its own disturbing memories.

Stealthily he rose to a sitting posture and, with a frown of humorous perplexity, took a swift and silent

inventory. Here he was, in a freight car, speeding somewhere or other, with a sore and damaged skull. The dog clearly belonged to him, or he to the dog—there was an old intimacy in the fawning fondness of the amber eyes. Yonder were two tramps, diverting themselves in their own way, irresponsible and questionable birds of passage. He scanned his own clothing. It was little better than theirs. His coat was threadbare, and with mud, oil and coal-dust, was in a more disreputable state. His wristbands were grimy, and one cuff-link had been torn away. He had no hat.

He bethought himself of his pockets, and went through them methodically one by one. They yielded several dollars in coin, a penknife and a tiny gold cross, but not a letter, not a scrap of paper, nothing to serve him. The gleam of a ring on his finger caught his eye; he rubbed away the dirt and carefully examined it, wondering if the stone was real. His hand was slightly cut and swollen, and the circlet would not come off, but by shifting it slightly he could see the white depression made by long wear. The setting was an odd one, formed of the twisted letters H. S. Those naturally should be his initials, but there he stopped. He repeated to himself all the names he could think of beginning with S, but they told him nothing.

He looked himself over again, carefully, reflectively—many a time of old he had regarded himself with the same amused, fastidious tolerance when dressed for a "slumming" expedition—his head a little to one side, the ghost of a smile on his lips. He put out his hand and laid it on the spaniel's head.

Its rough tongue licked his fingers; it held up one forepaw mutely and lamely. He drew the feverish, dirty little creature into his lap and examined the limp member. It was broken.

"Poor little beggar!" said he under his breath. "So you've been knocked out, too!" With his knife he cut a piece from the lining of his coat and with a splinter of wood from the floor he set the fractured bone and wrapped the leg tightly. The dog submitted without a whimper, and when he set it down, it lay quietly beside him, watching him with affectionate canine solicitude.

"I wonder who we are, you and I," muttered Harry Sanderson whimsically. "I wonder!"

His gaze turned to where he could see the sunshine dancing and shimmering from the tremulous water. He sniffed the warm air—it was clear and sweet. Not a cloud was in the perfect sky. How fine he felt, broken head and all!

He looked across the car, where the card players were still absorbed. Over the shoulder of one he could see the hand he held—a queen, two aces, a seven and a deuce. For an instant something in his brain snapped and crackled like the sputtering spark of an incomplete insulation—for an instant the fingers almost touched the latch of the closed door. Then the sensation faded, and left a blank as before. He rose to his feet and walked forward.

The players looked around. One of them nodded approvingly.

"Right as a trivet!" he said. "I made a pretty good job of that cut of yours. Hurt you much?"

"No," said Harry. "I'm obliged to you for the attention."

"Foolish to walk on a railroad track," the other went on. "By your looks, you've been on the road long enough to know better. We figgered it out that you was just a-going to cross the railroad bridge when the freight raised merry hell with you. We stopped to tank there and we picked you up, you and your four-legged mate. Must have been a bit squiffy, eh?"

He winked, and took a flask from his pocket. "Have a hair of the dog that bit you?" he said.

Harry took the flask, and, wiping the top on his sleeve, uncorked it. Something in the penetrating odor of the contents seemed to cleave through far mental wastes to an intimate, though mysterious goal. He put it to his lips and drank thirstily.

As the burning liquid scorched his throat, a recrudescence of old impulses surged up through the crust of more modern usage. Mentally, characteristically, he was once more the incongruous devil-may-care figure in whom conspicuous achievement and contradictory excesses had walked hand in hand. The Harry Sanderson of the new, remorseful, temperate life, of chastened impulses, of rote and rule and reformed habit—the rector of St. James—had been lost on that wild night ride. The man who had awakened in the freight car was the Satan Sanderson of four years before, who, under stress of mental illness and its warped purview, in that strenuous scene in the chapel, had regained his ancient governance.

Harry handed back the flask with a long breath. There was a composed yet reckless light in his eye—the old veiled gleam of vagary, and paradox, and escapade. He seated himself beside them.

"Thank you," he said. "With your permission, gentlemen, I will take a hand in the game."

CHAPTER XIV THE WOMAN WHO REMEMBERED

Since that tragical wedding-day at the white house in the aspens, Jessica had passed through a confusion of experiences. She had always lived much in herself, and to her natural reserve her blindness had added. As a result her knowledge both of herself and of life had been superficial. She had been drawn to Hugh by both the weakest and the noblest in her, in a self-obliterating worship that had counted her restored sight only an ornament and glory for her love. In the baleful hour of enlightenment she had been lost, whirled away, out into the storm and void, every landmark gone, every light extinguished, her feet set in the "abomination of desolation." The first bitter shock of the catastrophe, however, seemed to burn up in her the very capacity for further poignant suffering, and she went through the motions of life apathetically.

Change of scene and the declining health of David Stires occupied, fortunately, much of her waking thoughts. After the first few months of travel he failed

steadily. His citric-acid moods were forgotten, his harsh tempers put aside. Hour after hour he lay in his chair, gazing out from the wide sun parlor of the sanatorium on the crest of Smoky Mountain, whither their journeying had finally brought them. He had never spoken of Hugh. But Jessica, sitting each day beside him, reading to him till he dropped asleep, seeing the ever-increasing sadness in his face, knew the hidden canker that gnawed his heart.

To the northward the slope of the mountain fell gradually to fields of violet-eyed alfalfa, and twice a day a self-important little donkey-engine drew a single car up and down between the great glass building on the ridge and the junction of the northern railroad. This view did not attract her; she liked best the southern exposure, with its flushed, serrated snow-peaks in the distance, the warmer brown shadows of the gulch-seamed hills unrolling at her feet, and at their base the treeless, busy little county-seat two miles away. In time her fiercer pain had dulled, and her imagination— naturally so importunate—had begun to seize upon her surroundings. In the summer season the sanatorium had few guests, and for this she was thankful. Doctor Brent, its head, rallying her on her paleness, drove her out of doors with good-natured severity, and when she

was not with David Stires she walked or rode for hours at a time over the mountain trails. Breathing in the crisp air of altitude her spirits grew more buoyant. The beauty of shrub and flower, of cloud and sky, began to call to her, and the breath of October found a tinge of color in her cheek. She fed the squirrels, listened to the pert chirp of the whisky-jack and the whirring drum of the partridge, or sat on a hidden elevation which she named "The Knob," facing across the shallow valley to the south.

The Knob overlooked a little grassy shelf a few hundred feet below, where stood a miner's cabin, with weed-grown gravel heaps near by, in front of which a tree bore the legend, painted roughly on a board: "The Little Paymaster Claim." From its point of vantage, too, unobserved, she could look down into the gulch far below, where yellowish-brown cones reared like gigantic ant-hills—the ear-marks of the placer miner—and gray streaks indicated the flumes in which, by tortuous meanderings, the water descended to do its work in the sluices. She could even watch the toiling miners, hoisting the gravel by windlasses, or shovelling it into the long narrow boxes through which the foaming water raced. So limpid was the air that in the little town she could distinguish each several building lining the single

straight street—a familiar succession of gilded café, general emporium and drug store, with the dull terra cotta "depot" at one end, and on the other, on a sunburned acre of its own, the glaring white court-house, flanked by the post-office and the jail. She could see the clouds of dust, the wagons hitched at the curb and the drab figures grouped at the corners or passing in and out of doorways.

Her interest had opened eagerly to these scenes. The solitudes soothed and the life of the community below, frankly primitive and uncomplicated, attracted her. Between the town of Smoky Mountain and the expensive sanatorium on the ridge a great social gulf was fixed; the latter's patrons for the most part came and went by the narrow-gage road that linked with the northern junction; the settlement far below was only a feature of the panorama for which they paid so well. Even Doctor Brent—who had perched this place of healing where his patients could breathe air fresh from the Pacific and cooled by the snow-peaks—knew it chiefly through two of its citizens, Mrs. Halloran, the capable, bustling wife of the proprietor of the Mountain Valley House, the town's single hostelry, who brewed old-fashioned blackberry wine and cordials for his patients, and Tom Felder, a young lawyer whom he had known on the

coast before ill health had sent him to hang out his shingle in a more genial altitude.

The latter sometimes came for a chat with the physician, and on one of these calls Jessica and he had met. She had liked his keen, good-humored face and waving, slightly graying hair. She had met him once since on the mountain road, and he had walked with her and told her quaint stories of the townspeople. She did not guess that more than once since then he had walked there hoping to meet her again. He had taken her to Mrs. Halloran, whose heart she had won by praise of her cherry cordial.

As Mrs. Halloran said afterward: "'Twas no flirt with the bottle and make love to the spoon! She ain't a bit set up. Take the word I give you, Tom Felder, an' go and swap lies with the doctor at the santaranium soon again. Ye can do worse."

This had been Jessica's first near acquaintance with the town, but since that time she had often reined up at the door of the neat hotel to pass a word with Mrs. Halloran or to ask for another bottle of the cherry cordial, which the sick man she daily tended found grateful to his jaded palate.

"It brings back my boyhood," David Stires said to her one afternoon, tapping the bottle by his wheel-chair.

"That was before the chemist married the vintner's daughter. Somehow this has the old taste."

"It is nearly gone," she said. "I'll get another bottle—I am going for a ride now. I think it does you good."

"Before you go," he said, "fetch my writing-case and I will dictate a letter."

She brought and opened it with a trouble at her heart, for the request showed his increasing weakness. Until to-day the few letters he had written had been done with his own hand. Thinking of this as she waited, her fingers nervously plucked at the inside of the leather cover. The morocco flap fell and disclosed a slip of paper. It was a canceled bank-draft. It bore Hugh's name, and across its face, in David Stires' crabbed hand, written large, was the venomous word *Forgery*.

The room swam before her eyes. Only by a fierce effort could she compel her pen to trace the dictated words. Hugh's misdeed, evil as it was, had been to her but an abstract crime; now it suddenly lay bare before her, a concrete expression of coarse thievery, a living symbol of crafty simulation. Scarce knowing why she did it, she drew the draft covertly from its receptacle, and slipped it into her bosom. Her fingers trembled as they replaced the flap, and her face was pale when she put away the writing-case and went to don her habit.

The evidence of Hugh's sin! As the horse pounded down the winding road, she held her hand hard against her breast, as though it were a live coal that she would press into her flesh in self-torture. That paper must remain, as the sin that made it remained—the sign-manual of her dishonor and loss! The man whose hand had penned its lying signature was the man she had thought she loved. By that act he had thrust himself from her for ever. Yet he lived. Somewhere in the world he walked, in shame and degradation, beyond the pale of honorable living—and she was his wife!

She was his wife! The words hummed in the hoof-beats and taunted her. The odors of the balsam boughs about her became all at once the scent of jasmin, the sigh of the wind turned to the chanting of choir voices, and beneath her closed eyelids came a face seen but once, but never to be erased or forgotten, a face startled, quivering with a strange, remorseful flush— which she had not guessed was guilt!

She was his wife! Though she called herself Jessica Holme, yet, in the law, his name and fame were hers. There was deep in her the unreasoned, intuitive regard, handed down through inflexible feminine generations, for the relentless mandate, "let not man put asunder;" but she had no finical conception of woman's duty to

convention. To break the bond? To divorce the husband to whom she was wife in name only? That would be to spread abroad the disgrace under which she cringed! She thought of the old man she had left— uncomplaining, growing feebler every day. To shame him before the world, whose ancestors had been upright and clean-handed? To add the final sting to his sufferings—who had done her only good? No, she could not do that. Time must solve the problem for her in some other way.

The main street of the town was busy, yet quiet withal, with the peculiar quiet which marks the absence of cobblestone and trolley-bell. Farmers from outlying fruit ranches gossiped on the court-house square; here and there a linen collar and white straw hat betokened the professional man or drummer; and miners in overalls and thong-laced boots kept a-swing the rattan half-doors of the saloons.

"Look at that steady hand, now, an' her hair as red as glory!" said Mrs. Halloran, gazing admiringly from the doorstep where she had been chatting with Tom Felder. "Ye needn't stare yer gray eyes out though, or she'll stop at th' joolry shop to buy ye a ring—to shame ye fer jest hankerin' and sayin' nothin'!"

Felder laughed as he crossed the street, raising his

felt hat gallantly to the approaching rider. Mrs. Halloran was a privileged character. The ravage of drudgery had not robbed her of comeliness that gave her face an Indian summer charm, and she was as kindly as her husband was morose. It was not Michael Halloran who kept the Mountain Valley House popular! The old woman hurried to the curb and tied the horse as Jessica dismounted.

"How did ye guess I made some more this day?" she exclaimed. "Sure, if ye drink it yerself, my dearie, them cheeks is all th' trade-mark I need!" She led the way into the little carpeted side room, by courtesy denominated "the parlor." "I'll go an' put it up in two shakes," she said. "Sit ye down an' I'll not be ten minutes." So saying she bustled away.

Left alone, Jessica gazed abstractedly about her. Her mind was still full of the painful reflections of her ride. A door opened from the room into the office. It was ajar; she stepped close and looked in.

A group of miners lounged in the space before the front windows— familiarly referred to by its habitués as "the Amen Corner"—chatting and watching the passers-by.

Suddenly she clapped her hand to her mouth to stifle a cry. A name had been spoken—the name that was in

her thought—the name of "Hugh Stires." She leaned forward, listening breathlessly.

"I wonder where the young blackleg's been," said one, peering through the windows. "He'd better have stayed away for good, I'm thinking. What does he want to come back for, to a place where there aren't three men who will take a drink with him?"

The reply was as contemptuous.

"We get some rare black sheep in the hills!" The voice spoke meaningly. "If I had my way, he'd leave this region almighty quick!"

Jessica looked about her an instant wildly, guiltily. She could not be mistaken in the name! Was Hugh here, whither by the veriest accident she had come—here in this very town that she had gazed down upon every day for weeks? *Was he?* She pressed her cold hands to her colder cheeks. The contempt in the voices had smitten through her like a sword.

A revulsion seized her. No, no, it could not be! She had not heard aright. It was only a fancy! But she had an overwhelming desire to satisfy herself with her own eyes. From where she stood she could not see the street. She bethought herself of the upper balcony.

Swiftly, on tiptoe, she crossed to the hall door, threw it open, and ran hastily up the stair.

CHAPTER XV THE MAN WHO HAD FORGOTTEN

If the man who had been the subject of the observations Jessica had heard had been less absorbed, as he walked leisurely along on the opposite side of the street, he would have noticed the look of dislike in the eyes of those he passed. They drew away from him, and one spoke—to no one in particular and with an oath offensive and fervid. But weather-beaten, tanned, indifferently clad, and with a small brown dog following him, the new-comer passed along, oblivious to the sidelong scrutiny. He did not stare about him after the manner of a stranger, though, so far as he knew, he had never been in the place before. So far as he knew—for Harry Sanderson had no memories save those which had begun on a certain day a month before in a box-car. He walked with eyes on the pavement, absorbed in thoughts of his own.

But Harry Sanderson now was not the man who had ridden into oblivion in the motor-car. The rector of St. James was in a strange eclipse. Mentally and externally

he had reverted to the old Satan Sanderson, of the brilliant flashing originality, of the curt risk and daring. The deeply human and sensitive side, that had developed during his divinity years, was in abeyance; it showed itself only in the affection he bestowed on the little nameless dog that followed him like a brown, shaggy shadow.

He was like that old self of his, and yet, if he had but known it, he was wonderfully like some one else, too—some one who had belonged to the long ago and garbled past that still eluded him; some one who had been a part also of the life of this very town, till a little over a month before, when he had left it with dread dogging his footsteps!

Curious coincidences had wrought together for this likeness. In the past weeks Harry had grown perceptibly thinner. A spare beard was now on his chin, and the fiery sun that had darkened his cheeks to sallow had lightened his brown hair a shade. The cut on his brow had healed to the semblance of a thin red birth-mark. Most of all, the renaissance of the old character had given his look, to the casual eye, a certain flare and jauntiness, which dissipation and license, unclogged now with memory or compunction, had matured and vitalized. His was now a replica of the face he had once seen, in that lost life of his, mirrored in his chapel study

—his own face, with the trail of evil upon it, and yet weirdly like Hugh Stires'.

Fate—or God!—was doing strange things for Harry Sanderson!

Harry's game of cards in the freight-car had been a sequent of the game in the chapel. It was an instinctive effort of the newly-stirring consciousness to relink the broken chain, utilizing the mental formula which had been stamped deeply upon it when the curtain of oblivion descended—which had persisted, as the photograph of the dead retina shows the scene upon which the living eye last looked. The weeks that followed were reversionary. Rebellion against convention, dissipation—these had been the mask through which the odd temperament of Satan Sanderson had looked at life. This mask had fallen before a career of new meanings and motives. These blotted suddenly out with their inspirations and habits, and, the old spring touched, the mind had automatically resumed its old viewpoint.

He had studied himself with a sardonic, *ex parte* interest. He had found at his disposal a well-stocked mind, a copious vocabulary. Terms of science, historic references, the thousand and one allusions of the daily newspaper that the unlearned pass over, all had their

significance for him. He was no superficial observer, and readily recognized the evidences of mental culture. But the cord that had bound all together into character had snapped. He was a ship without a rudder; a derelict, drifting with the avid winds of chance on the tide of fate. A thousand ways he had turned and turned. A thousand tricks he had tried to cajole the unwilling memory. All were vain. When he had awakened in the freight-car, many miles had lain between him and his vanished history, between him and St. James parish, the town he had impressed, the desolate white house in the aspens, the chapel service and surplice, and the swift and secret-keeping river. Between him and all that these things had meant, there lay a gulf of silence and blankness as wide as infinity itself.

But drifting, adventuring, blown by the gipsy wind of chance, learning the alphabet and the rule of three of "the road," the man was at once a part of it and apart from it. The side that rejoiced in the liberty and madcap adventure was overlaid by another darkling side whose fingers were ever feeling for the lost latch. In the nomad weeks of wind and sun, as the tissues of the brain grew slowly back to a state of normal action, the mind seized again and again upon the bitter question of his identity. It had obtruded into clicking leagues on

steel-rails, into miles afoot by fruit-hung lanes, on white Pacific shell-roads under cedar branches, on busy highways. It had stalked into days of labor in hop-fields, work with hand and foot that brought dreamless sleep and generous wage; into nights of less savory experience in city purlieus, where a self-forgotten man gamed and drank, recklessly, audaciously, forbiddingly. Who was he? From what equation of life had he been eliminated? Had he loved anything or anybody? Had he a friend, any friend, in the world? At first it was not often that he cared; only occasionally some deep-rooted instinct would stir, subtly conscious, without actual contrast, of the missed and evaded. But he came to ask it no longer quizzically or sardonically, but gloomily and fiercely. And lacking answer, the man of no yesterdays had plunged on toward the ardent, alien to-morrow, and further into audacious folly. He had drunk deeper, the sign-posts of warning were set in his countenance, and his smile had grown as dangerous as a sunstroke.

The man of no memories gave no heed to the men on the street who looked at him askance. He sauntered along unconsciously, his hands thrust deep in his pockets. With a casual glance at the hotel across the way, he entered a saloon, where a score of patrons were standing

at the bar, or shaking dice noisily at the tables ranged against the wall. The bartender nodded to his greeting—the slightest possible nod. The dog who had followed him into the place leaped up against him, its forepaws on his knee.

"Brandy, if you please," said the new arrival, and poured indolently from the bottle set before him.

The conversation in the room had chilled. To its occupants the man who had entered was no stranger; he was Hugh Stires, returned unwelcome to a place from which he had lately vanished. Moreover, what they felt for him was not alone the crude hatred which the honest toiler feels for the trickster who gains a living by devious knaveries. There was an uglier suspicion afloat of Hugh Stires! A blue-shirted miner called gruffly for his score, threw down the silver and went out, slamming the swing-door. Another glowered at the new arrival, and ostentatiously drew his glass farther along the bar.

The new-comer regarded none of them. He poured his glass slowly full, sipped from it, and holding it in his hand, turned and glanced deliberately about the place. He looked at everybody in the room, suddenly sensible of the hostile atmosphere, with what seemed a careless amusement. Then he raised his glass.

"Will you join me, gentlemen?" he said.

There was but one response. A soiled, shambling figure, blear, white-haired and hesitating, with a battered violin under its arm, slouched from a corner and grasped eagerly for the bottle the bartender contemptuously pushed toward him. No one else moved.

The man who waited studied the roomful with a disdainful smile, with eyes sparkling like steel points. He as wholly misunderstood their dislike as they misconstrued his effrontery—did not guess that to them he stood as one whom they had known and had good reason to despise. Their attitude struck him as so manifestly unreasonable and absurd—so primarily the sulky hatred of the laborious boor for the manifestly more flippant member of society—that it diverted him. He had drunk at bar-rooms in many strange places; never before had he encountered a community like this. His veiled, insolent smile swept the room.

"A spirit of brotherhood almost Christian!" he said. "If I observe that the town's brandy is of superior vintage to its breeding, let me not be understood as complimenting the former without reservation. I have drunk better brandy; I have never seen worse manners!"

He looked smilingly at the soiled figure beside him—a fragment of flotsam tossed on the tide of failure. "I erred in my general salutation," he said. "Gentility is,

after all, less a habit than an instinct." He lifted his glass—to the castaway. "I drink to the health of the only other gentleman present," he said, and tossed the drink off.

A snort and a truculent shuffle came from the standing men. Their faces were dark. Tom Felder, the lawyer, entered the saloon just in time to see big Devlin, the owner of the corner dance-hall, rise from a table, rolling up flannel sleeves along tattooed arms. He saw him stride forward and, with a well-directed shove, send the shambling inebriate reeling across the floor.

"Two curs at the bar are enough at a time!" quoth Devlin.

Then the lawyer saw an extraordinary thing. The emptied glass rang sharply on the bar, the arm that held it straightened, the lithe form behind it seemed to expand—and the big bulk of Devlin went backward through the doorway, and collapsed in a sprawling heap on the pavement.

"For my part," said an even, infuriate voice from the threshold, "I prefer but one."

The face the roomful saw now as they pushed to the outer air, and which turned on the flocking crowd, bore anything but the slinking look they had been used to see on the face of Hugh Stires. The smile that meant danger played over it; there was both calculation and savagery in it. It was the look of the man to whom all risks are alike, to whom nothing counts. In the instant confusion, every one there recognized the element of hardihood dumfounded. Here was one who, as Barney McGinn, the freighter, said afterward, "hadn't the sand of a sick coyote," bearding a bully and the most formidable antagonist the town afforded. Devlin himself was not overpopular; his action had been plainly enough a play to the galleries; and courage—that animal attribute which no circumstance or condition can rob of due admiration—had appeared in an unexpected quarter. But the man they despised had infuriated them with insult, and Devlin had the sympathy that clings to a fair cause. An ugly growl was running through the crowd, and several started forward. Even when Tom Felder put up his hand with a sharp, indignant exclamation, they fell back with an unwilling compulsion.

The prostrate man was on his feet in an instant, wiping the blood from a cleft lip, and peeled off his vest with a vile epithet.

"That is incidentally a venturesome word to select from your vocabulary," said the even voice, a sort of detonation in it. "You will feel like apologizing presently."

Devlin came on with a bull-like rush. The lawyer's eye, shrewdly gaging the situation, gave the slighter man short shrift, and for several intense seconds every breath stopped. Those seconds called up from some mysterious covert all the skill and strength of the old hard-hitting Satan Sanderson, all the science of parry and feint learned in those bluff college bouts with the gloves with Gentleman Jim. And this hidden reserve rushed into combat with an avid thirst and wild ferocity as strange as the steady eye and hand that cloaked them beneath a sardonic coolness.

It was a short, sharp contest. Not a blow broke the guard of the man whose back was to the doorway—on the other hand, Devlin's face was puffed and bleeding. When for a breath he drew back, gulping, a sudden glint of doubt and fear had slipped beneath the blood and sweat.

The end came quickly. Harry stepped to meet him, there was a series of swift passes—then one, two, lightning-like blows, and Devlin went down white and stunned in the dust of the roadway.

So high was the tension and so instantaneous the close, that for a moment the crowd was noiseless, the spell still upon them. In that moment Tom Felder came hastily forward, for, though sharing the general dislike, admiration was strong in him, and, knowing the temper of the bystanders, he expected trouble.

The man who had administered Devlin's punishment, however, did not see his approach. He was looking somewhere above their heads—at the upper balcony of the hotel opposite—staring, in a kind of strained and horrified expectancy, at a girl who leaned forward, her hands clenching the balustrade, her eyes fixed on his face. The late sunlight on her hair made it gleam like burnished copper over her green riding-habit, and her cheeks were blanched.

There was something in that face, in that intense look, that seemed to cleave the gray veil that swathed Harry Sanderson's past. Somewhere, buried in some cell of his brain, a forgotten memory tugged at its shackles—a memory of a time when, thousands and thousands of years ago, he had been something more than the initials "H. S." The look pierced through the daredevil present in which the mind astray had roved reckless and insensate, to a deeper stratum in which slept maturer qualities of refined taste, of dignity and of repute. It stripped off the protecting cicatrice and left him enveloped in an odd embarrassment. A flush burned his face.

Only an instant the gaze hung between them. It

served as a distraction, for other eyes had raced to the balcony. Loud voices were suddenly hushed, for there was not wanting in the crowd that instinctive regard for the proprieties which belongs to communities where gentlewomen are few. In that instant Felder put his hand on the arm of the staring man and drew him to the door of the hotel.

"Inside, quickly!" he said under his breath, for a rumble from the crowd told him the girl had left the balcony above. He pushed the other through the doorway and turned for a second on the threshold.

"Whatever private feelings you may have," he said in a tone that all heard, "don't disgrace the town. Fair play—no matter who he is! McGinn, I should think you, at least, were big enough to settle your grudges without the help of a crowd."

The freighter reddened angrily for a second, then with a shame-faced laugh, shrugged his shoulders and turned away. The lawyer went in, shutting the hotel door behind him.

CHAPTER XVI THE AWAKENING

The man whose part the lawyer had taken had yielded to his touch almost dazedly as the girl disappeared. The keen, pleasurable tang of danger which had leaped in his blood when he faced the enmity of the crowded street—the reckless zest with which he would have met any odds and any outcome with the same smile, and gone down if need be fighting like the tiger in the jungle—had been pierced through by that look from the balcony. His poise for a puzzling moment had been shaken, his self-command overthrown. Feeling a dull sense of anger at the curious embarrassment upon him, he went slowly through the office to the desk, and with his back to the room, lit a cigar.

The action was half mechanical, but to the men gathered at the windows, as they got down from the chairs on which they had been standing, interested spectators of the proceedings outside, it seemed a pose of gratuitous insolence. Tom Felder, entering, saw it with something of resentment.

"That was a close squeak," he said. "Do you realize that? In five minutes more you'd have been handled a sight worse than you handled your man, let me tell you!"

The man of no memories smiled, the same smile that had infuriated the bar-room—and yet somehow it was more difficult to smile now.

"Is it possible," he asked, "that through an unlucky error I have trounced the local archbishop?"

Felder looked at him narrowly. Beneath the sarcasm he distinguished unfamiliarity, aloofness, a genuine astonishment. The appearance in the person of Hugh Stires of the qualities of nerve and courage had surprised him out of his usual indifference. The "tinhorn gambler" had fought like a man. His present *sang-froid* was as singular. Had he been an absolute stranger in the town he might have acted and spoken no differently. Felder's smooth-shaven, earnest face was puzzled as he answered curtly:

"You've trounced a man who will remember it a long time."

"Ah?" said the man addressed easily. "He has a better memory than I, then!"

He gazed over the heads of the silent roomful to the simmering street where Devlin, with the aid of a supporting arm, was staggering into the saloon in which

his humiliation had begun. "They seem agitated," he said. The feeling of embarrassment was passing, the old daring was lifting. His glance, scanning the room, set itself on a shabby, blear figure in the background, apologetic yet keenly and pridefully interested. A whimsical light was in his eye. He crossed to him and, reaching out his hand, drew the violin from under his arm.

"Music hath charms to soothe the savage breast," he said, and, opening the door, he tucked the instrument under his chin and began to play.

What absolute contempt of danger, what insane prompting possessed him, can scarcely be imagined. As he stood there on the threshold with that veiled smile, he seemed utterly careless of consequence, beckoning attack, flaunting an egregious impertinence in the face of anger and dislike. Felder looked for a quick end to the folly, but he saw the men in the street, even as they moved forward, waver and pause. With almost the first note, it had come to them that they were hearing music such as the squeaking fiddles of the dance-halls never knew. Those on the opposite pavement crossed over, and men far down the street stood still to listen.

More than the adept's cunning, that had at first tingled in his fingers at sight of the instrument, was in

Harry Sanderson's playing. The violin had been the single passion which the old Satan Sanderson had carried with him into the new career. The impulse to "soothe the savage breast" had been a flare of the old character he had been reliving; but the music, begun in bravado, swept him almost instantly beyond its bounds. He had never been an indifferent performer; now he was playing as he had never played in his life, with inspiration and abandon. There was a diabolism in it. He had forgotten the fight, the crowd, his own mocking mood. He had forgotten where he was. He was afloat on a fluctuant tide of melody that was carrying him back—back—into the far-away past—toward all that he had loved and lost!

"It's *Home, Sweet Home*," said Barney McGinn,—"no, it's *Annie Laurie*. No, it's—hanged if I know what it is!"

The player himself could not have told him. He was in a kind of tranced dream. The self-made music was calling with a sweet insistence to buried things that were stirring from a long sleep. It sent a gulp into the throat of more than one standing moveless in the street. It brought a suspicious moisture to Tom Felder's eyes. It drew Mrs. Halloran from the kitchen, wiping her hands on her apron. It called to a girl who crouched in

the upper hall with her miserable face buried in her hands, drew her down the stair to the office door, her eyes wide with a breathless wonder, her face glistening with feeling.

From the balcony Jessica had witnessed the fight without understanding its meaning. A fascination she could not gainsay had glued her eyes to the struggle. It was he—it was the face she knew, seen but once for a single moment in the hour of her marriage, but stamped indelibly upon her memory. It was no longer smooth-shaven, and it was changed, evilly changed. But it was the same! There was recklessness and mockery in it, and yet strength, not weakness. Shunned and despised as he might be—the chief actor, as it seemed to her, in a cheap and desperate bar-room affray, a coarse affair of fisticuffs in the public street—yet there was something intrepid in his bearing, something splendid in his victory. In spite of the sharp, momentary sense of antagonism that had bruised her inmost fiber, when the brutal bulk of his opponent fell she could have wept with relief! Then, suddenly, she had found that look chaining her own. It had given her a strange thrill, had both puzzled and touched her. She had dragged her eyes away with a choking sensation, a sense of helplessness and capture. When the violin sounded, a resistless

rush of feeling had swept her to the lower door, where she stood behind the spectators, spellbound.

In the man who played, weird forces were contending. The feel of the polished wood on his cheek, the odor of the resined catgut in his nostrils, were plucking, plucking at the closed door. A new note crept to the strings. They had spoken pathos—now they told of pain. All the struggle whose very meaning was forgotten, the unrequital, the baffled quest, the longing of that last year which had been born of a woman's kiss in a darkened room, never voiced in that lost life, poured forth broken, inarticulate.

To Jessica, standing with hands close-clasped, it seemed the agony of remorse for a past fall, the cry of a forlorn soul, knowing itself cast out, appealing to its good angel for pity and pardon. Hugh had often played to her, lightly, carelessly, as he did all things. She had deemed it only one of his many clever, amateurish accomplishments. Now it struck her with a pang that there had been in him a deeper side that she had not guessed. Since her wedding-day she had thought of her marriage as a loathed bond, from which his false pretense had absolved her. Now a doubt of her own position assailed her. Had loneliness and outlawry driven him into the career that had made him shunned even in this

rough town—a course which she, had she been faithful to her vow "for better, for worse," might have turned to his redemption? God forgave, but she had not forgiven! Smarting tears scorched her eyelids.

For Harry Sanderson the music was the imprisoned memory, crying out strongly in the first tongue it had found. But the ear was alien, the mind knew no by-path of understanding. It was a blind wave, feeling round some under-sea cavern of suffering. Beneath the pressure the closed door yielded, though it did not wholly open. The past with its memories remained hidden, but through the rift, miraculously called by the melody, the real character that had been the Reverend Henry Sanderson came forth. The perplexed phantom that had been moving down the natural declivity of resurrected predisposition, fell away. The slumbering qualities that had stirred uneasily at sight of the face on the balcony, awoke. Who he was and had been he knew no more than before; but the new writhing self-consciousness, starting from its sleep, with almost a sense of shock, became conscious of the gaping crowd, the dusty street, the red sunset, and of himself at the end of a vulgar brawl, sawing a violin in silly braggadocio in a hotel doorway.

The music faltered and broke off. The bow dropped at his feet. He picked it up fumblingly and turned back

into the office, as a man entered from a rear door. The new-comer was Michael Halloran, the hotel's proprietor, short, thick-set and surly. Asleep in his room, he had neither seen the fracas nor heard the playing. He saw instantly, however, that something unusual was forward, and, blinking on the threshold, caught sight of the man who was handing the violin back to its owner. He clenched his fist with a scowl and started toward him.

His wife caught his arm.

"Oh, Michael, Michael!" she cried. "Say nothing, lad! Ye should have heard him play!"

"Play!" he exclaimed. "Let him go fiddle to his side-partner Prendergast and the other riffraff he's run with the year past!" He turned blackly to Harry. "Take yourself from this house, Hugh Stires!" he said. "Whether all's true that's said of you I don't say, but you'll not come here!"

Harry had turned very white. With the spoken name—a name how familiar!—his eyes had fallen to the ring on his finger—the ring with the initials H. S. A sudden comprehension had darted to his mind. A score of circumstances that had seemed odd stood out now in a baleful light. The looks of dislike in the bar-room—the attitude of the street—this angry diatribe—all smacked of acquaintance, and not alone acquaintance, but

obloquy. His name was Hugh Stires! He belonged to this very town! And he was a man hated, despised, forbidden entrance to an uncouth hostelry, an unwelcome visitant even in a bar-room!

An hour earlier the discovery would not so have appalled him. But the violin music, in the emergence of the real Harry Sanderson, had, as it were, flushed the mind of its turgid silt of devil-may-care and left it quick and quivering. He turned to Felder and said in a low voice—to him, not to the hotel-keeper, or to the roomful:

"When I entered this town to-day, I did not know my name, or that I had ever set foot in it before. I was struck by a train a month ago, and remember nothing beyond that time. It seems that the town knows me better than I know myself."

Halloran looked about him with a laugh of derision and incredulity, but few joined in it. Those who had heard the playing realized that in some eerie way the personality of the man they had known had been altered. Before the painful, shocked intensity of his face, the lawyer felt his instant skepticism fraying. This was little like acting! He felt an inclination to hold out his hand, but something held him back.

Harry Sanderson turned quietly and walked out of the door. Pavement and street were a hubbub of excited talk. The groups parted as he came out, and he passed between them with eyes straight before him.

As he turned down the street, a fragment of quartz, thrown with deliberate and venomous aim, flew from the saloon doorway. It grazed his head, knocking off his hat.

Tom Felder had seen the flying missile, and he leaped to the center of the street with rage in his heart. "If I find out who threw that," he said, "I'll send him up for it, so help me God!"

Harry stooped and picked up his hat, and as he put it on again, turned a moment toward the crowd. Then he walked on, down the middle of the street, his eyes glaring, his face white, into the dusky blue of the falling twilight.

CHAPTER XVII AT THE TURN OF THE TRAIL

The scene in the hotel office had left Jessica in a state of mental distraction in which reason was in abeyance. In the confusion she had slipped into the little sitting-room unnoticed, feeling a sense almost of physical sickness, to sit in the half-light, listening to the diminishing noises of the spilling crowd. She was wind-swept, storm-tossed, in the grip of primal emotions. The surprise had shocked her, and the strange appeal of the violin had disturbed her equipoise.

The significant words of awakening spoken in the office had come to her distinctly. In their light she had read the piteous puzzle of that gaze that had held her motionless on the balcony. Hugh had forgotten the past—all of it, its crime, its penalty. In forgetting the past, he had forgotten even her, his wife! Yet in some mysterious way her face had been familiar to him; it had touched for an instant the spring of the befogged memory.

As she spurred through the transient twilight past

the selvage of the town and into the somber mountain slope, she struck the horse sharply with her crop. He who had entrapped her, who had married her under the shadow of a criminal act, who had broken her future with his, when his whole bright life had crashed down in black ruin—could such a one look as he had looked at her? Could he make such music that had wrung her heart?

All at once the horse shied violently, almost unseating her. A man was lying by the side of the road, tossing and muttering to himself. She forced the unwilling animal closer, and, leaning from the saddle, saw who it was. In a moment she was off and beside the prostrate form, a spasm of dread clutching at her throat at sight of the nerveless limbs, the chalky pallor of the brow, the fever spots in the cheeks.

A wave of pity swept over her. He was ill and alone; he could not be left there—he must have shelter. She looked fearfully about her. What could she do? In that town, whose intolerance and dislike she had seen so actively demonstrated, was there no one who would care for him? She turned her head, listening to a nearing sound—footsteps were plodding up the road. She called, and presently a pedestrian emerged from the half-dark and came toward her.

He bent over the form she showed him.

"It's Stires," he said with a chuckle. "I heard he'd come back." The chuckle turned to a cough, and he shook his head. "This is sad! You could never believe how I have labored with the boy, but"—he turned out his hands—"you see, there is the temptation. It is his unhappy weakness."

Jessica remembered the yellow, smirking face now. She had passed him on the day Tom Felder had walked with her from the Mountain Valley House, and the lawyer had told her he lived in the cabin just below the Knob, where she so often sat. She felt a quiver of repulsion.

"He is not intoxicated," she said coldly. "He is ill. You know him, then?"

"Know him!" he echoed, and laughed—a dry, cackling laugh. "I ought to. And I guess he knows me." He shook the inert arm. "Get up, Hugh!" he said. "It's Prendergast!"

There flashed through her mind the phrase of the surly hotel-keeper: "His side-partner, Prendergast!" Could it be? Had Hugh really lived in the cabin on which she had so often peered down during those past weeks? And with this chosen crony!

She touched Prendergast's arm. "He is ill, I say,"

she repeated. "He must be cared for at once. Your cabin is on the hillside, isn't it?"

"*His* cabin," he corrected. "A rough place, but it has sheltered us both. I am but guide, philosopher and friend."

She bit her lips. "Lift him on my horse," she said. She stooped and put her hands under the twitching shoulders. "I will help you. I am quite strong."

With her aid he lifted the swaying form on to the saddle and supported it while Jessica led the way up the darkening road.

"Here is the cut-off," he said presently. "Ah, you know it!" for she had turned into the side-path that led along the hill, under the gray, snake-like flume—the shortest route to the grassy shelf on which the cabin stood.

The by-way was steep and rugged, and rhododendron clumps caught at her ankles, and once she heard a snake slip over the dry rustle of leaves, but she went on rapidly, dragging at the bridle, turning back now and then anxiously to urge the horse to greater speed. She scarcely heard the offensively honied compliments which Prendergast offered to her courage and resource. Her pulses were throbbing unsteadily, her mind in a ferment.

It seemed an eternity they climbed; in reality it was

scarcely twenty minutes before they reached the grassy knoll and the cabin whose crazy swinging door stood wide to the night air. She tied the horse, went in and at Prendergast's direction found matches and lit a candle. The bare, two-room interior it revealed, was unkempt and disordered.

Rough bunks, a table and a couple of hewn chairs were almost its only furniture. The window was broken and the roof admitted sun and rain. Prendergast laid the man they had brought on one of the bunks and threw over him a shabby blanket.

"My dear young lady," he said, "you are a good Samaritan. How shall we thank you, my poor friend here and I?"

Jessica had taken money from her pocket and now she held it out to him. "He must have a doctor," she said. "You must fetch one."

The yellow eyes fastened on the bill, even while his gesture protested. "You shame me!" he exclaimed. "And yet you are right; it is for him." He folded it and put it into his pocket. "As soon as I have built a fire, I will go for our local *medico*. He will not always come at the call of the luckless miner. All are not so charitable as you."

He untied her horse and extended a hand, but she mounted without his help. "He will thank you one

day—this friend of mine," he said, "far better than I can do."

"It is not at all necessary to tell him," she replied frigidly. "The sick are always to be helped, in every circumstance."

She gave her horse the rein as she spoke and turned him up the steep path that climbed back of the cabin, past the Knob, and so by a narrow trail to the mountain road.

Emmet Prendergast stood listening to the dulling hoof-beats a moment, then reëntered the cabin. The man on the bunk had lifted to a sitting position, his eyes were open, dazed and staring.

"That's right," the older man said. "You're coming round. How does it feel to be back in the old shebang? Can't guess how you got here, can you? You were towed on horseback by a beauty, Hughey, my boy—a rip-staving beauty! I'll tell you about it in the morning, if you're good."

The man he addressed made no answer; his eyes were on the other, industrious and bewildered.

"I heard about the row," went on Prendergast. "They didn't think it was in you, and neither did I." He looked at him cunningly. "Neither did Moreau, eh, eh? You're a clever one, Hugh, but the lost-memory racket

won't stand you in anything. You hadn't any call to get scared in the first place—*I* don't tell all I know!"

He shoved the candle nearer on the table. "There's a queer look in your face, Hugh!" he said, with a clumsy attempt at kindness. "That rock they threw must have hurt you. Feel sort of dizzy, eh? Never mind, I'll show you a sight for sore eyes. You went off without your share of the last swag, but I've saved it for you. Prendergast wouldn't cheat a pal!"

From a cranny in the clay-chinked wall he took a chamois-skin bag. It contained a quantity of gold-dust and small nuggets, which he poured into a miner's scales on the table and proceeded to divide in two portions. This accomplished, he emptied one of the portions on to a paper and pushed it out.

"That's yours," he said.

Harry's eyes were on his with a piercing intensity now, as though they looked through him to a vast distance beyond. He was staring through a gray mist, at something far off but significant that eluded his direct vision. The board table, the yellow gold, the flickering candle-light recalled something horrifying, in some other world, in some other life, millions of ages ago.

He lurched to his feet, overturning the table. The gold-dust rattled to the floor.

"Your deal!" he said. Then with a vague laugh, he fell sidewise upon the bunk.

Emmet Prendergast stared at him with a look of amazement on his yellow face. "He's crazy as a chicken!" he said.

He sat watching him a while, then rose and kindled a fire on the unswept hearth. From a litter of cans and dented utensils in a corner he proceeded to cook himself supper, after which he carefully brushed up the scattered gold-dust and returned it all to its hiding-place. Lastly he rummaged on a shelf and found a phial; this proved to be empty, however, and he set it on the table.

"I guess you'll do well enough without any painkiller," he said to himself. "Doctors are expensive. Anyway, I'll be back by midnight."

He threw more wood on the fire, blew out the candle, and, closing the door behind him, set off down the trail to the town—where a faro-bank soon acquired the bill Jessica had given him.

CHAPTER XVIII THE STRENGTH OF THE WEAK

It was pitch-dark when Jessica reached the sanatorium, though she went like a whirlwind, the chill damp smell of the dewy balsams in her nostrils, the dust rising ghost-like behind the rapid hoofs. She found David Stires anxious and peevish over her late coming.

Sitting beside him as he ate his supper, and reading to him afterward, she had little time for coherent thought; all the while she was maintaining her self-control with an effort. Since she had ridden away that afternoon, she felt as if years had gone over her with all their changes. She was oppressed with a new sense of fate, of power beyond and stronger than herself, and her mind was enveloped in a haze of futurity. She felt a relief when the old man grew tired and was wheeled to his bedroom.

Left alone, her reflections returned. She began to be tortured. She tried to read—the printed characters swam beyond her comprehension. At length she drew a hood over her head and stole out on to the wide porch.

It was only nine o'clock, and along the gravel paths that wound among the shrubbery a few dim forms were strolling—she caught the scent of a cigar and the sound of a woman's laugh. The air was crisp and bracing, with a promise of frost and painted leaves. She gazed down across the dark gulches toward the town, a straggling design pricked in blinking yellow points. Halfway between, folded in the darkness, lay the green shelf and the cabin to which her thought recurred with a kind of compulsion.

Her eyes searched the darkness anxiously. He had seemed dangerously ill; he might die, perhaps. If he did, what would it be for her, his wife, but freedom from a galling bond? She thought of the violin playing. Had that been but the soul's swan-song, the last cry of his stained and desolate spirit before it passed from this world that knew its temptation and its fall? If she could only know what the doctor had said!

There was no moon, but the stars were glowing like tiny, green-gilt coals, and the yellow road lay plain and clear. With a sudden determination she drew her light cloak closely about her, stepped down, sped across the grass to a footpath, and so to the road.

As she ran on down the curving stretch under the trees, moving like a hastening, gray phantom through a
purple world of shadows, the crackling slip of bank-paper that lay in her bosom seemed to burn her flesh. She was stealing away to gaze upon the outcast who had shamed and humbled her—going, she knew not why, with burning cheeks and hammering heart.

She slipped through the side trail to the cabin with a choking sensation. She stole to the window and peered in—in the firelight she could see the form on the bunk, tossing and muttering. Otherwise the place was empty. She lifted the latch softly and entered.

The strained anxiety of Jessica's look relaxed as she gazed about her. She saw the phial on the table—the doctor had been there, then. If he were in serious case, Prendergast would be with him. She threw back her hood, drew one of the chairs to the side of the bunk and sat down, her eyes fixed on his face. The weakness and helplessness of his posture struck through and through her. Two sides of her were struggling in a chaotic combat for mastery.

"I hate you! I hate you!" she said under her breath, clenching her cold hand. "I *must* hate you! You stole my love and put it under your feet! You have disgraced my present and ruined my future! What if you have forgotten the past—your crime? Does that make you the less guilty, or me the less wretched?"

But withal a silent voice within her gave the lie to her vehemence. Some element of her character that had been rigid and intact was crumbling down. An old, sweet something, that a dreadful mill had ground and crushed and annihilated, was rising whole and undefiled, superior to any petty distinction, regardless of all that lifted combative in her inheritance, not to be gainsaid or denied.

She leaned closer, listening to the incoherent words and broken phrases borne on the turbid channels of fever. But she could not link them together into meaning. Only one name he spoke clearly over and over again—the name Hugh Stires—repeated with the dreary monotony of a child conning a lesson. She noted the mark across his brow. Before her marriage, in her blindness, she had used to wonder what it was like. It was not in the least disfiguring—it gave a touch of the extraordinary. It was so small she did not wonder that in that ecstatic moment of her bride's kiss she had not seen it.

Slowly, half fearfully, she stretched out her hand and laid it on his. As if at the touch the mutterings ceased. The eyes opened, and a confused, troubled look crept to them. Then they closed again, and the look faded out into a peace that remained.

Jessica dropped to her knees and buried her face in the blanket, burning and chilling with an indescribable sensation of mingled pain and pleasure. She scarcely knew what she was thinking. It seemed to her that his very weakness and helplessness voiced again the something that had sounded in the music of the violin, when the buried, forgotten past had cried out its pain and shame and plea, half unconsciously—to her! A thrill ran through her, the sense of moral power of the weak over the strong, of the feminine over the masculine.

A rising flush stained her cheeks. With a sudden impulse, and with a guilty backward glance, she bent and touched her lips to his forehead.

She drew back quickly, her face flooded with color, caught her breath, then, drawing her hood over her head, went swiftly to the door and was swallowed up in the darkness.

CHAPTER XIX THE EVIL EYE

Harry Sanderson, harking back from the perilous pathway of fever, was to see himself in the light of reawakened instincts. The man of no memories, in his pointless wanderings, had felt dissatisfaction, a fierce resentment, a savage unrest, but morally he had not suffered. The spiritual elements of the maturer growth had slept. At a woman's look they had awakened, to rise to full stature under the strange spell of melody. When the real, remorseful nature, newly emerged, found itself an object of animadversion and contempt, face to face with a past of shame and reproach, the shock had been profound. The stirring of the old conscience was as painful as is the first gasp of air to the drowned lung. It had thrown the brain into a fever to whose fierce onslaught the body had temporarily succumbed.

When, toward midnight, the fever ebbed, he had fallen into a deep sleep of exhaustion, from which he opened his eyes next morning upon the figure of Prendergast, sitting pipe in mouth in the sunny doorway.

He lifted himself on his elbow. That crafty face had been inexplicably woven with the delirious fantasies of his fever. Where and when had he known it? Then in a great wave welled over him the memory of his last conscious hours—the scene in the saloon, the fight, the music, the sudden appalling discovery of his name and repute. He remembered the sickening wave of self-disgust, the fierce agony of resentment that had beat in his every vein as he walked up the darkening street. He remembered the thrown quartz. No doubt another missile had struck home, or he had been set upon, kicked and pommelled into insensibility. This old man—a miner probably, for there were picks and shovels in the corner—had succored him. He had been ill, there was lassitude in every limb, and shadowy recollections tantalized him. As in the garish day one mistily recalls a dream of the night before, he retained a dim consciousness of a woman's face—the face he had seen on the balcony—leaning near him, bringing into a painful disorder a sense of grateful coolness, of fragrance, and of rest.

He turned his head. Through the window he could see the blue, ravined mountain—a slope of verdure soaked in placid, yellow sunshine, rising gradually to the ridge, peaceful and Arcadian.

As he stared again at the seated figure, the grim fact reared like a grisly specter, deriding, thrusting its haggard presence upon him. In this little community, which apparently he had forsaken and to which he had by chance returned, he stood a rogue and a scoundrel, a thing to point the finger at and to avoid! The question that had burned his brain to fire flamed up again. The town despised him. What had been his career? How had he become a pariah? And by what miracle had he been so altered as to look upon himself with loathing?

He was dimly conscious withal that some fundamental change had passed over him, though how or when he could not tell. Some mysterious moral alchemy had transmuted his elements. What he had been he was no more. He was no longer even the man who had awakened in the box-car. Yet the debts of the unknown yesterday must be paid in the coin of the known to-day!

He lifted himself upright, dropping his feet to the floor. At the movement the man on the doorstep rose quickly and came forward.

"You're better, Hugh," he said. "Take it easy, though. Don't get up just yet—I'm going to cook you some breakfast." He turned to the hearth, kicked the smoldering log-ends together and set a saucepan on

them. "You'll be stronger when you've got something between your ribs," he added.

"How long have I been lying here?" asked Harry.

"Only since last night. You've had a fever."

"Where is my dog?"

"Dog?" said the other. "I never knew you had one."

Harry's lips set bitterly. It had fared more hardly, then, than he. It had been a ready object for the crowd to wreak their hatred upon, because it belonged to him—because it was Hugh Stires' dog! He leaned back a moment against the cabin wall, with closed eyes, while Prendergast stirred the heating mixture, which gave forth a savory aroma.

"Is this your cabin, my friend?"

The figure bending over the hearth straightened itself with a jerk and the blinking yellow eyes looked hard at him. Prendergast came close to the bunk.

"That's the game you played in the town," he said with a surly sneer. "It's all right for those that take it in, but you needn't try to bamboozle me, pretending you don't know your own claim and cabin! I'm no such fool!"

A dull flush came to Harry's face. Here was a page from that iniquitous past that faced him. His own cabin? And his own claim? Well, why not?

"You are mistaken," he said calmly. "I am not pretending. I can not remember you."

Prendergast laughed in an ugly, derisive way. "I suppose you've forgotten the half-year we've lived here together, and the gold-dust we've gathered in now and again—slipped it all, have you?"

Harry stood up. The motion brought a temporary dizziness, but it passed. He walked to the door and gazed out on the pleasant green of the hillside. On a tree near-by was nailed a rough, weather-beaten board on which was scrawled "The Little Paymaster Claim." He saw the grass-grown gravel-trenches, evidence of abandoned work. He had been a miner. That in itself was honest toil. Across the waving foliage he could look down to the distant straggling street with its huddles of houses and its far-off swinging signs. Some of these signs hung above resorts of clicking wheels and green baize tables; more than once in the past month on such tables he had doubled many times over a paltry stake with that satiric luck which smiles on the uncaring. His eye ran back up the slope.

"The claim is good, then," he said over his shoulder. "We found the pay?"

Prendergast contemplated him a moment in grim silence, with a scowl. "You're either really fuddled,

Hugh," he said then, "or else you're a star play-actor, and up to something deep. Well, have it your own way—it's all the same to me. But you can't pull the wool over my eyes long!"

There was mockery and threat in his tone, but more than both, the evil intimacy in his words gave Harry a qualm of disgust. This man had been his associate. That one hour in the town had shown him what his own life there had been.

What should he do? Forsake for ever the neighborhood where he had made his blistering mark? Fling all aside and start again somewhere? And leave behind this disgraceful present, with that face that had looked into his from above the dusty street?

If fate intended that, why had it turned him back? Why had he been plucked rudely from his purpose and set once more here, where every man's hand was against him—every one but this sorry comrade? There was in him an intuitive obstinacy, a steadfastness under stress which approved this drastic coercion. If such was the bed he had made, he would lie in it. He would drink the gall and vinegar without whimpering. Whatever lay behind, he would live it down. This man at least had befriended him.

He turned into the room. "Perhaps I shall remember

after a while." He took the saucepan from Prendergast's hand. "I'll cook the breakfast," he said.

Prendergast filled his pipe and watched him. "I guess there *are* bats in your belfry, sure enough, Hugh," he said at length. "You never offered to do your stint before."

CHAPTER XX MRS. HALLORAN TELLS A STORY

From the moment her kiss fell upon the forehead of the delirious man in the cabin, Jessica began to be a prey to new emotions, the significance of which she did not comprehend. She was no longer a child; she had attained to womanhood on that summer's wedding-day that seemed so far away. But her woman's heart was untried, and it felt itself opening to this new experience with a strange confusion.

That kiss, she told herself that night, had been given to her dead ideal, that had lain there in its purifying grave-clothes of forgetfulness. Yet it burned on her lips, as that other kiss in a darkened room had burned afterward, but with a sense of pleasure, not of hurt. It took her back into crimson meadows with her lost girlhood and its opaled outlook—and Hugh. Then the warring emotions racked her again; she felt a whirl of anger at herself, of hot impatience, of mortification, of self-pity, and of stifled longing for she knew not what.

But largest of all in her mind next day was anxiety.

She must know how he fared. In the open daylight she could not approach the cabin, but she reflected that the doctor had been there, and no doubt had carried some report of him to the town. So, as the morning grew, she rode down the mountain, ostensibly to get the cherry cordial she had left behind her the day before—really to satisfy her hunger for news.

As it happened, Mrs. Halloran's first greeting set her anxiety at rest. Prendergast had bought some tobacco at the general store an hour before, while she had been making her daily order, and the store-keeper had questioned him. Prendergast had a fawning liking for the notice of his fellows—save for his saloon cronies, few enough in the town, where it was currently reported that he had a prison record in Arkansas, ever exchanged more than a nod with him—and he had responded eagerly to the civil inquiries. To an interested audience he had told of the finding of Hugh on the mountain road in a sort of crazy fever, and enlarged upon the part the girl on horseback had played. Hugh was all right now, he said, except that he didn't remember him, or the cabin, or Smoky Mountain.

Here was new interest. Though her name was known to few, Jessica had come to be a familiar figure on the streets—she was the only lady rider the place knew

—and the description was readily recognizable without the name which Mrs. Halloran supplied. In an hour the story had found a hundred listeners, and as Jessica rode by that day, many a passer-by had turned to gaze after her.

What Prendergast had said Mrs. Halloran told her in a breath. Before she finished she found that Jessica had not heard of the incident in the saloon which had precipitated the fight with Devlin, and with sympathetic rhetoric Mrs. Halloran told this, too.

"He deserved it, ye see, dearie," she finished. "But no less was it a brave thing that—what ye did last night, alone on the mountain with them two, an' countin' yerself as safe as if ye were in God's pocket! To hear that scalawag Prendergast talk, he's been Hugh Stires' good angel—the oily hypocrite! An' do ye think it's true that he's lost his memory—Stires, I mean—an' don't know nothin' that's ever happened with him? Could that be, do ye think?"

"I've often heard of such a thing, Mrs. Halloran," responded Jessica. Her heart was throbbing painfully. "But why does Smoky Mountain hate him so? What has he done?"

Mrs. Halloran shook her head. "I never knew anything myself," she said judiciously. "I reckon the town

allus counted him just a general low-down. The rest is only suspicion an' give the dog a bad name."

There had been comfort for Jessica in this interview. The burden of that illness off her mind—she had not realized how great a load this had been till it was lifted—she turned eagerly toward this rift in the cloud of infamy that seemed to envelop the reputation of the man whose life her own had again so strangely touched. She was feeling a new kinship with the town; it was now not alone a spot upon which she had loved to gaze from the height; it was the place wherein the man she had once loved had lived and moved.

Mrs. Halloran's story had materially increased the poignant force of her pity. What had seemed to her a vulgar brawl, had been in reality a courageous and unselfish championship of a defenseless outcast. Thinking of this, the self-blame and contrition which she had felt when she listened to the violin assailed her anew, till she seemed a very part of the guilt, an equal sinner by omission.

Yet she rode homeward that day with almost a light heart.

CHAPTER XXI A VISIT AND A VIOLIN

Prendergast's first view had been one of suspicion, but this had been shaken, and thereafter he had studied Harry with a sneering tolerance. There had been little talk between them during the meal which the younger man had cooked, taking the saucepan from the other's hands. Shrinking acutely from the details of the dismal past which he must learn, Harry had asked no questions and Prendergast had maintained a morose silence. The latter had soon betaken himself down the mountain—to his audience in the general store.

As Harry stood in the cabin doorway, looking after him, toward the town glistening far below in the morning sunlight, he thought bitterly of his reception there.

"They all knew me," he thought; "every one knew me, on the street, in the hotel. They know me for what I have been to them. Yet to me it is all a blank! What shameful deeds have I done?" He shrank from memory now! "What was I doing so far away, where was I going, on the night when I was picked up beside the

railroad track? I may be a drunkard," he said to himself. "No, in the past month I have drunk hard, but not for the taste of the liquor! I may be a gambler—the first thing I remember is that game of cards in the box-car! I may be a cheat, a thief. Yet how is it possible for bad deeds to be blotted out and leave no trace? Actions breed habit, if they do not spring from it, and habit, automatically repeated, becomes character. I feel no inherent propensity to rob, or defraud. Shall I? Will these things come back to me if my memory does? Shall I become once more one with this vile old man, my 'side-partner,' to share the evil secrets that I see in his eyes—as I must once have shared them?" He shuddered.

There welled over him again, full force, the passionate resentment, the agony of protest, that had been the gift of the resuscitated character. He found himself fighting a wild desire to fling his resolution behind him and fly from his reputation and its penalties.

In the battle that he fought now he turned, even in his weakness, to manual labor, striving to dull his thought with mechanical movement. He cleaned and put to rights both rooms and sorted their litter of odds and ends. But at times the inclination to escape became well-nigh insupportable. When the conflict was

fiercest he would think of a girl's face, once seen, and the thought would restrain him. Who was she? Why had her look pierced through him?

In that hateful career that seemed so curiously alien, could she have had a part?

He did not know that she of whom he wondered, in the bitterest of those hours had been very near him—that on her way up the mountain she had stolen down to the Knob to look through the parted bushes to the cabin with the blue spiral rising from its chimney. He could not guess that she gazed with a strained, agitated interest, a curiosity even more intense than his own, the look of a heart that was strangely learning itself with mingled and tremulous emotions.

Though the homely task to which he turned failed to allay his struggle, by nightfall Harry had put the warring elements under. When Prendergast returned at supper-time the candle was lighted in its wall-box, the dinted tea-kettle was singing over a crackling fire, and Harry was perspiring over the scouring of the last utensil.

Prendergast looked the orderly interior over on the threshold with a contemptuous amusement. "Almost thought I was in church," he said. He took off his coat and lazily watched the other cook the frugal evening meal. "Excuse my not volunteering," he observed; "you do it so nicely I'm almost afraid you'll have another attack of that forgettery of yours, and go back to the old line."

Presently he looked at the bunk, clean and springy with fresh cut spruce-shoots. He went to it, knelt down and thrust an arm into the empty space beneath it. He got up hastily.

"What have you done with that?" he demanded with an angry snarl.

"With what?" Harry turned his head, as he set two tin plates on the bare table.

"With what was under here."

"There was nothing there but an old horse skin," said Harry. "It is hanging on the side of the cabin."

With an oath Prendergast flung open the door and went outside. He reëntered quickly with the white hide in his arms, wrapped it in a blanket and thrust it back under the bunk.

"Has any one been here to-day—since you put it out there?" he asked quickly.

"No," said Harry, surprised. "Why?"

Prendergast chuckled. The chuckle grew to a guffaw and he sat down, slapping his thigh. Presently he went to the wall, took the chamois-skin bag from its hiding-place and poured some of its yellow contents into his palm. "That's why. Do you remember that, eh?"

Harry looked at it. "Gold-dust," he said. "I seem to recall that. I am going to begin work in the trench to-morrow; there should be more where that came from."

Prendergast poured the gold back into the bag with a cunning look. The other had asked for no share of it. At that moment he decided to say nothing of the evening before, of the girl or the horseback journey—lest Hugh, cudgelling his brains, might remember he had been offered a half. If Hugh's peculiar craziness wanted to dig in the dirt, very well. It might be profitable for them both. He put the pouch into his pocket with a grin.

"There's plenty more where that came from, all right," he said, "and I'll teach you again how to get it, one of these days."

Prendergast said little during the meal. When the table was cleared he lit his pipe and took from a shelf a board covered with penciled figures and scrutinized it.

"Hope you remember how to play old sledge," he said. "When we stopped last game you owed me a little over seventeen thousand dollars. If you forget it isn't a cash game some day and pay up, why, I won't kick," he added

with rough jocularity. He threw a pack of cards on to the table and drew up the chairs.

Harry did not move. As they ate he had been wondering how long he could abide that sinister presence. The garish cards themselves now smote him with a shrinking distaste. As he was about to speak a knock came at the cabin door and Prendergast opened it.

The visitor Harry recognized instantly; it was the man who had called for fair play at the fight before the saloon, who had drawn him into the hotel.

Felder carried a bundle under his arm. He nodded curtly to Prendergast and addressed himself to Harry.

"I am the bearer of a gift from some one in the town," he said. "I have been asked to deliver this to you." He put the bundle into the other's hands.

Harry drew up one of the chairs hastily. "Please sit down," he said courteously. He looked at the bundle curiously. "*Et eos dona ferentes*," he said slowly. "A gift from some one in the town!"

A keen surprise flashed into the lawyer's glance. "The quotation is classic," he said, "but it need not apply here." He took the bundle, unwrapped it and disclosed a battered violin. "Let me explain," he continued. "For the owner of this you fought a battle yesterday. You tested its tone a little later—it seems that you are a

master of the most difficult of instruments. There was a time, I believe, when the old man was its master also; he was once, they say, the conductor of an orchestra in San Francisco. Drink and the devil finally brought him down. For three years past he has lived in Smoky Mountain. Nobody knows his name—the town has always called him 'Old Despair.' You did him what is perhaps the first real kindness he has ever known at its hands. He has done the only thing he could to requite it."

Harry had colored painfully as Felder began to speak. The words brought back that playing and its strange rejuvenescence of emotion, with acute vividness. His voice was unsteady as he answered:

"I appreciate it—I am deeply grateful—but it is quite impossible that I accept it from him."

"You need not hesitate," said the lawyer. "Old Despair needs it no longer. He died last night in Devlin's dance-hall, where he played—when he was sober enough—for his lodging. I happened to be near-by, and I assure you it was his express wish that I give the violin to you."

Rising, he held out his hand. "Good night," he said. "I hope your memory will soon return. The town is much interested in your case."

The flush grew deeper in Harry's cheek, though he saw there was nothing ironical in the remark. "I scarcely hope so much," he replied. "I am learning that forgetfulness has its advantages."

As the door closed behind the visitor, Prendergast kicked the chair back to the table.

"You're getting on!" he sneered, his oily tone forgotten. "Damn his impertinence! He didn't offer to shake with *me*! Come on and play."

Harry opened the door again and sat down on the cool step, the violin in his hands.

"I think I don't care for the cards to-night," he said. "I'd rather play this."

CHAPTER XXII THE PASSING OF PRENDERGAST

The little town had been unconsciously grateful for its new sensation. The return of Hugh Stires and his apparent curious transformation was the prime subject of conversation. For a half-year the place had known but one other event as startling: that was the finding, some months before, of a dead body—that of a comparative stranger in the place—thrust beneath a thicket on Smoky Mountain, on the very claim which now held Prendergast and his partner.

The "Amen Corner" of the Mountain Valley House had discussed the pros and cons exhaustively. There were many who sneered at the loss of memory and took their cue from Devlin who, smarting from his humiliation and nursing venom, revamped suspicions wherever he showed his battered face. In his opinion Hugh Stires was "playing a slick game."

"Your view is colored by your prejudices, Devlin," said Felder. "He's been a blackleg in the past—granted.

But give the devil his due. As for the other ugly tale, there's no more evidence against him than there is against you or me!"

"They didn't find the body on *my* ground," had been the other's surly retort, "and *I* didn't clear out the day before, either!"

The phenomenon, however, whether credited or pooh-poohed, was a drawing card. More than a few found occasion to climb the mountain by the hillside trail that skirted the lonely cabin. These, as likely as not, saw Prendergast lounging in the doorway smoking, while the younger man worked, leading a trench along the brow of the hill to bring the water from its intake—which Harry's quick eye had seen was practicable—and digging through the shale and gravel to the bed-rock, to the sparse yellow grains that yielded themselves so grudgingly. Some of the pedestrians nodded, a few passed the time of day, and to each Harry returned his exact coin of salutation.

The spectacle of Hugh Stires, who had been used to pass his days in the saloons and his nights in even less becoming resorts, turned practical miner, added a touch of *opera bouffe* to the situation that, to a degree, modulated the rigor of dispraise. It was the consensus of opinion that the new Hugh Stires seemed vastly

different from the old; that if he were "playing a game," it was a curious one.

The casual espionage Prendergast observed with a scowl, as he watched Harry's labors—when he was at the cabin, for after the first few days he spent most of his time in haunts of his own in the town, returning only at meal-time, gruff and surly. Harry, however, recognized nothing unusual in the curious glances. He worked on, intent upon his own problem of dark contrasts.

On the one side was a black record, exemplified in Prendergast, clouded infamy, a shuddering abhorrence of his past self as he saw it through the pitiless lens of public opinion; on the other was a grim constancy of purpose, a passionate wish to reconstruct the warped structure of life of which he found himself the tenant, days of healthful, peace-inspiring toil, a woman's face that threaded his every thought. As he wielded his pick in the trench or laboriously washed out the few glistening grains that now were to mean his daily sustenance, he turned often to gaze up the slope where, set in its foliage, the glass roof of the sanatorium sparkled softly through the Indian haze. Strange that the sight should mysteriously suggest the face that haunted him!

Emmet Prendergast saw the abstracted regard as he came up the trail from the town. He was in an ugly humor. The bag of gold-dust which he had shown to Harry he had not returned to the hiding-place in the wall, and with this in his pocket the faro-table had that day tempted him. The pouch was empty now.

Harry's back was toward him, and the gold-pan in which he had been washing the gravel lay at his feet. With a noiseless, mirthless laugh Prendergast stole into the cabin and reached down from the shelf the bottle into which each day Harry had poured his scanty findings. He weighed it in his hand—almost two ounces, a little less than twenty dollars. He hastily took the empty bag from his pocket.

But just then a shadow darkened the doorway and Harry entered. He saw the action, and, striding forward, took the bottle from the other's hand.

Prendergast turned on him, a sinister snarl under his affectation of surprise. "Can't you attend to your own rat-killing?" he growled. "I guess I've got a right to what I need."

"Not to that," said Harry quietly. "We shall touch the bottom of the flour sack to-morrow. You expect to get your meals here, I presume."

"I still look forward to that pleasure," answered Prendergast with an evil sneer. "Three meals a day and a rotten roof over my head. When I think of the little I have done to deserve it, the hospitality overcomes me! All I have done is to keep you from starving to death and out of quod at the same time. I only taught you a safe way to beat the game—an easier one than you seem to know now—and to live on Easy Street!"

"I am looking for no easy way," responded Harry, "whatever you mean by that. I expect to earn my living as I'm earning it now—it's an honest method, at all events."

"You've grown all-fired particular since you lost your memory," retorted Prendergast, his eyes narrowing. "You'll be turning dominie one of these days! Perhaps you expect to get the town to take up with you, and to make love to the beauty in the green riding-habit that brought you here on her horse the night you were out of your head!"

Harry started. "What do you mean?" he asked thickly.

Prendergast's oily manner was gone now. His savage temper came uppermost.

"I forgot you didn't know about that," he scoffed. "I made a neat story of it in the town. They've been gabbling about it ever since."

Harry caught his breath. As through a mist he saw

again that green habit on the hotel balcony—that face that had haunted his waking consciousness. It had not been Prendergast alone, then, who had brought him here. And her act of charity had been made, no doubt, a thing for the tittering of the town, cheapened by chatter, coarsened by joke!

"I wonder if she'd done it if she'd known all I know," continued the other malevolently. "You'd better go up to the sanatorium, Hugh, and give her a nice sweet kiss for it!"

A lust of rage rose in Harry's throat, but he choked it down. His hand fell like iron on Prendergast's shoulder, and turned him forcibly toward the open door. His other hand pointed, and his suppressed voice said:

"This cabin has grown too small for us both. The town will suit you better."

Prendergast shrank before the wrath-whitened face, the dangerous sparkle in the eyes. "You've got through with me," he glowered, "and you think you can go it alone." The old suspicion leaped in the malicious countenance. "Well, it won't pay you to try it yet. I know too much! Do you understand? *I know too much!*"

Harry went out of the cabin. At the door he turned. "If there is anything you own here," he said, "take it with you. You needn't be here when I come back."

His fingers shaking with the black rage in his heart, Prendergast gathered his few belongings, rolled them in the white horse-skin which he drew from beneath his bunk, and wrapped the whole in a blanket. He fastened the bundle in a pack-strap, slung it over his shoulder, and left the cabin. Harry was seated on one of the gravel-heaps, some distance away, looking out over the valley, his back toward him. As he took the steep path leading toward the little town Prendergast shot the figure an envenomed look.

"What's your scheme, I wonder?" he muttered darkly. "Whatever it is, I'll find out, never fear! And if there's anything in it, you'll come down from that high horse!" He settled his burden and went rapidly down the trail, turning over in his mind his future schemes.

As it chanced, there was one who saw his vindictive face. Jessica, crouched on the Knob, had seen him come and now depart, pack on back, and guessed that the pair had parted company. Her whole being flamed with sympathy. She could see his malignant scowl plainly from where she leaned, screened by the bushes. It terrified her. What had passed between them in the cabin? She left the Knob wondering.

All that evening she was ill at ease. At midnight, sleepless, she was looking out from her bedroom window

across the phantom-peopled shadows, where on the face of the pale sky the stars trembled like slow tears. Anxiety and dread were in her heart; a pale phantom of fear seemed lurking in the shadows; the night was full of dread.

CHAPTER XXIII A RACE WITH DEATH

On the day following the expulsion of Prendergast, Harry woke restless and unrefreshed. Fleeting sensations mocked him—a disturbing conviction that the struggling memory in some measure had succeeded in reasserting itself in the shadowy kingdom of sleep. Waking, the apparitions were fled again into their obscurity, leaving only the wraiths of recollection to startle and disquiet.

A girl's face hovered always before him—ruling his consciousness as it had ruled his sleeping thought. "Is it only fancy?" he asked himself. "Or is it more? It was there—my memory—in shreds and patches, on my sleep; now when I wake, it is only the fraying mist of dreams.... Dreams!" He drew a deep breath. "Yet the overmastering sense of reality remains. Last night I walked in intimate, forgotten ways—and she was in them—*she!*" He flushed, an odd, sensitive flush. "Dreams!" he said. "All dreams and fancies!"

At length he took down from its shelf the bottle he

had rescued from Prendergast's intention and emptied it of its glistening grains—enough to replenish his depleted stock of provisions. He paused a moment as he put on his hat, smiling whimsically, a little sadly. He dreaded entering the town. But there could be no remedy in concealment. If he was to live and work there, appear he must on the streets sooner or later. Smoky Mountain must continue to think of him as it might; what he was from that time on, was all that could count to him.

If he had but known it, there was good reason for hesitation to-day. Early that morning an angry rumor had disturbed the town; the sluice of the hydraulic company had been robbed again. Some two months previously there had occurred a series of depredations by which the company had suffered. The boxes were not swept of their golden harvest each day, and in spite of all precautions, coarse gold had disappeared mysteriously from the riffles—this, although armed men had watched all night. There had been much guess-work. The cabin on the hillside was the nearest habitation—the company's flume disgorged its flood in the gulch beneath it—and suspicion had eventually pointed its way. The sudden ceasing of the robberies with the disappearance of Hugh Stires had given focus to this

suspicion. Now, almost coincident with his return, the thievery had recommenced. It had been a red-letter day for Devlin and his ilk who cavilled at the more charitable. Of all this, however, the object of their "I-told-you-so" was serenely ignorant.

As Harry walked briskly down the mountain, a feeling of unreality stole upon him. The bell was ringing in the steeple of the little Catholic church below, and the high metallic sound came to him with a mysterious and potential familiarity. With the first note, his hand in his pocket closed upon an object he always carried—the little gold cross he had found there when he awakened in the freight-car, the only token he possessed of his vanished past. More than once it had been laid for a mascot on the faro-table or the roulette-board with his last coin. Always it had brought the stake back, till he had gained a whimsical belief in its luck.

He drew it out now and looked at it. "Strange that the sound of a bell always reminds me of that," he muttered. "Association of ideas, I fancy, since there is a cross on the church steeple. And what is there in that bell? It is a faint sound even from here, yet night after night, up there in the cabin, that far-off peal has waked me suddenly from sleep. Why is it, I wonder?"

Entering the town, there were few stirring on the sunny streets, but he could not but be aware that those he met stopped to gaze after him. Some, indeed, followed. His first objective point was a jeweler's, where he could turn his gold-dust into readier coin for needful purchases. He saw a sign next the Mountain Valley House, and entered.

The jeweler weighed the dust with a distrustful frown, but Harry's head was turned away. He was reading a freshly printed placard tacked on the wall—an offer of reward for the detection of the sluice thief. He read it through mechanically, for as he read there came from the street outside a sound that touched a muffled chord in his brain. It was the exhaust of a motor-car.

He thrust the money the goldsmith grudgingly handed him into his pocket and turned to the door. A long red automobile had stopped at the curb. Two men whom it carried were just entering the hotel.

Harry had seen many such machines in his wanderings, and they had aroused no baffling instinct of habitude. But the old self was stirring now, every sense alert. Hour by hour he had found himself growing more delicately susceptible to subtle mental impressions, haunted by shadowy reminders of things and places. Something in the sight of the long, low "racer" reminded him—of what? His eye traced its polished lines, noting its cunning mechanism, its build for silent speed, with the eager lighting of a connoisseur. He took a step toward it, oblivious to all about him.

He did not note that men were gathering, that the nearest saloon was emptying of its occupants. Nor did he see a girl on horseback, with a tiny child before her on the saddle, who reined up sharply opposite.

The rider was Jessica; the child, an ecstatic five-year-old she had picked up on the fringe of the town, to canter in with her hands gripping the pommel of the saddle. She saw Harry's position instantly and guessed it perilous. What did the men mean to do? She leaned forward, a swift apprehension in her face.

Harry came back suddenly to a realization of his surroundings. He looked about him, startled, his cheek darkening its red, every muscle instinctively tightening. He saw danger in the lowering faces, and the old lust of daring leaped up instantly to grapple with the rejuvenated character.

Devlin's voice came over the heads of the crowd as, burly and shirt-sleeved, he strode across the street:

"Hand over the dust you've stolen before you are tarred and feathered, Hugh Stires!"

Harry looked at him surprised, his mind instantly
recurring to the placard he had seen. Here was a tangible accusation.

"I have stolen nothing," he responded quietly.

"Where did he get what he just sold me?" The jeweler's sour query rose behind him from the doorway.

"We'll find that out!" was the rough rejoinder.

In face of his threatening peril, Jessica forgot all else—the restive horse, the child. She sprang to the ground, her face pained and indignant, and started to run across the street. But with a cry of dismay she turned back. The horse had caught sight of the red automobile, and, snorting and wild-eyed, had swung into the roadway.

"It's Devlin's kid!" some one cried out, and Devlin, turning, went suddenly ashen. The baby was the one soft spot in his ruffianly heart. He sprang toward the animal, but the movement and the hands clutching at the bridle sent it to a leaping terror. In another instant it had broken through the ring of bystanders, and, frenzied at its freedom, dashed down the long, level street with the child clinging to the saddle-pommel.

It was all the work of a moment, one of panic and confusion, through which rang Jessica's scream of remorse and fright. Torpor held the crowd—all save one, whose action followed the scream as leap follows the spur. In a single step Harry gained the automobile. With an instantaneous movement he pushed the lever down and jerked the throttle wide. The machine bounded into its pace, the people rolling back before it, and, gathering headway, darted after the runaway.

The spectators stood staring. "He'll never catch him," said Michael Halloran, who had joined the crowd. "Funeral Hollow's only a mile away." With others he hurried to the hotel balcony, where he could watch the exciting race. Jessica stood stock-still, as blanched as Devlin, wringing her hands.

Harry Sanderson had acted with headlong intention, without calculation, almost without consciousness of mental process. Standing on the pavement, with the subtle lure of the motor creeping in his veins, his whole body responding—as his fingers had tingled at sight of the violin—to the muffled vibrations of that halted bundle of steel, in the sharp exigency he had answered an overmastering impulse. In the same breath he had realized Jessica's presence and the child's peril, both linked in that anguished cry. With the first bound of the car under him, as the crowd was snatched behind, a weird, exultant thrill shot through every nerve. Each bolt and bar he knew as one would tell his fingers. Somewhere, at some time, he had known such flight—through mellow sunlight, with the air singing past. Where? When?

Not for the fraction of a second, however, did his gaze waver. He knew that the flat on which the town was built fell away in a hollow ravine to the southward—he could see it from the cabin doorway—a stretch of breakneck road only a mile ahead. Could the child hold on? Could he distance those frenzied hoofs in time? The arrow of the indicator stole forward on the dial.

Far behind, as the crowd watched, a cry rose from the hotel balcony. It was Barney McGinn, the freighter, with a glass at his eye. "He's gaining!" he shouted. "He has almost overtaken the horse!"

The horse's first fury of speed was tiring. The steel steed was creeping closer. A thunder of hoofs in pursuit would have maddened the flying animal, but the gliding thing that was now so close to him came on with noiseless swiftness. Harry had reserved, with the nicety of a practised hand, a last increment of speed. With the front wheels at the horse's flank, he drew suddenly on this. As the car responded, he swerved it sharply in, and, holding with one hand, leaned far out from the step, and lifted the child from the saddle.

The automobile halted again before the hotel amid a hush. The men who a little while before had been ripe

for violence, now stood in shamefaced silence. It was Jessica who ran forward and took the child, still sobbing a little, from Harry's hands. One long look passed between them—a look on her part brimming with a great gratitude for his lifting of her weight of dread and compunction, and with something besides that mantled her cheeks with rich color. She kissed the child and placed her in her father's arms.

Devlin's countenance broke up. He struggled to speak, but could not, and, burying his face in the child's dress and crying like a baby, he crossed the street hastily to his own door.

Harry stepped to the pavement with a dull kind of embarrassment at the manifold scrutiny. He had misconstrued Jessica's flushing silence, and the inference stung. The fierce zest was gone, and the rankling barb of accusation smarted. He should apologize to the owner, he reflected satirically, for helping himself to the automobile—he who stole gold-dust, he at whose door the town laid its unferreted thieveries! He who was the scapegoat for the town's offenses!

That owner, in very fact, stood just then in the hotel doorway regarding him with interest. He was the sheriff of the county. He was about to step forward, when an interruption occurred. A scuffle and a weak

bark sounded, and a lean brown streak shot across the pavement.

"Rummy!" cried Harry. "Rummy!"

Through some chink of the dead wall in his brain the name slipped out, a tiny atom of flotsam retrieved from the wreck of memory. That was all, but to the animal which had just found its lost master, the word meant a sublimation of delight, the clearing of the puzzle of namelessness that had perplexed its canine brain. The dog's heaven was reached!

Down on his knees on the pavement went Harry, with his arms about the starved, palpitating little creature, and his cheek against its shaggy coat. In another moment he had picked it up in his arms and was walking up the street.

Late that night Tom Felder, sitting in his office, heard the story of the runaway from the sheriff's lips. He himself had been in court at the time.

"And the horse?" he asked.

"In the Hollow, with his back broken," said the sheriff.

The lawyer sprang from his chair. "Good God!" he exclaimed. "How can a man like that ever have been a scoundrel?"

The sheriff relit his dead cigar reflectively. "It's a

curious thing," he said. "They are saying on the street that he's sent Prendergast packing. He'll have to watch out—the old tarantula will sting him if he can!"

Harry Sanderson went back to his cabin with a strange feeling of exaltation and disappointment—exaltation at the recurrence of something of his old adventures, disappointment at the flushed silence with which Jessica had received the child.

CHAPTER XXIV ON SMOKEY MOUNTAIN

Jessica bore back from the town that afternoon a spirit of tremulous gladness. In the few moments of that thrilling ride and rescue, a mysterious change had been wrought in her.

In the past days her soul had been possessed by a painful agitation which she did not attempt to analyze. At moments the ingrained hatred of Hugh's act, the resentment that had been the result of that year of pain, had risen to battle for the inherent justice of things. At such times she was restless and *distraite*, sitting much alone, and puzzling David Stires by meaningless responses.

She could not tell him that the son whose name he never took upon his lips was so near: that he whose crime his father's pride of name had hidden, through all the months since then, had gone down with the current, shunned by honest folk, adding to his one dismal act the weight of persistent repetition! She could not tell him this, even though that son now lived without

memory of the evil he had done; though he struggled under a cloud of hatred, reaching out to clean deed and high resolve.

Now, however, all distrust and trepidation had vanished. Strangely and suddenly the complex warfare in her mind had stilled. Standing with Mrs. Halloran, she had listened to the comment with shining eyes. Not that she distinguished any sudden and violent *volte-face* of opinion to turn persecution to popularity and make the reprobate of to-day the favorite of to-morrow. But in its very reserve she instinctively felt a new tension of respect. Suspicion and dislike aside, there was none there who would again hinder the man who had made that race with death!

For her own part, she only knew that she had no longer fear of soul or sense of irrevocable loss, or suffering. What were those old Bible words about being born again? What was that rebirth but a divine forgetting, a wiping out, a "remembering no more?" If it was the memory of his shame that had dragged him down, that memory was gone, perhaps for ever. The Hugh she now loved was not the Hugh who had sinned!

She sat by David Stires that evening chatting gaily—he had been much weaker and more nervous of late and she would not have him told of the runaway—talking

of cheerful things, radiating a glow from her own happiness that warmed the softly-lighted sick-room. All the while her heart was on the hillside where a rough cabin held him who embodied for her all the mystery and meaning of life. By a kind of clairvoyance she saw him sitting in the snug firelight, thinking perhaps of the instant their eyes had met. She did not guess that for him that moment had held an added pang.

So the hours had passed, and the sun, when it rose next day, shone on a freshly created world. The wind no longer moaned for the lost legends of the trees. There was a bloom on every flowering bush, a song in the throat of every bird. She was full of new feelings that yielded in their sway only to new problems that loomed on her mental horizon. As the puzzle of the present cleared, the future was become the all-dominating thing. She knew now that she had never hated, had never really ceased to love. And Hugh? Love was not a mere product of times and places. It was only the memory that was gone, his love lived on underneath. Surely that was what the violin—what the look on his face had said! When the broken chain was welded, he would know her! Would it be chance—some sudden mental shock—that would furnish the clue? She had heard of such things.

But suppose he did not recover his memory. In the very nature of the case, he must sometime learn the facts of his past. Was it not better to know the very worst it contained now, to put all behind him, and face a future that held no hidden menace? She alone could tell him what had clouded his career—the thing whose sign and symbol was the forged draft. She carried the slip of paper in the bosom of her dress, and every day she took it out and looked at it as at some maleficent relic. It was a token of the old buried misery that, its final purpose accomplished, should be forgotten for ever. How to convey the truth with as little pain as might be—this was the problem—and she had found the solution. She would leave the draft secretly in the cabin, where he must see it. It bore his own name, and the deadly word David Stires' cramped fist had written across it, told its significant story. How it got there Hugh would not question; it would be to him only a detail of his forgotten life there.

She was glad when in the late afternoon Doctor Brent came for his chat with David Stires, and the latter sent her out for a walk. It was a garlanded day, a day of clear blue spaces between lavender clouds lolling in the sky, and over all the late summer landscape a dull gold wash of sun. There had long ceased to be for her any

direction save one—down the mountain road to where a rambling, overgrown path led to the little grassy plateau with its jutting rock, which was her point of observation. She did not keep to the main road, but chose a short-cut through the thick underbrush that brought her more quickly to the Knob. There she sat down, and, parting the bushes, peered through them.

All was quiet. No wisp of smoke curled from the cabin chimney, no work was forward; for Harry had climbed far up the mountain, alone with his thoughts. It was a favorable opportunity.

Jessica had the fateful draft in her hand as she ran quickly down the trail and across the cleared space to the cabin door. It was wide open. Peering warily she saw that both rooms were empty, and, with a guilty last glance about her, she entered. A smile curved her lips as she saw the plain neatness of the interior; the scoured cooking-utensils, the coarse Mackinaw clothing hung from wooden pegs, the clean bacon suspended from the rafters. A nail in the wall held an old violin, and beneath it was a shelf of books.

To these, battered and dog-eared novels rescued from the mildewed litter of the cabin, Harry had turned eagerly in the long evenings for lack of mental pabulum. She took one from the meager row, and opened it curiously. It was *David Copperfield*, and she saw with kindling interest that heavy lines were drawn along certain of the pages. The words that had been marked revealed to the loving woman something of his soul.

She looked about her. Where should she put the draft? He had left a marker in the book; he would open it again, no doubt. She laid the draft between the printed leaves, beyond the marker. Then, replacing the volume on the shelf, she ran from the door and hastened back up the steep trail to the Knob.

Leaning back against the warm rock, lapped in the serene peacefulness of the spot, Jessica fell into reverie. Never since her wedding-day had she said to herself boldly: "I love him!"—never till yesterday. Now all was changed. Her thought was a tremulous assurance: "I shall stay here near him day after day, watching. Some day his memory will come back, and then my love will comfort him. The town will forget it has hated, and will come to honor him. Sometime, seeing how he is changed, his father will forgive him and take him back, and we shall all three go home to the white house in the aspens. If not, then my place will still be with Hugh! Perhaps we shall live here. Perhaps a cabin like that will be home, and I shall live with him, and work with him, and care for him."

Thus she dreamed—a new day-dream, unravaged by the sordid tests of verity.

So absorbed was she that she did not hear a step approaching over the springy moss—a sharply drawn breath, as the intruder stifled an exclamation. She had drawn her handkerchief across her eyes against the dancing glimmer of sunlight. Suddenly it dropped to her lap, and she half turned.

In the instant of surprise, as Harry's look flashed into hers, a name sprang unbidden to her lips—a name that struck his strained face to sudden whiteness, ringing in his ears like the note of a sunken bell. All that was clamoring in him for speech rushed into words.

"You call my name!" he cried. "You know me! Have I ever been 'Hugh' to you? Is that what your look said to me? Is that why your face has haunted me? Tell me, I pray you!"

She had struggled to her feet, her hands pressed to her bosom. The surprise had swung her from her moorings. Her heart had been so full in her self-communings that now, between the impulse toward revealment and the warning of caution, she stood confused.

"I had never seen you in the town before that day," she said. "I am stopping there"—she pointed to the ridge above, where the roof of the sanatorium glistened

in the sunlight. "I was at the hotel by merest accident when—you played."

The light died in his eyes. He turned abruptly and stared across the foliaged space. There was a moment's pause.

"Forgive me!" he said at length, in a voice curiously dull. "You must think me a madman to be talking to you like this. To be sure, every one knows me. It is not strange that you should have spoken my name. It was a sudden impulse to which I yielded. I had imagined ... I had dreamed ... but no matter. Only, your face—that white band across your eyes—your voice—they came to me like something far away that I have known. I was mistaken. I was crazy to think that you—"

He stopped. A wave of sympathy passed over her. She felt a mad wish to throw all aside, to cry to him: "You *did* know me! You loved me once! I am Jessica—I am your wife!" So intense was her emotion that it seemed to her as if she had spoken his name again audibly, but her lips had not moved, and the tap of a woodpecker on a near-by trunk sounded with harsh distinctness.

"I have wanted to speak to you," she said, after an instant in which she struggled for self-control. "You

did a brave thing yesterday—a splendid thing. It saved me from sorrow all my life!"

He put aside her thanks with a gesture. "You saved me also. You found me ill and suffering and your horse carried me to my cabin."

"I want to tell you," she went on hastily, her fingers lacing, "that I do not judge you as others do. I know about your past life—what you have forgotten. I know you have put it all behind you."

His face changed swiftly. To-day the determination with which he had striven to put from his mind the problem of his clouded past had broken down. In the light of the charge which had been flung in his teeth the afternoon before, his imagination had dwelt intolerably on it. "Better to have ended it all under the wheels of the freight-engine," he had told himself. "What profit to have another character, if the old lies chuckling in the shadow, an old-man-of-the-sea, a lurking thing, like a personal devil, to pull me down!" In these gloomy reflections her features had recurred with a painful persistence. He had had a bad half-hour on the mountain, and now, before her look and tone, the ever-torturing query burst its bonds.

"You know!" he said hoarsely. "Yet you say that? They stoned me in the street the day I came back.

Yesterday they counted me a thief. It is like a hideous nightmare that I can't wake from. Who am I? Where did I come from? I dare not ask, for fear of further shame! Can you imagine what that means?"

He broke off, leaning an unsteady hand against a tree. "I've no excuse for this raving!" he said, in a moment, his face turned away. "I have seen you but twice. I do not even know your name. I am a man snatched out of the limbo and dropped into hell, to watch the bright spirits passing on the other side of the gulf!"

Pain lay very deep in the words, and it pierced her like a bodily pang, so close did she seem to him in spirit. She felt in it unrest, rebellion, the shrinking sensibility that had writhed in loneliness, and the longing for new foothold on the submerged causeway of life.

She came close to him and touched his arm.

"I know all that you suffer," she said. "You are doing the strong thing, the brave thing! The man in you is not astray now; it was lost, but it has found its way back. When your memory comes, you will see that it is fate that has been leading you. There was nothing in your past that can not be buried and forgotten. What you have been you will never be again. I know that! I saw you fight Devlin and I know why you did it. I

heard you play the violin! Whatever has been, I have faith in you now!"

She spoke breathlessly, in very abandon, carried away by her feeling. As she spoke he had turned toward her, his paleness flushed, his eyes leaping up like hungry fires, devouring her face. At the look timidity rushed upon her. She stopped abruptly and took a startled step from him.

He turned from her instantly, his hands dropped at his sides. The word that had almost sprung to speech had slipped back into the void.

"I thank you for the charity you have for me," he said, "which I in no way deserve. I ... I shall always remember it."

She hesitated an instant, made as if to speak. Then, turning, she went quickly from him. At the edge of the bushes she stopped with a sudden impulse. She looked at the handkerchief she held in her hand. Some tiny lettering was embroidered in its corner, the word *Jessica*. She looked back—he had not moved. Rolling it into a ball, she threw it back, over the bushes, then ran on hastily through the trees.

After a time Harry turned slowly, his shoulders lifting in a deep respiration. He drew his hand across his brow as though to dispel a vision. This was the first

time he had hit upon the place. He saw the flat ledge, with the bushes twisted before it for a screen. She had known the place before, then! The white and filmy cambric caught his eye, lying at the base of the great, knob-like rock. He went to it, picked it up, and looked at it closely.

"Jessica!" he whispered. The name clung about him; the very leaves repeated it in music. He had a curious sensation as if, while she spoke, that very name had half framed itself in some curtained recess of his thought. He pressed the handkerchief to his face. The faint perfume it exhaled, like the dust of dead roses, gave him a ghostly impression of the familiar.

He thought of what she had said; she had not known him! And yet that look, the strange dreaming sense of her presence, his name on her lips in the moment of bewilderment!

He struck his forehead sharply with his open hand.

"Fool!" he said, with a bitter laugh. "Fool!"

CHAPTER XXV THE OPEN WINDOW

Over the sanatorium on the ridge sleep had descended. On its broad grounds there was no light of moon or stars, and its chamber windows were dark, save where here and there the soft glow of a night-lamp sifted through a shutter. The evening had closed gloomily, breeding storm. The air was sultry and windless, and now and then sheet-lightning threw into blunt relief the dark bodies of the trees. Inside the building all slumbered, soundly or fitfully as health or illness decreed, carrying the humors of the stirring day into the wider realm of sleep.

Jessica had closed her eyes, thinking of a time when secrecy would all be ended, disguise done, when she would wear again the ring she had taken off in bitterness, when indeed and in name she would be a wife before the world. She had picked a great bowl of wild star-jasmin and set it by her bedside and the room was sweet with the delicate scent. The odor carried her irresistibly back to the far-away mansion that had since

seemed a haunted dwelling, to the days of her blindness and of Hugh's courtship. Before she extinguished the light she searched in a drawer and found her wedding-ring—the one she had worn for less than an hour. It was folded away in a box which she had not opened since the dreadful day when she had broken in pieces her model of the Prodigal Son. When she crept into bed, the ring was on her finger. She had fallen asleep with her cheek resting on it.

She awoke with a start, with a vague, inexplicable uneasiness, an instinct that the night had voiced an unusual sound. She sat up in bed, staring into the dark depths of the room. Her instant thought had been of David Stires, but the tiny bell on the wall whose wire led to his bedroom was not vibrating. She listened a moment, but there was only a deep silence.

Slipping out of bed, she crossed the room and parted the curtain from before the tall French window. The room was on the ground floor and the window gave directly on the lawn. The wind seemed dead, and the world outside—the broad, cleared expanse of trees and shrubs, and the descending forest that closed it round—was wrapped in a dense blackness. While she gazed there came a sudden yellow flare of lightning and far-distant mutter of thunder spoke behind the hills.

Still with the unreasoning uneasiness holding her, she groped to the door, drew the bolt and looked out into the wide, softly carpeted hall, lighted dimly by a lamp set just at the turn of the staircase. All at once a shiver ran through her. There, a dozen steps away, the light full upon him, stood the man who filled her thoughts.

He stood perfectly still, without movement or gesture, gazing at her. She could see his face distinctly, silhouetted on the pearl-gray wall. It wore an expression of strained concern and of deep helplessness. The instant agitation and surprise blotted the puzzle of his presence there. She forgot that it was the dead of night, that she was in her nightgown. It flashed across her mind that some near and desperate trouble had befallen him. All the protective and maternal in her love welled up. She went quickly toward him.

He did not move or stir, and then she realized that though his eyes seemed to look at her, it was with a passive tranced fixity. They saw nothing. He was asleep.

It was the mind which was conscious, the action of the brain was at rest. The body, through the operation of some irreducible law of the subjective self, was moving in an automatic somnambulism. The intermittent

memory that had begun to emerge in sleep, that had given him on waking the eerie impression of a dual identity, had led him, involuntarily and unerringly, to her.

She halted, a deep compassion and a painful wonderment holding her, feeling with a thrill the power she possessed over him. Then, like a cold wave, surged over her a numbing sense of his position. How had he entered? Had he broken locks like a burglar? The situation was anomalous. What should she do? Waked abruptly, the result might be disastrous. Discovered, his presence there when all slumbered, suspected as he had been, would be ruinous. She must get him away, out of the house, and quickly.

A breath of cool air swept past her, putting out the lamp—an outer door was open. At the same instant she heard steps beyond the curve of the hall, Doctor Brent's voice peremptory and inquiring. Her nerves chilled; he blocked the sole avenue of retreat. No, there was one other, and only one— a single way to shield him. Quiet and resourceful now, though her cheeks were hot, she took the hand of the unconscious man, drew him silent and unresisting into the friendly shadow of her room, closed the door noiselessly and bolted it.

For a moment she stood motionless, her heart beating violently. Had he been seen? Or had the open door created an alarm? Releasing his hand gently, she found her way softly to a stand, lighted a tiny night-taper, and threw a shawl about her. Through its ground-glass the light cast a wan glimmer which showed the shadowy outlines of the room, its white rumpled bed, its scattered belongings eloquent of a woman's ownership, and the pallid countenance of the sleeping man. He had stopped still; a troubled frown was on his face, and his head was bent as if listening.

A sudden confusion tingled through her veins, a sense of maidenly shame that she could be there beside him *en déshabille*, opposing the sweet reminder of their real relationship—was he not in fact her husband?—that lay ever beneath her thought to justify and explain. He must wake before he left that room. What would he think? She flushed scarlet in the semi-darkness; she could not tell him—that! Not there and then! The blood forsook her heart as footsteps sounded outside the door. They paused, passed on, returned and died away.

Suddenly, in the tense silence of the room, the mantel-clock struck three, a deep chime, like the vibration of a far-off church bell. The tone was not loud—indeed the low roll of the thunder had been well-nigh as loud—but there was in the intrusive metallic cadence a peculiar suggestion to the dormant mind. As the sound of the

church bell in the town had done so often, it penetrated the crust of sleep; it touched the inner ear of the conscious intelligence that stirred so painfully, throbbing keenly to sights and sounds and odors that to the wakeful mind left only a cloudy impression eddying to some unfamiliar center. Harry started, a shudder ran through his frame, he swayed dizzily, his hand went to his forehead.

In the instant of shocked awakening, Jessica was at his side in an agony of apprehension, her arm thrown about him, her hand pressed across his lips, her own lips at his ear in an agonized warning:

"Hush, do not speak! It is I, Jessica. Make no noise."

She felt her wrist caught in a grasp that made her wince. His whole body was trembling violently. "Jessica!" he said in a painfully articulated whisper. "You? Where am I?"

"This is my room," she breathed. "You have been walking in your sleep. Make no sound. We shall be heard."

A low exclamation broke from his lips. He looked bewilderedly about him, his eyes returning to her face with a horrified realization. "I ... came here ... to your room?" The voice was scarcely audible.

"It was I who brought you here. You were in the

hall—you would have been found. The house is roused."

He turned abruptly to the door, but she caught his arm. "What are you going to do? You will be seen!"

"So much the better; it will be at my proper measure—as a prowler, a housebreaker, a disturber of honest sleep!"

"No, no!" she protested in a panic. "You shall not; I will not have you taken for what you are not! I know—but they would not know! No one must see you leave this room! Do you not think of me?"

He caught his breath hard. "Think of you!" he repeated huskily. "Is there ever an hour when I do not think of you? Is there a day when I would not die to serve you? Yet in my very sleep—"

He paused, gazing at her where she stood in the half-light, a misty, uncertain figure. She was curiously happy. The delicious and pangless sense of guilt, however—the guilt of the hidden, not the blameworthy thing—that was tingling through her was for him a shrinking and acute self-reproach.

"Here!" he said under his breath. "To have brought myself here, of all places, for you of all women to risk yourself for me! I only know that I was wandering for years and years in a shadowy desert, searching for

something that would not be found—and then, suddenly I was here and you were speaking to me! You should have left me to be dragged away where I could trouble no one again."

She was silent. "Forgive me," he said, "if you can. I—I can never forgive myself. How can I best go?"

For answer she moved to the window, slender and wraith-like. He followed silently. A million vague new impressions were clutching at him; the fragrance in the room was like a hypnotic incense veiling shadowy forms. Lines started from the blank:

As she parted the curtain, a second of bright lightning revealed the landscape, the dark hedges and clustered trees. It blackened, and she drew him back with a hushed word, pointing where a lantern was flashing through the shrubbery.

"It is a watchman," she said. "He will be gone presently."

Looking at her, where she stood in the dim light, half turned away, one hand against her cheek, there welled through him a wave of that hopeless longing which her

kiss had awakened in that epoch moment of the Reverend Henry Sanderson. The clinging white gown, with the filmy lace at its throat, the taper's faint glow glimmering to a numbus in her loosened hair, the sweet intangible suggestions of the room—all these called to him potently, through the lines that raced in his brain.

"God help me!" he whispered, the pent passion of his dreams rushing to utterance. "Why did I ever see your face? I was reckless and careless then. I had damned the decent side of me that now is quivering alive! I have tried to blot your face from my memory. But it is useless. I shall always see it."

A rumble of nearer thunder sounded and a tentative dash of rain struck the pane. She was shaken to her depths. She stood in a whirlwind of emotion. She seemed to feel his arms clasping her, his lips on hers, his adjuring words in her ears. The odor of the flowers wreathed them both. The beating of her heart seemed to fill all the silent room.

On the lawn just outside the window, low voices were heard through the increasing rain. They passed, and after a moment he softly unlatched the window.

"Good-by," he said.

She stretched out her hand. He touched it, then drew the window wide. As he stepped noiselessly down on to the springy turf, the lightning flashed again—a pale-green glow that seemed almost before her face. She drew back, and the same instant, through the thunder, the electric bell on the wall rang sharply. She threw on her dressing-gown, thrust her feet into slippers, and hastened from the room.

The same flash that had startled Jessica lighted brightly the physician and the watchman, who stood at the corner of the building, having finished their tour of inspection. It was the latter who had found the open door and who had aroused the doctor, insisting that he had seen a man in the hall. The other had pooh-poohed this, but now by the lightning both saw the figure emerge from the French window and disappear in the darkness.

They ran back, the physician ahead. The window was not locked, and they stepped through it into an empty room.

"To be sure!" said the doctor disgustedly. "He was here all the time—heard us searching the halls, and took the first unlocked door he found. Miss Holme, no doubt, is sitting up with Mr. Stires. Not a word of

this," he added as they walked along the hall. "Unless she misses something, there is no need of frightening her."

He barred the outer door behind the watchman and went on. As he reached David Stires' room, the door opened and Jessica came out. She spoke to him in a low, anxious voice. "I was coming for you," she said. "I am afraid he is not so well. I can not rouse him. Will you come in and see what you can do?"

The doctor entered, and a glance at his patient alarmed him. Until dawn he sat with Jessica watching. When the early sunlight was flooding the room, however, David Stires opened his eyes and looked upon her quite naturally.

"Where is Harry Sanderson?" he asked. "I thought he was here."

She looked at him with a forced smile. "You have been dreaming," she answered.

He seemed to realize where he was. "I suppose so," he said with a sigh, "but it was very real. I thought he came in and spoke your name."

She stroked his hand. "It was fancy, dear." If he but knew who had really been there that night! If she could only tell him all the happy truth!

He lay silent a moment. Then he said: "If it could

only have been Harry you married instead of Hugh! For he loved you, Jessica."

She flushed as she said: "Ah, that was fancy, too!"

It was the first time since the day of her marriage that he had spoken Hugh's name.

CHAPTER XXVI LIKE A THIEF IN THE NIGHT

Dawn had come with an unleashed wind and the crash of thunder. The electric storm, which had muttered and menaced like a Sabbath of witches till daylight, had broken at length and turned the world to a raving turmoil, pitilessly scarring the mountain and deluging the gulches with cloud-burst.

In the cabin on the hillside Harry had watched the rage of the elements with a dull sense of accord; it typified the wild range of feeling in which his soul had been harried. Battle had been the keynote of a series of days and doings of which the tense awakening in Jessica's chamber, with its supreme moment of passion and longing, had been a weird culmination.

As he made his way down the mountain in the blank and heavy dark, correcting his path by the lightning, he had faced squarely the question that in that dim room had become an imminent demand.

"*What if I love her!* What right have I to love her, with a wretched name like mine? She has refinement,

a measure of wealth, no doubt, and I am poor as poverty, dependent on the day's grubbing in the ditch for to-morrow's bacon and flour. Yet that would not stand in the way! I am no venal rogue, angling for the loaves and fishes. Whatever else she cursed me with, Nature gave me a brain, and culture and experience have educated it. With hand or brain I can hew my own niche to stand in! Must I put away the longing that drove me to her in sleep, with her dawning love that shielded me? And if, knowing all, she love me, must the past, that is so unreal to me, block my way to happiness? I am putting it deep underground, and its ghost shall not rise! Time passes, reputations change. Mine will change. And when I have squared my living here, the world is wide. What does it matter who she is, if she is the one woman for me? What does it matter what I have been, if I shall be that no longer?"

So he had argued, but his argument ended always with the same stern and unanswerable conclusion: "To drag her down in order to lift myself! Because she pities me—pity is akin to love!—shall I take advantage of her interest and innocence? Shall I play upon divine compassion and sinister propinquity, like any mean adventurer who inveigles a romantic girl into marrying a rascal to reform him?"

In the cabin, through the long hours till the dawn began to infiltrate the dark hollows of the wood he had lain wide-eyed, thinking. When day came he had cooked his breakfast and thereafter sat watching the havoc of the storm through the window. Hours passed thus before the fury of the wind had spent itself, and with the diminution of the rain, a crouching mist had crept over the range from the west, from which Smoky Mountain jutted like a drenched emerald island. At length he rose, threw open the door and stood looking out upon the wind-whipped foliage and the drab desolation of the fog. Then he threw on his Mackinaw coat, picked up his gold-pan and climbed down the slope. Beneath all other problems must lie the sordid problem of his daily food. He had uncovered a crevice in the bed-rock at the end of his trench the day before, and now he scraped a pailful of the soggy gravel it contained and carried it back to the cabin. A fresh onslaught of rain came just then, and setting the heaped-up pan on the doorstep, he reëntered the room.

With a sigh he took off his damp coat and threw a log on the fire. He abstractedly watched it kindle, then filled and lit his pipe and turned to the book-shelf. He ran his hand absently along the row. Where had been that wide, dim expanse of library walls that hovered

like a mirage beyond his visual sight? He chose a volume he had been reading, and turned the pages.

All at once his hand clenched. He gave a choked cry. He was staring at a canceled bank-draft bearing his own name—a draft across whose face was written, in the cramped hand resembling the signature, a word that seemed etched in livid characters of shame—*Forgery!*

"Pay to Hugh Stires"—"the sum of five thousand dollars"—he read the phrases in a hoarse, husky monotone, every vein beating fiercely, his body hot with the heat of a forge. There it was, a hideous chapter of it, the damnable truth from which he had shrunk! "I may be a thief!"—he had said that to himself long ago. His mind had revolted at the idea, yet the thought had clung. It had made him a coward. When the allegation had passed before the jeweler's shop, it had stung the deeper for his dread. He had been the beneficiary of that forgery. He alone could have perpetrated it. The popular suspicion was well grounded: he was a common criminal!

Did the town know? He snatched at the draft and read the date. More than a year ago, and it had been presented for payment in a distant city, the city near which he had been picked up beside the railroad track. The forged name was the same as his own. Who was

David Stires? His father? Had that city been his home once, and that infamous act the forerunner of his flight or exile? He looked at the paper again with painful intentness. It was canceled—therefore had been paid without question. Yet the man it had robbed had stamped it with that venomous hall-mark. Clearly the law had not stepped in—for here he was at liberty, owning his name. He had been let go, then, disowned, to carry his badge of crime here into the wilderness! And how had he lived since then? Harry shuddered.

What now? It was no longer a question only of his life and repute here at Smoky Mountain. The trail led infinitely further; it led to the greater world, into which he had fondly dreamed of going. The words Jessica had spoken on the hillside sounded in his ears: "*Whatever has been* I have faith in you now." His face lightened. That assurance had swept the past utterly aside, had leaned only on the present. His present, at least, was clean!

He drew a sudden breath and the color faded from his cheek; a baleful suggestion had insinuated itself with a harrowing pain. *Was* it clean? He had forced an entrance in the dead of night to tread dark halls like a thief— and he had laid that flattering unction to his soul! Suppose he had not gone there innocent of

purpose? What if, not alone the memory, but the lusts and vices of the former man were reasserting themselves in sleep? What if the new Hugh Stires, unknown to the waking consciousness, was carrying on the deeds of the old? What if the town was right? What if there was, indeed, good reason for suspecting him?

He stumbled to a chair and sat down, his frame rigid. He thought of the robbed sluice in the gulch below, of his own unhappy adventure of the night. How could he tell what he had done—what he might do? Minutes went by as he sat motionless, his mind catching strange kaleidoscopic pictures that fled past him into the void. At length he rose and went to the window. Far down the hillside, a faint line through the mist spanned the gulch bottom. A groan burst from his lips:

"That is the hydraulic flume," he said aloud. "Gold has been stolen there in the past, again and again. Some was stolen two nights ago. *How do I know but that I am the thief?*" Was that what Prendergast had meant by the "easier way"? A shiver ran over him. "How do I know!" he thought. "I can see myself—the evil side of me—when the dark had fallen, waking and active ... I see myself creeping down there, stealing from shadow to shadow, to scoop the gold from the riffles when the moon is under a cloud. I see men sitting from

dark to daylight, with loaded rifles across their knees, watching. I see a flash of fire ... I hear a report. I see myself there by the sluice-boxes, dead, shot down in the act of a thief, making good the name men know me by!"

The figure of Jessica came before him, standing in her soft white gown, her hand against her cheek and the jasmin odors about her. The dream he had dreamed could not be—never, never, never! All that was left was surrender, ignominious flight to scenes barren of suggestion.

To a place where he could work and save and repay! He looked at the slip of bank-paper in his hand.

At that instant a shining point caught his eye. It came from the pan of gravel on the doorstep on which the rain had been beating. He thrust the draft into his pocket and seized a double handful of the gravel. He plunged it into a pail of water and held it to the light. It sparkled with coarse, yellow flakes of gold. He dropped the handful with a sharp exclamation, threw on his coat and rushed from the cabin.

All day, alone on the fog-soaked hillside, Harry toiled in the trench without food or rest.

CHAPTER XXVII INTO THE GOLDEN SUNSET

It was a fair, sweet evening, and the room where Jessica sat beside David Stires' bed, reading aloud to him, was flooded with the failing sunlight. The height was still in brightness, but the gulches below were wine-red and on their rims the spruces stood shadow-straight against the golden ivory of the southern sky. Since the old man's seizure in the night he had been much worse and she had scarcely left his room. To-day, however, he had sat propped by pillows, able to read and chat, and the deep personal anxiety that had numbed her had yielded. She was reading now from a life of that poetess whose grave has made a lonely Colorado mountain a place of pilgrimage. She read in a low voice, holding the page to the dimming light:

"The spot she chose was a bare knoll, facing out across the curved chasm, the wide empty gulf on three sides, a plot hounded by a knot of noble trees that whispered softly together. Here above the sky was beautifully blue, the searching fall wind that numbed the fingers in the draw of the gorge was gone, and the warm sunshine was mellow and

pleasant. It was a spot to dream in, leaning upon the great facts of God that He teaches best to those who love His Nature. A spot in which to be laid at last for the long sleep, when mortal dreams are over and work is done."

"That is beautiful," he said. "I should choose a spot like that." He pointed down the long slope, where a red beam of the sun touched the gray face of the Knob and turned it to a spot of crimson-lake. "That must be such a place."

Her cheeks flushed. She knew what he was thinking. He would not wish to lie in the far-away cemetery that looked down on the white house in the aspens, the theater of his son's downfall! The Knob, she thought with a thrill, overlooked the place of Hugh's regeneration.

A knock came at the door. It was a nurse with letters for him from the mail, and while he opened them Jessica laid aside the book and went slowly down the hall to the sun-parlor, where the doctor stood with the group gathered after the early supper, chatting of the newest "strike" on the mountain.

"We'll be famous if we keep on," he was saying, as she looked out of the wide windows across the haze where the sunlight drifted down in dust of gold. "I've a mind to stake out a claim myself."

"We pay you better," said one of the occupants

grimly. "Anyway, the whole of Smoky Mountain was staked in the excitement a year ago. There's no doubt about this find, I suppose?"

"It's on exhibition at the bank," the doctor replied. "More than five thousand dollars, *cached* in a crevice in the glacial age, as neat as a Christmas stocking!"

"Wish it was *my* stocking," grunted the other. "It would help pay my bill here."

The man of medicine laughed and nodded to Jessica where she stood, her cheeks reddened by the crimsoning light. She had scarcely listened to the chatter, or, if she did, paid little heed. All her thoughts were with the man she loved. Watching the luminous purple shadows grow slowly over the landscape, she longed to run down to the Knob, to sit where she had first spoken to him, perhaps by very excess of yearning to call him to her side. She had a keen sense of the compunction he must feel, and longed, as love must, to reassure him.

The talk went on about her.

"Where is the lucky claim?" some one asked.

"Just below this ridge," the doctor replied. "It is called the 'Little Paymaster.'"

The name caught her ear now. The Little Paymaster? That was the name on the tree—on Hugh's claim! At that instant she thought she heard David Stires calling.

She turned and ran quickly up the long hall to his open door.

The sight of his face at first startled her, for it was held captive of emotion; but it was an emotion of joy, not of pain. A letter fluttered in his grasp. He thrust it into her hands.

"Jessica!" he exclaimed. "Hugh has paid it! He has sent the five thousand dollars, interest and principal, to the bank, to my account."

For a moment she stood transfixed. The talk she had mechanically heard leaped into significance, and her mind ran back to the hour when she had left the draft at the cabin. She caught the old man's hand and knelt by his chair, laughing and crying at once.

"I knew—oh, I knew!" she cried, and hid her face in the coverlet.

"It is what I have prayed for," he said, after a moment, in a shaking voice. "I said I hoped I would never see his face again, but I was bitter then. He was my only son, after all, and he is your husband. I have thought it all over lying here."

Jessica lifted her eyes, shining with a great thankfulness. During these last few days the impulse to tell all that she had concealed had been almost irresistible; now the barrier had fallen. The secret she had repressed so long came forth in a rush of sentences that left him mute and amazed.

"I should have told you before," she ended, "but I didn't know—I wasn't sure—" She broke down for very joy.

He looked at her with eyes unnaturally bright. "Tell me everything, Jessica!" he said. "Everything from the beginning!"

She drew the shade wider before the open window, where he could look down across the two miles of darkening foliage to the far huddle of the town—a group of toy houses now hazily indistinct—and, seated beside him, his hand in hers, poured out the whole. She had never framed it into words; she had pondered each incident severally, apart, as it were, from its context. Now, with the loss of memory and the pitiful struggle of recollection as a background, the narrative painted itself in vivid colors to whose pathos and meaning her every instinct was alive. Her first view of Hugh, the street fight and the revelation of the violin—the part she and Prendergast had taken—the rescue of the child—the leaving of the draft in the cabin, and the strange sleep-walking that had so nearly found a dubious ending—she told all. She did not realize that she was revealing the depths of her own heart without reserve. If she omitted to tell of his evil reputation and the neighborhood's hatred, who could blame? She was a woman, and she loved them both.

Dusk came before the moving recital was finished. The rose of sunset grew over the trellised west, faded, and the gloom deepened to darkness, pricked by stars. The old man from the first had scarcely spoken. When she ended she could hardly see his face, and waited anxiously to hear what he might say. Presently he broke the silence.

"He was young and irresponsible, Jessica," he said. "Money always came so easily. He didn't realize what he was doing when he signed that draft. He has learned a lesson out in the world. It won't hurt his career in the end, for no one but you and I and one other knows it. Thank God! If his memory comes back—"

"Oh, it will!" she breathed. "It must! That day on the Knob he only needed the clue! When I tell him who I am, he will know me. He will remember it all. I am sure—sure! Will you let me bring him to you?" she added softly.

"Yes," he said, pressing her hand, "to-morrow. I shall be stronger in the morning."

She rose and lighted the lamp, shading it from his eyes.

"Do you remember the will, Jessica?" he asked her presently. "The will I drew the day he came back? You never knew, but I signed it—the night of your wedding. Harry Sanderson was right, my dear, wasn't he?

"I wish now I hadn't signed it, Jessica," he added. "I must set it right— I must set it right!" He watched her with a smile on his face. "I will rest now," he said, and she adjusted the pillows and turned the lamp low.

Crossing the room, she stepped through the long window on to the porch, and stood leaning on the railing. From the dark hedges where the brown birds built came a drowsy twitter as from a nest of dreams. A long time she stood there, a thousand thoughts busy in her brain—of Hugh, of the beckoning future. She thought of the day she had destroyed the model that her fingers longed to remold, now that the Prodigal was indeed returned. The words of the biblical narrative flashed through her mind: *And he arose and came to his father. But when he was yet a great way off, his father saw him, and had compassion, and ran, and fell on his neck, and kissed him.* So Hugh's father would meet him now! The dewed odors of the jasmin brought the memory of that stormy night when he had come to her in his sleep. She imagined she heard again his last word—his whispered "Good-by" in the sound of the rain.

She thought it a memory, but the word that flashed into her mind was carried to her from the shadow, where a man stood in the shrubbery watching her dim figure and her face white and beautiful in the light from a near-by window, with a passionate longing and rebellion.

Harry was seeing her, he told himself, for the last time. He had made up his mind to this on that stormy morning when he had found the lucky crevice. For days he had labored, spurred by a fierce haste to make requital. Till the last ounce of the rich "pocket" had been washed, and the whole taken to the bank in the town, no one had known of the find. It had repaid the forgery and left him a handful of dollars over—enough to take him far away from the only thing that made life worth the effort. He had climbed to the ridge on the bare chance of seeing Jessica—not of speaking to her. Watching her, it required all his repression not to yield to the reckless desire that prompted him to go to her, look into her eyes, and tell her he loved her. He made a step forward, but stopped short, as she turned and vanished through the window.

Standing on the porch, a gradual feeling of apprehension had come to Jessica—an impression of blankness and chill that affected her strangely. Inside the room she stood still, frightened at the sudden sense of utter soundlessness.

She caught up the lamp, and, turning the wick, approached the bed. She put out her hand and touched the wasted one on the coverlet. Then a sobbing cry came from her lips.

David Stires was gone. A crowning joy had goldened his bitterness at the last moment, and he had gone away with his son's face in his heart and the smile of welcome on his lips.

CHAPTER XXVIII THE TENANTLESS HOUSE

Dark was falling keen and cool, for frost was in the air, touching the fall foliage on the hills to crimson and amber, silvering the long curving road that skirted the river bluff, and etching delicate hoar tracery on the spidery framework of the long black railroad bridge that hung above "the hole." The warning light from a signal-post threw a crimson splash on the ground. Its green pane cast a pallor on a bearded face turned out over the gloomy water.

The man who had paused there had come from far, and his posture betokened weariness, but his features were sharp and eager. He turned and paced back along the track to the signal-post.

"It was here," he said aloud. He stood a moment, his hands clenched. "The new life began here. Here, then, is where the old life ended." From where he stood he could see blossoming the yellow lights of the little city, five miles away. He set his shoulders, whistled to the small dog that nosed near-by, and set off at a quick pace down the road.

What had brought him there? He scarcely could have told. Partly, perhaps, a painful curiosity, a flagellant longing to press the iron that had seared him to his soul. So, after a fortnight of drifting, the dark maelstrom of his thoughts had swept him to its dead center. This was the spot that held the key to the secret whose shame had sent him hither by night, like a jailbird revisiting the haunts that can know him no more. He came at length to a fork in the road; he mechanically took the right, and it led him soon to a paved road and to more cheerful thoroughfares.

Once in the streets, a bar to curious glances, he turned up his coat collar and settled the brim of his felt hat more closely over his eyes. He halted once before a shadowed door with a barred window set in its upper panel—the badge of a gambling-house. As he had walked, baffling hints of pictures, unfilled outlines like a painter's studies had been flitting before him, as faces flit noiselessly across the opaque ground of a camera-obscura. Now, down the steps from that barred door, a filmy, faded, Chesterfieldian figure seemed to be coming toward him with outstretched hand—one of the ghosts of his world of shadows.

He walked on. He crossed an open square and presently came to the gate of a Gothic chapel, set well back

from the street. Its great rose-window was alight, for on this evening was to be held a memorial service for the old man whose money had built the pile, who had died a fortnight before in a distant sanatorium. A burnished brass plate was set beside the gate, bearing the legend: "St. James Chapel. Reverend Henry Sanderson, Rector." The gaze with which the man's eye traced the words was as mechanical as the movement with which his hand, in his pocket, closed on the little gold cross; for organ practice was beginning, and the air, throbbing to it, was peopled with confused images—but no realization of the past emerged.

He turned at the sound of wheels, and the blur shocked itself apart to reveal a kindly face that looked at him for an instant framed in the window of a passing carriage. With the look a specter plucked at the flesh of the wayfarer with intangible fingers. He shrank closer against the palings.

Inside the carriage Bishop Ludlow settled back with a sigh. "Only a face on the pavement," he said to his wife, "but it reminded me somehow of Harry Sanderson."

"How strange it is!" she said—the bishop had no secrets from his wife—"never a word or a sign, and everything in his study just as he left it. What can you

do, John? It is four months ago now, and the parish needs a rector."

He did not reply for a moment. The question touched the trouble that was ever present in his mind. The whereabouts of Harry Sanderson had caused him many sleepless hours, and the look of frozen realization which had met his stern and horrified gaze that unforgetable night—a look like that of a tranced occultist waked in the demon-constrained commission of some rueful impiety—had haunted the good man's vigils. He had knowledge of the by-paths of the human soul, and the more he reflected the less the fact had fitted. The wild laugh of Hugh's, as he had vanished into the darkness, had come to seem the derisive glee of the tempter rejoicing in his handiwork. Recollection of Harry's depression and the insomnia of which he had complained had deepened his conviction that some phase of mental illness had been responsible. In the end he had revolted against his first crass conclusion. When the announced vacation had lengthened into months, he had been still more deeply perplexed, for the welfare of the parish must be considered.

"I know," he said at length. "I may have failed in my whole duty, but I haven't known how to tell David Stires, especially since we heard of his illness. I had

written to him—the whole story; the ink was not dry on the paper when the letter came from Jessica telling us of his death."

Behind them, as they talked, the man on the pavement was walking on feverishly, the organ music pursuing him, the dog following with a reluctant whine.

At last he came to a wide, dark lawn set thick with aspens clustering about a white house that loomed grayly in the farther shadow. He hesitated a moment, then walked slowly up the broad, weed-grown garden path toward its porch. In the half light the massive silver door-plate stood out clearly. He had known instinctively that that house had been a part of his life, and yet a tremor caught him as he read the name—STIRES. The intuition that had bent his steps from the street, the old stirring of dead memory, had brought him to his past at last. This house had been his home!

He stood looking at it with trouble in his face. He seemed now to remember the wide colonnaded porch, the tall fluted columns, the green blinds. Clearly it was unoccupied. He remembered the scent of jasmin flowers! He remembered—

He started. A man in his shirt-sleeves was standing by a half-open side door, regarding him narrowly.

"Thinking of buying?" The query was

good-humoredly satiric. "Or maybe just looking the old ranch over with a view to a shake-down!"

The trespasser smiled grimly. It was not the first time he had seen that weather-beaten face. "You have given up surgery as a profession, I see," he said.

The other came nearer, looked at him in a puzzled way, then laughed.

"If it isn't the card-sharp we picked up on the railroad track!" he said, "dog and all! I thought you were far down the coast, where it's warmer. Nothing much doing with you, eh?"

"Nothing much," answered the man he addressed. Others might recognize him as the black sheep, but this nondescript watchman whom chance had set here could not. He knew him only as the dingy vagabond whose broken head he had bandaged in the box-car!

"I'm in better luck," went on the man in shirt-sleeves. "I struck this about two months ago, as gardener first, and now I'm a kind of a sort of a watchman. They gave me a bunk in the summer-house there"—he jerked his thumb backward over his shoulder—"but I know a game worth two of that for these cold nights. I'll show you. I can put you up for the night," he added, "if you like."

The wayfarer shook his head. "I must get away to-night, but I'm much obliged."

"Haven't done anything, have you?" asked his one-time companion curiously. "You didn't seem that sort."

The bearded face turned away. "I'm not 'wanted' by the police, no. But I'm on the move, and the sooner I take the trail the better. I don't mind night travel."

"You'd be better for a rest," said the watchman, "but you're the doctor. Come in and we'll have a nip of something warm, anyhow."

He led the way to the open door and beckoned the other inside, closing it carefully to. "It's a bully old hole," he observed, as he lit a brace of candles. "It wasn't any trick to file a key, and I sleep in the library now as snug as a bug in a rug." He held the light higher. "You look a sight better," he said. "More flesh on your bones, and the beard changes you some, too. That scar healed up fine on your forehead—it's nothing but a red line now."

His guest followed him into a spacious hall, scarce conscious of what he did. A double door to the left was shut, but he nevertheless knew perfectly that the room it hid had a tall French window, letting on to a garden where camelias had once dropped like blood. The open door to the right led to the library.

There the yellow light touched the dark wainscoting, the marble mantelpiece, dim paintings on the wall, and

a great brass-bound Korean desk in a corner. What black thing had once happened in that room? What face had once looked at him from that wheel-chair? It was an old face, gray and lined and passionate—his father, doubtless. He told himself this calmly, with an odd sense of apartness.

The other's glance followed his pridefully. "It's a fine property," he said. "The owner's an invalid, I hear, with one leg in the grave. He's in some sanatorium and can't get much good of it. Nice pictures, them," he added, sweeping a candle round. "That's a good-looker over there—must be the old man's daughter, I reckon. Well, I'll go and get you a finger or two to keep the frost out of your lungs. It'll be cold as Billy-be-dam to-night. Make yourself at home." The door closed behind him.

The man he left was trembling violently. He had scarcely repressed a cry. The portrait that hung above the mantelpiece was Jessica's, in a house-dress of soft Romney-blue and a single white rose caught in her hair. "The old man's daughter!"—the words seemed to echo and reëcho about the walls, voicing a new agony without a name. Then Jessica was his sister!

The owner of the house, his father, an invalid in a sanatorium? It was a sanatorium on the ridge of Smoky

Mountain where she had stayed, into which he had broken that stormy night! Had his father been there then, yearning in pain and illness over that evil career of his in the town beneath? Was relationship the secret of Jessica's interest, her magnanimity, that he had dreamed was something more? A dizzy sickness fell upon him, and he clenched his hands till the nails struck purple crescents into the palms.

As he stared dry-eyed at the picture in the candle-light, the misery slowly passed. He must *know*. Who she was, what she was to him, he must learn beyond peradventure. He cast a swift glance around him; orderly rows of books stared from the shelves, the mahogany table held only a pile of old magazines. He strode to the desk, drew down its lid and tried the drawers. They opened readily and he rapidly turned over their litter of papers, written in the same crabbed hand that had etched the one damning word on the draft he had found in the cabin on Smoky Mountain.

This antique desk, with its crude symbols and quaint brass-work, a gift to him once upon a time from Harry Sanderson, had been David Stires' carry-all; he had been spending a last half-hour in sorting its contents when the bank-messenger, on that fateful day, had brought him the slip of paper that had told his son's disgrace.

Most of the papers the searcher saw at a glance were of no import, and they gave him no clue to what he sought. Then, mysteriously guided by the subtle memory that seemed of late to haunt him, though he was but half conscious of its guidance, his nervous fingers suddenly found and pressed a spring—a panel fell down, and he drew out a folded parchment.

Another instant and he was bending over it with the candle, his fingers tracing familiar legal phrases of a will laid there long ago. He read with the blood shrinking from his heart:

"To my son Hugh, in return for the care and sorrow he has caused me all the days of his life, for his dissolute career and his graceless desertion, I do give and bequeath the sum of one thousand dollars and the memory of his misspent youth. The residue of my estate, real and personal, I do give and bequeath to my ward, Jessica Holme—"

The blood swept back to his heart in a flood. Ward, not daughter! He could still keep the one sweet thing left him. His love was justified. Tears sprang to his eyes, and he laid the parchment back and closed the desk. He hastily brushed the drops away, as the rough figure of the watchman entered and set down two glasses and a bottle with a flourish.

"There you are; that'll be worth five miles to you!" He poured noisily. "Here's how!" he said.

His guest drank, set down the glass and held out his hand. "Good luck," he said. "You've got a good, warm berth here; maybe I shall find one, too, one of these days."

The dog thrust a cold muzzle into his hand as he walked down the gravel path slowly, feeling the glow of the liquor gratefully, with the grudging release it brought from mental tension. He had not consciously asked himself whither now. In some subconscious corner of his brain this had been asked and answered. He was going to his father. Not to seek to change the stern decree; not to annul those bitter phrases: *his dissolute career—the memory of his misspent youth!* Only to ask his forgiveness and to make what reparation was possible, then to go out once more to the world to fight out his battle. His way was clear before him now. Fate had guided him, strangely and certainly, to knowledge. He was thankful for that. He had come a silent shadow; like a shadow he would go.

He retraced his steps, and again stood on the square near where the rose-window of the Gothic chapel cast a tinted luster on the clustering shrubbery. The audience-room was full now, a string of carriages waited at the

curb, and as he stood on the opposite pavement the treble of the choir rose full and clear:

He drew his hat-brim over his eyes, and mingled with the hurrying street.

CHAPTER XXIX THE CALL OF LOVE

The bell was tapping in the steeple of the little Catholic church on the edge of the town, and the mellow tone came clearly up the slope of the mountain where once more the one-time partner of Prendergast stood on the threshold of the lonely cabin, sentinel over the mounds of yellow gravel that marked his toil.

The returned wanderer had met with a distinct surprise in the town. As he passed through the streets more than one had nodded, or had spoken his name, and the recognition had sent a glow to his cheek and a lightness to his step.

Since the daring feat in the automobile, the tone of the gossip had changed. His name was no longer connected with the sluice robberies. The lucky find, too, constituted a material boom for Smoky Mountain and bettered the stock in its hydraulic enterprises, and this had been written on the credit side of the ledger. Opinion, so all-powerful in a new community, had altered. Devlin had abruptly ordered from his place one who had

done no more than to repeat his own earlier gibes, and even Michael Halloran, the proprietor of the Mountain Valley House, had given countenance to the more charitable view championed by Tom Felder. All this he who had been the outcast could not guess, but he felt the change with satisfaction.

As he gazed up the slope, all gloriously afire with the marvellous frost-hues of the autumn—dahlia crimsons, daffodil golds and maple tints like the flames of long-sought desires—toward the glass roof that sparkled on the ridge above, one comfort warmed his breast. If it had been the subtle stirring of blood kinship, the blind instinct of love, that had drawn him to that nocturnal house-breaking, not the lawless appetence of the natural criminal! Whether his father was indeed there he must discover.

Till the sun was low he sat in the cabin thinking. At length he called the dog and fastened it in its accustomed place, and began slowly to climb the steep ascent. When he came to a certain vine-grown trail that met the main path, he turned aside. Here lay the spot where he had first spoken with her, face to face. Here she had told him there was nothing in his past which could not be buried and forgotten!

As he parted the bushes and stepped into the narrow space beside the jutting ledge, he stopped short with an exclamation. The place was no longer a tangle of vines. A grave had been lately made there, and behind it, fresh-chiseled in the rock, was a statue: a figure seated, chin on hand, as if regarding the near-by mound. As in a dream he realized that its features were his own. Awestruck, the living man drew near.

It was Jessica's conception of the Prodigal Son, as she had modelled it in Aniston in her blindness, after Hugh's early return to the house in the aspens. That David Stires should have pointed out the distant Knob as a spot in which he would choose to be buried had had a peculiar significance to her, and the wish had been observed. Her sorrow for his death had been deepened by the thought that the end had come too suddenly for David Stires to have reinstated his son. This sorrow had possessed one comfort— that he had known at the last and had forgiven Hugh. Of this she could assure him when he returned, for she could not really believe—so deep is the heart of a woman—that he would not return. In the days of vigil she had found relief in the rough, hard work of the mallet. None had intruded in that out-of-the-way spot, save that one day Mrs. Halloran, led by curiosity to see the grave of the rich man whose whim it had been to be buried on the mountain side,

had found her at her work, and her Jessica had pledged to silence. She was no fool, was Mrs. Halloran, and to learn the name of the dead man was to put two and two together. The guess the good woman evolved undershot the mark, but it was more than sufficient to summon all the romance that lurked beneath that prosaic exterior; nevertheless she shut her lips against temptation, and all her motherly heart overflowed to the girl who worked each day at that self-appointed task. Only the afternoon before Jessica had finished carving the words on the base of the statue on which the look of the startled man was now resting: *I will arise and go unto my father*.

The gazer turned from the words, with quick question, to the mound. He came close, and in the fading light looked at the name on the low headstone. So he had come too late!

And the son said unto him, Father, I have sinned against heaven and in thy sight, and am no more worthy to be called thy son. Though for him there could have been no robe or ring, or fatted calf or merriment, yet he had longed for the dearer boon of confession and understanding. If he could only have learned the truth earlier! If he might only put back the hands of the clock!

Hours went by. The shadows dreamed themselves

away and dark fell, cloudless and starry. The half-moon brightened upon him sitting moveless beside the stone figure. At length he rose to his feet, his limbs cramped and stiffened, and made his way back to the lonely cabin on the hillside.

There he found fuel, kindled a blaze in the fireplace and cooked his frugal supper. The shock of surprise past, he realized his sorrow as a thing subjective and cerebral. The dead man had been his father; so he told himself, but with an emotion curiously destitute of primitive feeling. The very relationship was a portion of that past that he could never grasp; all that was of the present was Jessica!

He thought of the losing battle he had fought there once before, when tempest shrieked without—the battle which had ended in *débacle* and defeat. He thought of the will he had seen, now sealed with the Great Seal of Death. He was the shorn beggar, she the beneficiary. What duty she had owed his father was ended now. Desolate she might be—in need of a hand to guide and guard—but she was beyond the reach of penury. This gave him a sense of satisfaction. Was she there on the mountain at that moment? There came upon him again the passionate longing that had held him in that misty sanatorium room when the odor of the jasmin had

wreathed them both—when she had protected and saved him!

At last he took Old Despair's battered violin from the wall, and, seating himself in the open doorway, looking across the mysterious purple of the gulches to the skyline sown with pale stars, drew the bow softly across the strings. In the long-past days, when he had been the Reverend Henry Sanderson, in the darker moods of his study, he had been used to seek the relief to which he now turned. Never but once since then had he played with utter oblivion of self. Now his struggle and longing crept into the music. The ghosts that haunted him clustered together in the obscurity of the night, and stood between his opening future and her.

Through manifold variations the music wandered, till at length there came from the hollowed wood an air that was an unconscious echo of a forgotten wedding-day—"O perfect love, all human thought transcending." After the fitful medley that had spoken, the placid cadence fell with a searching pathos that throbbed painfully on the empty silence of the mountain.

Empty indeed he thought it. But the light breeze that shook the pine-needles had borne the sound far to an ear that had grown tense with listening—to one on the ridge above to whom it had sounded the supreme call of youth

and life. He did not feel her nearer presence as she stole breathless across the dark path, and stood there behind him with outstretched hands, her whole being merged in that mute appeal.

The music died, the violin slipped from beneath his chin, the bow dropped and his head fell on his arms. Then he felt a touch on his shoulder and heard the whisper: "Hugh! Hugh!"

"Jessica!" he cried, and sprang to his feet.

In those three words all was asked and answered. It did not need the low cry with which she flung herself on her knees beside the rough-hewn steps, or the broken sentences with which he poured out the fear and hope that he had battled with.

"I have watched every day and listened every night," she said. "I knew that you would come—that you *must* come back!"

"If I had never gone, Jessica!" he exclaimed. "Then I might have seen my father! But I didn't know—"

She clasped her hands together. "You know now—you remember it all?"

He shook his head. "I have been there"—he pointed to the hillside—"and I have guessed who it is that lies there. I know I sinned against him and against myself, and left him to die unforgiving. That is what the statue said to me—as he must have said: *I am no more worthy to be called thy son.*"

"Ah," she cried, "he knew and he forgave you, Hugh. His last thought was of your coming! That is why I carved the figure there."

"You carved it?" he exclaimed. She bent her forehead to his hands, as they clasped her own.

"The prodigal is yourself," she said. "I modelled it once before when you came back to him, in the time you have forgotten. But I destroyed it,"—the words were very low now—"on my wedding-day."

His hands released hers, and, looking up, she saw, even in the moonlight, that with the last word his face had gone ghastly white. At the sight, timidity, maidenly reserve, fell, and all the woman in her rushed uppermost. She lifted her arms and clasped his face.

"Hugh," she cried, "can't you remember? Don't you understand? Think! I was blind, dear, blind—a white bandage was across my eyes, and you came to me in a shaded room! Why did you come to me?"

A spark seemed to dart through his brain, like the prickling discharge from a Leyden jar. A spot of the mental blackness visualized, and for an instant sprang out in outlines of red. He smelled the odor of jasmin flowers. He saw himself standing, facing a figure with bandaged eyes. He saw the bandage torn off, felt that yielding body in his arms, heard a voice—her voice—crying, "Hugh—Hugh! My husband!" and felt those lips pressed to his own in the tense air of a darkened room.

A cry broke from his lips: "Yes, yes! I remember! Jessica, my wife!" His arms went round her, and with a little sob she nestled close to him on the doorstep.

The blank might close again about him now! He had had that instantaneous glimpse of the past, like lightning through a rifted pall, and in that glimpse was joy. For him there was now no more consciousless past or remorseful present. No forgery or exile, no Prendergast, or hatred, or evil repute. For her, all that had embittered, all that stood for loss and grieving, was ended. The fire on the hearth behind them domed and sank, and far below the lights of the streets wavered unheeded.

The shadowed silence of the cathedral pines closed them round. Above in the calm sky the great constellations burned on and swung lower, and in that dim confessional she absolved him from all sin.

CHAPTER XXX IN A FOREST OF ARDEN

Keen, morning sunlight, a sky clean as a hound's tooth, and an air cool and tinctured with the wine of perfect autumn! Jessica breathed it deeply as her buoyant step carried her along the mountain trails, brave in the pageant of the passing year. Her face reflected the rich color and her eyes were deep as the sky.

Only last night had been that sweet unfolding in which the past had been swept away for ever. To-day her heart was almost too full to bear, beating to thought of the man to whose arms the violin had called her. That had been the hour of confidence, of love's sacrament, the closure of all her distrust and agony. Now she longed inexpressibly for the further assurance she knew would look from his eyes to hers; yet her joy was so poignant that it was near to pain, and withal was so enwound with maidenly consciousness that, knowing him near, she must have fled from him. She walked rapidly on, losing herself in the windings of blind wood-paths, revelling in the beauty of the silent, empty forest.

The morning had found the man whose image filled her mental horizon no less a prey to conflicting emotions than herself. That hour on the mountain-side, under the stars, had left Harry possessed of a mêlée of perplexing emotions. Dreaming and waking, Jessica's face hung before his eyes, her voice sounded in his ear. Yet over his happiness more than once a chill had fallen, an odd shrinking, an unexplainable sense of flush, of fastidiousness, of mortification. This subtle conflict of feeling, not understood, had driven him, in sheer nervousness, to the peaceful healing of the solitudes.

The future held no longer any doubt—it held only her. Where was that future to be? Back in the city to which his painful curiosity had so lately driven him? This lay no longer in his own choice; it was for her to decide now, Jessica—his wife. He said the word softly, under his breath, to the sweet secret grasses, as something mysterious and sacred. How appealing, how womanly she was—how incommunicably dear, how—

He looked up transfixed, for she stood there before him, ankle-deep in a brown whirlwind of leaves from a frost-stung oak, her hand to her cheek in an adorable gesture that he knew, her lips parted and eager. She said no word, nor did he, but he came swiftly and caught her to him, and her face buried itself on his breast.

As he looked down at her thus folded, the trouble, the sense of vexing complexity vanished, and the primitive demand reasserted its sway.

Presently he released her, and drew her gently to a seat on the sprawling oak roots.

"I wanted so to find you," she said. "I have so many, many things to say."

"It is all wonderfully strange and new!" he said. "It is as though I had rubbed Aladdin's lamp, and suddenly had my heart's desire."

"Ah," she breathed, "am I that?"

"More than that, and yet once I—Jessica, Jessica! When I woke this morning in the cabin down there, it seemed to me for a moment that only last night was real, and all the past an ugly dream. How could you have loved me? And how could I have thrown my pearl away?"

"We are not to think of that," she protested, "never, never any more."

"You are right," he rejoined cheerfully; "it is what is to come that we must think of." He paused an instant, then he said:

"Last night, when you told me of the white house in the aspens, I did not tell you that I had just come from there—from Aniston."

She made an exclamation of wonder. "Tell me," she said.

Sitting with her hand in his, he told of that night's experiences, the fear that had held him as he gazed at her portrait in the library, the secret of the Korean desk that had solaced his misery and sent him back to the father he was not to see.

At mention of the will she threw out her hand with a passionate gesture. "The money is not mine!" she cried. "It is yours! He intended to change it—he told me so the day he died. Oh, if you think I—"

"No, no," he said gently. "There is no resentment, no false pride in my love, Jessica. I am thinking of you—and of Aniston. You would have me go back, would you not?"

She looked up smiling and slowly shook her head. "You are a blind guesser," she said. "Don't you think I know what is in your mind? Not Aniston, Hugh. Sometime, but not now—not yet. It is nearer than that!"

His eyes flowed into hers. "You understand! Yes, it is here. This is where I must finish my fight first. Yesterday I would have left Smoky Mountain for ever, because you were here. Now—"

"I will help you," she said. "All the world besides counts nothing if only we are together! I could live in a cabin here on the mountain always, in a Forest of Arden, till I grow old, and want nothing but that—and you!" She paused, with a happy laugh, her eye turned away.

A log cabin, but a home glorified by her presence! In a dozen words she had sketched a sufficient Paradise. As he did not answer, she faced him with crimsoning cheeks, then reading his look she suddenly threw her arms about his neck.

"Hugh," she cried, "we belong to each other now. There is no one else to consider, is there? I want to be to you what I haven't been—to bear things with you, and help you."

He kissed her eyes and hair. "You *have* helped, you *do* help me, Jessica!" he urged. "But I am jealous for your love. It must not be offended. The town of Smoky Mountain must not sneer—and it would sneer now."

"Let it!" she exclaimed resentfully. "As if I would care!"

"But *I* would care," he said softly. "I want to climb a little higher first."

She was silent a moment, her fingers twisting the fallen leaves. "You don't want them to know that I am your wife?"

"Not yet—till I can see my way."

She nodded and smiled and the cloud lifted from her face. "You must know best," she said. "This is what I shall do, then. I shall leave the sanatorium to-morrow. The people there are nothing to me, but the town of Smoky Mountain is yours, and I must be a part of it, too. I am going to the Mountain Valley House. Mrs. Halloran will take care of me." She sprang to her feet as she added: "I shall go to see her about it now."

He knew the dear desire her determination masked—to do her part in softening prejudice, in clearing his way—and the thought of her great-heartedness brought a mist to his eyes. He rose and walked with her through the bracken to the road. They came out to the driveway just below the trail that led to the Knob. The bank was high, and leaping first he held up his arms to her and lifted her lightly down. In the instant, as she lay in his arms, he bent and kissed her on the lips.

Neither noted two figures walking together that at that moment rounded the bend of the road a little way above. They were Tom Felder and Doctor Brent, the latter swinging a light suit-case, for he was on his way to the station of the valley railroad. He had chosen to walk that he might have a longer chat with his friend. Both men saw the kiss and instinctively drew back, the

lawyer with a sudden color on his face, the doctor with a look of blank astonishment.

The latter, in one way, knew little about the town. Beside Felder and Mrs. Halloran, whose surly husband he had once doctored when the town's practitioner was away—thereby earning her admiration and gratitude— there were few with whom he had more than a nodding acquaintance. He had liked David Stires, and Jessica he genuinely admired, though he had thought her at times somewhat distant. He himself had introduced Felder to her, on one of the latter's visits. He had not observed that the young lawyer's calls had grown more frequent, nor guessed that he had more than once loitered on the mountain trails hoping to meet her.

The doctor noted now the telltale flush on his companion's face.

"We have surprised a romance," he said, as the two unconscious figures disappeared down the curving stretch. "Who is the man?"

"He is the one we have been talking about."

The other stared. "Not your local Jekyll and Hyde, the sneak who lost his memory and found himself an honest man?"

Felder nodded. "His cabin is just below here, on the hillside."

"Good Lord!" ejaculated the doctor. "What an infernal pity! What's his name?"

"Hugh Stires."

"Stires?" the other repeated. "Stires? How odd!" He stood a moment, tapping his suit-case with his stick. Suddenly he took the lawyer's arm and led him into the side-path.

"Come," he said, "I want to show you something."

He led the way quickly to the Knob, where he stopped, as much astonished as his companion, for he had known nothing of the statue. They read the words chiselled on its base. "The prodigal son," said Felder.

"Now look at the name on the headstone," said the physician.

Felder's glance lifted from the stone, to peer through the screening bushes to the cabin on the shelf below, and returned to the other's face with quick comprehension. "You think—"

"Who could doubt it? *I will arise and go unto my father.* The old man's whim to be buried here had a meaning, after all. The statue is Miss Holme's work—nobody in Smoky Mountain could do it—and I've seen her modelling in clay at the sanatorium. What we saw just now is the key to what might have been a pretty riddle if we had ever looked further than our noses.

It's a case of a clever rascal and damnable propinquity. The ward has fallen in love with the black sheep!"

They betook themselves down the mountain in silence, the doctor wondering how deep a hurt lay back of that instant's color on his friend's now imperturbable face, and more than disturbed on Jessica's account. Her care for the cross-grained, likable invalid had touched him.

"A fine old man to own a worthless son," he said at length, musingly. "A gentleman of the old school. Your amiable blackleg has education and good blood in him, too!"

"I've wondered sometimes," said Felder, "if the old Hugh Stires, that disreputable one that came here, wasn't the unreal one, and the Hugh Stires the town is beginning to like, the real one, brought back by the accident that took his memory. You medical men have cases of such double identity, haven't you?"

"The books have," responded the other, "but they're like Kellner's disease or Ludwig's Angina—nobody but the original discoverer ever sees 'em."

As they parted at the station the doctor said: "We needn't take the town into our confidence, eh? Some one will stumble on the statue sooner or later, but we won't help the thing along." He looked shrewdly in the other's face as they shook hands.

"You know the old saying: There's as many good fish in the sea as ever were caught."

The lawyer half laughed. "Don't worry," he said. "If I had been in danger, the signal was hung out in plenty of time!"

CHAPTER XXXI THE REVELATION OF HALLELUJAH JONES

Hallelujah Jones was in his element. With his wheezy melodeon, his gasoline flare and his wild earnestness, he crowded the main street of the little mining-town, making the engagement of the "San Francisco Amazons" at the clapboard "opera house" a losing venture. The effete civilization of wealthy bailiwicks did not draw forth his powers as did the open and unveneered debaucheries of less restricted settlements. Against these he could inveigh with surety, at least, of an appreciative audience.

He had not lacked for listeners here, for he was a new sensation. His battered music-box, with its huge painted text, was far and away more attractive than the thumping pianolas of the saloons or the Brobdignagian gramophone of the dance-hall, and his old-fashioned songs were enthusiastically encored. When he lit his flare in the court-house square at dusk on the second evening, the office of the Mountain Valley House was emptied and the bar-rooms and gaming-tables well-nigh deserted of their patrons.

Jessica had seen the mustering crowd from the hotel entrance. Mrs. Halloran had welcomed her errand that day and given her her best room, a chamber overlooking the street. She had persuaded her visitor to spend the afternoon and insisted that she stay to supper, "just to see how she would like it for a steady diet." Now, as Jessica passed along toward the mountain road, the spectacle chained her feet on the outskirts of the gathering. She watched and listened with a preoccupied mind; she was thinking that on her way to the sanatorium she would cross to the cabin for a good-night word with the man upon whom her every thought centered.

As it happened, however, Harry was at that moment very near her. Alone on the mountain, the perplexing conflict of feeling had again descended upon him. He had fought it, but it had prevailed, and at nightfall had driven him down to the town, where the street preacher now held forth. He stood alone, unnoted, a little distance away, near the court-house steps, where, by reason of the crowd, Jessica could see neither him nor the dog which sniffed at the heels of the circle of bystanders as if to inquire casually of salvation.

Numbers were swelling now, and the street preacher, shaking back his long hair, drew a premonitory, wavering chord from his melodeon, and struck up a gospel song:

The song ended, he mounted his camp-stool to propound his usual fiery text.

The watcher by the steps was gazing with a strange, alert intentness. Something in the scene—the spluttering, dripping flame, the music, the forensic earnestness of the pilgrim—held him enthralled. The dormant sense that in the recent weeks had again and again stirred at some elusive touch of memory, was throbbing. Since last night, with its sudden lightning flash of the past that had faded again into blankness, he had been as sensitive as a photographic plate.

Hallelujah Jones knew the melodramatic value of contrast. As his mood called, he passed abruptly from exhortation to song, from prayer to fulmination, and he embellished his harangue with anecdotes drawn from his lifelong campaign against the Arch-Enemy of Souls.

Of what he had said the solitary observer had been quite unconscious. It was the *ensemble*—the repetition of something experienced somewhere before—that appealed to him. Suddenly, however, a chance phrase pierced to his understanding.

Another moment and he was leaning forward, his eyes fixed, his breath straining at his breast. For each word of the speaker now was knocking a sledge-hammer blow upon the blank wall in his brain. Hallelujah Jones had launched into the recital of an incident which had become the *chef d'ouvre* of his repertory—a story which, though the stern charge of a bishop had kept him silent as to name and locality, yet, possessing the vividness of an actual experience, had lost little in the telling. It was the tale of an evening when he had peered through the tilted window of a chapel, and seen its dissolute rector gambling on the table of the Lord.

Back in the shadow the listener, breathless and staring, saw the scene unroll like the shifting slide of a stereopticon—the epitaph on his own dead self. Nerve and muscle and brain tightened as if to withstand a shock, for the man who moved through the pictures was himself! He saw the cards and counters falling on the table, the entrance of the two intruding figures, heard Hugh's wild laugh as he fled, and the grate of the key

in the lock behind him as he stood in his study. He heard the rush of the wind past the motor-car, the rustle of dry corn in the hedges, and felt the mist beating on his bare head—

He did not know that it was the voice of the street preacher which was singing now. The words shrieked themselves through his brain. Harry Sanderson, not Hugh Stires! Not an outcast! Not criminal, thief and forger! The curtain was rent. The dead wall in his brain was down, and the real past swept over him in an ungovernable flood. Hallelujah Jones had furnished the clue to the maze. His story was the last great wave, which had crumbled, all at once, the cliff of oblivion that the normal process of the recovered mind had been stealthily undermining. The formula, lost so long in the mysterious labyrinth of the brain, had reëstablished itself, and the thousand shreds of recollection that he had misconstrued had fallen into their true place in the old pattern. Harry Sanderson at last knew his past and all of puzzlement and distress that it had held.

Shaking in every limb and feeling all along the court-house wall like a drunken man, he made his way to the further deserted street. A passer-by would have shrunk at sight of his face and his burning eyes.

For these months, he, the Reverend Henry Sanderson, disgraced, had suffered eclipse, had been sunk out of sight and touch and hearing like a stone in a pool. For these months—through an accidental facial resemblance and a fortuitous concurrence of circumstances—he had owned the name and ignominy of Hugh Stires. And Jessica? Deceived no less than he, dating her piteous error from that mistaken moment when she had torn the bandage from her eyes on her wedding-day. She had never seen the real Hugh in Smoky Mountain. She must learn the truth. Yet, how to tell her? How could he tell her *all*?

At any hour yesterday, hard as the telling must have been, he could have told her. Last night the hour passed. How could he tell her now? Yet she was the real Hugh's wife by law and right; he himself could not marry her! If God would but turn back the universe and give him yesterday!

Why not *be* Hugh Stires? The wild idea came to him to throw away his own self for ever, never to tell her, never to return to Aniston, to live on here or fly to

some distant place, till years had made recognition impossible. He struck his forehead with his closed hand. He, a priest of God, to summon her to an illegal union? To live a serial story of hypocrisy, with the guilty shadow of the living Hugh always between them, the sword of Damocles always suspended above their heads, to cleave to the heart of his Fool's Paradise? The mad thought died. Yet what justice of Heaven was it that Jessica, whose very soul had been broken on the wheel, should now, through no conscious fault, be led by his hand through a new Inferno of suffering?

His feet dragging as though from cold, he climbed the mountain road. As he walked he took from his pocket the little gold cross, and his fingers, numb with misery, tied it to his thong watch-guard. It had been only a bauble, a pocket-piece acquired he knew not when or how; now he knew it for the badge of his calling. He remembered now that, pressed a certain way, it would open, and engraved inside were his name and the date of his ordination.

He might shut the cabin door, but he could not forbid the torturer that came with him across the threshold. He might throw himself upon his knees and bury his face in the rough skin of the couch, but he could not shut out words that blent in golden-lettered flashes

across his throbbing eyeballs: *Thou shalt not covet thy neighbor's wife.*

So he crouched, a man under whose feet life had crashed, leaving him pinned beneath the wreck, to watch the fire that must creep nearer and nearer.

CHAPTER XXXII THE WHITE HORSE SKIN

Curiosity held Jessica until the evangelist closed his melodeon preparatory to a descent upon the dance-hall. Then, thinking of the growing dark with some trepidation—for the recent "strike" had brought its influx of undesirable characters to the town—she started toward the mountain.

Ahead of her a muffled puff-puff sounded, and the dark bulk of an automobile—the sheriff's, the only one the town of Smoky Mountain boasted—was moving slowly in the same direction, and she quickened her pace, glad of this quasi-company. It soon forged ahead, but she had passed the outskirts of the town then and was not afraid.

A little way up the ascent a cumbrous shadow startled her. She saw in a moment that it was the automobile, halted at the side of the road. Her footsteps made no sound and she was close upon it when she saw the three men it had carried standing near-by. She made to pass them, and had crossed half the intervening space, when

some instinct sent her to the shade of the trees. They had stopped opposite the hydraulic concession, where a side path left the main road— it was the same path by which she and Emmet Prendergast had taken their unconscious burden on a night long ago—leading along the hillside, overlooking the snake-like flume, and forming a steeper short-cut to the cabin above. They were conversing in low tones, and as they talked they pointed, she thought toward it.

Jessica had never in her life been an eavesdropper, but her excited senses made her anxious. Moreover, she was in a way committed, for she could not now emerge without being seen. As she waited, a man came from the path and joined the others. The sky had been overcast and gloomy, but the moon drew out just then and she saw that the new-comer, evidently a patrol, carried a rifle in the hollow of his arm. She also saw that one of the first three was the automobile's owner.

For some minutes they conversed in undertones, whose very secrecy inflamed her imagination. It seemed to her that they made some reference to the flume. Had there been another robbery of the sluice-boxes, and could they still suspect Hugh?

Dread and indignation made her bold. When they turned into the path she followed, treading noiselessly,

till she was close behind them. They had stopped again, and were looking intently at a shadowy gray something that moved in the bottom below.

She heard the man who carried the rifle say, with a smothered laugh:

"It's only Barney McGinn's old white horse taking a drink out of the sluice-box. He often does that."

Then the sheriff's voice said: "McGinn's horse is in town to-night, with Barney on her back. Horse or no horse, I'm going to"—the rest was lost in the swift action with which he snatched the firearm from the first speaker, sighted, and fired.

In the still night the concussion seemed to rock the ground, and roused a hundred echoes. It startled and shocked the listening girl, but not so much as the sound that followed it—a cry that had nothing animal-like, and that sent the men running down the slope toward an object that lay huddled by the sluice-box.

In horrified curiosity Jessica followed, slipping from shadow to shadow. She saw the sheriff kneel down and draw a collapsed and empty horse's skin from a figure whose thieving cunning it would never cloak again.

"So it was you, after all, Prendergast!" the sheriff said contemptuously.

The white face stared up at them, venomous and

writhing, turning about the circle as though searching for some one who was not there.

"How did—you guess?"

The sheriff, who had been making a swift examination, answered the panted question. "You have no time to think of that now," he said.

A sinister look darted into the filming yellow eyes, and hatred and certainty rekindled them. Prendergast struggled to a sitting posture, then fell back, convulsed. "Hugh Stires! He was the only—one who knew—how it was done. He's clever, but he can't get the best of Prendergast!" A spasm distorted his features. "Wait—wait!"

He fumbled in his breast and his fingers brought forth a crumpled piece of paper. He thrust it into the sheriff's hands.

"Look! Look!" he gasped. "The man they found murdered on the claim there"—he pointed wildly up the hillside—"Doctor Moreau. I found him—dying! Stires—"

Strength was fast failing him. He tried again to speak, but only inarticulate sounds came from his throat.

A blind terror had clutched the heart of the girl leaning from the shadow. "Doctor Moreau"

—"murdered." Why, he had been one of Hugh's friends! Why did this man couple Hugh's name with that worst of crimes? What dreadful thing was he trying to tell? She hardly repressed a desire to scream aloud.

"Be careful what you say, Prendergast," said the sheriff sternly.

The wretched man gathered force for a last effort. His voice came in a croaking whisper:

"It was Stires killed him. Moreau wrote it down—and I—kept the paper. Tell Hugh—we break—even!"

That was all. His head fell back with a shiver, and Emmet Prendergast was gone on a longer journey than ever his revenge could warm him.

CHAPTER XXXIII THE RENEGADE

While the man whom the town knew as Hugh Stires listened to the tale of the street preacher, another, unlike yet curiously like him in feature, had slowly climbed the hilly slope from the north by the sanatorium road. He walked with a jaunty swagger bred of too frequent applications to a flask in his pocket.

Since the evening of the momentous scene in the chapel with Harry Sanderson, Hugh had had more and more recourse to that black comforter. It had grown to be his constant companion. When, late on the night of the game, some miles away, he had gloatingly counted the money in his pockets, he had found nearly a thousand dollars in double-eagles, and a single red counter—the last he had had to stake against Harry's gold. He put the crimson disk into his pocket, "to remember the bishop by," he thought with a chuckle, but the fact that for each of the counters Harry had won he had sworn to render a day of clean and decent living, he straightway forgot. For the other's position he had wasted no

pity. Harry would find it difficult to explain the matter to the bishop! Well, if it "broke" him, served him right! What business had he to set himself so far above every one else?

For some time thereafter Hugh had seriously contemplated going abroad, for a wholesome fear had dogged him in his flight from Smoky Mountain. For weeks he had travelled by night, scanning the daily newspapers with a desperate anxiety, his ears keen for hue and cry. But with money in his pocket, courage returned, and in the end fear lulled. There had been no witness to that deed on the hillside. There might be suspicion, but no more! At length the old-time attraction of the race-course had absorbed him. He had followed the horses in "the circuit," winning and losing, consorting with the tipsters, growing heavier with generous living, and welcoming excitement and change. But the ghost of Doctor Moreau haunted him, and would not be exorcized.

Money, however, could not last always, and a persistent run of ill luck depleted his store. When poverty again was at his elbow a vagrant rumor had told him, with the usual exaggerations, of the rich "find" on the Little Paymaster Claim on Smoky Mountain. Too late he cursed the reasonless panic that had sent him into

flight. Had the ground been "jumped" by some one who now profited? Nevertheless, it was still his own to claim; miners' law gave him a year, and he had left enough possessions in the cabin, he thought cunningly, to disprove abandonment. He dreaded a return, but want and cupidity at length overcame his fears. He had arrived at Smoky Mountain on this night to claim his own.

As he walked unsteadily along, Hugh drank more than once from the flask to deaden the superstitious dread of the place which was stealing over him. On the crest of the ridge he skirted the sanatorium grounds and at length gained the road that twisted down toward the lights of the town. In the dubious moonlight he mistook the narrow trail to the Knob for the lower path to the cabin. As he turned into it, the report of a rifle came faintly from the gulch below. It seemed to his excited senses like the ghostly echo of a shot he had himself fired there on a night like this long before—a hollow echo from another world.

He quickened his steps and stumbled all at once into the little clearing that held the new-made grave and Jessica's statue. The sight terrified his intoxicated imagination. His hair rose. The name on the headstone was Stires, and there was himself—no, a ghost

of himself!—sitting near! He turned and broke into a run down the steep slope. In his fear—for he imagined the white figure was pursuing him—he tripped and fell, regained his feet, rushed across the level space, threw his weight against the cabin door, and burst into the room.

A dog sprang up with a growl, and in the light of the fire that burned on the hearth, a man sitting at the rough-hewn table lifted a haggard face from his arms and each recognized the other.

The ghost was gone now before firelight and human presence, and Hugh, with a loud laugh of tipsy incredulity, stood staring at the man before him.

"Harry Sanderson!" he cried. "By the great horn spoon!" His shifty eyes surveyed the other's figure—the corduroys, the high laced boots, the soft blue flannel shirt. "Not exactly in purple and fine linen," he said—the impudent swagger of intoxication had slipped over him again, and his boisterous laugh broke with a hiccough. "I thought the gospel game was about played out that night in the chapel. And now you are willing to take a hint from the prodigal. How did you find my nest? And perhaps you can tell me who has been making himself so infernally at home here lately?"

"*I* have," said Harry evenly.

Hugh's glance, that had been wavering about the neat interior, returned to Harry, and knowledge and anger leaped into it. "So it was you, was it? You are the one who has been trying his hand as a claim-jumper!" He lurched toward the table and leaned upon it. "I've always heard that the devil took care of his own. The runaway rector stumbles on my manor, and with his usual luck—'Satan's luck' we called it at college—steps in just in time to strike it rich!"

He stretched his hand suddenly and caught a tiny object that glittered against Harry's coat—the little gold cross, which the other had tied to his watch-guard. The thong snapped and Hugh sent the pendant rattling across the doorway.

"You were something of a howling swell as a parson," he said insolently, "but you don't need the jewelry now!"

Harry Sanderson's eyes had not left Hugh's face; he was thinking swiftly. The bolt from the blue had been so recent that this sudden apparition seemed a natural concomitant of the situation. Only the problem was no longer imminent; it was upon him. Jessica was not for him—he had accepted that. Though the clock might not turn backward, this man must stand between them. Yet his presence now in the predicament was

intolerable. This drunken, criminal maligner had it in his power to precipitate the climax for her in a coarse and brutal *exposé*. Hugh had no idea of the true tangle, else he had not been seen in the town. But if not to-night, then to-morrow! Harry's heart turned cold within him. If he could eliminate Hugh from the problem till he could see his way!

"Well," said Hugh with a sneer, "what have you got to say?"

Harry rose slowly and pushed the door shut. "When we last met," he said, "what you most wanted was to leave the country."

"I changed my mind," retorted Hugh. "I've got a right to do that, I suppose. I've come back now to get what is mine, and I'll have it, too!" He rapped the table with his knuckles.

Hugh had no recollection now of past generosities. His selfish materialism saw only money that might be his. "I know all about the strike," he went on, "and there's no green in my eye!"

"How much will you take for the property?"

Hugh laughed again jeeringly. "That's your game, is it? But I'm not such a numskull! Whatever you could offer, it's worth more to me. You've found a good thing here, and you'd like to skin me as a butcher skins

a sheep." In the warmer air of the cabin the liquor he had drunk was firing his brain, and an old suspicion leaped to his tongue.

"I know you, Satan Sanderson," he sneered. "You were always the same precious hypocrite in the old days, pretending to be so almighty virtuous, while you looked out for number one. I saw through you then, too, when you were posing as my friend and trying your best all along to queer me with the old man! I knew it well enough. I knew what the reason was, too! You wanted Jessica! You—"

Self-control left Harry suddenly, as a ship's sail is whipped from its gaskets in a white squall. Before the words could be uttered, his fingers were at Hugh's throat.

At that instant there was the sound of running feet outside, a hurried knock at the door and an agitated voice that chilled Harry's blood to ice.

His hands relaxed their hold; he dragged Hugh to the door of the inner room, thrust him inside, shut and bolted it upon him.

Then he went and opened the outer door.

CHAPTER XXXIV THE TEMPTATION

Jessica's eyes met Harry's in a look he could not translate, save that it held both yearning and anguish.

The accusation of Prendergast had stunned her faculties. As in an evil dream, with the low breeze murmuring by and the fitful moon overhead, she had seen the sheriff rise to his feet and methodically put the fragment of paper into his pocket-book. A moment later she was running up the dark path, her thoughts a confusion in which only one coherent purpose stood distinct—to warn him. They would know no need to hasten. If the man she loved had reached the cabin, she would be before them.

Not that she believed him guilty; in his lost past there could be no stain so dark as that! She recalled the look of personal hatred she had once surprised on Prendergast's face. He hated Hugh, and dying, had left this black lie behind to do him a mischief. He was innocent, innocent! But would the charge not be believed? They would arrest him, drag him down to the

town, to the brick jail on the court-house square. The community was prejudiced. Innocent men had been convicted before of crimes they never committed. In those breathless minutes she did not reason further; she knew only that a vital danger threatened him, and that he must fly from it. The lighted pane had told her the occupant of the cabin had returned.

She stood before the door, her hands clasped tightly, her eyes on Harry's face, even in this crucial moment drinking in thirstily what she saw there; for in this crisis, hanging on the narrow verge of catastrophe, when he had need to summon all his store of poise and contained strength, his look melted over her in a mist of tenderness.

"What has happened?" he asked.

He did not offer to touch or to kiss her, but this she did not remember till afterward. In what words could she tell him? Would he think she believed him guilty when she besought him to fly? She answered simply, directly, with only a deep appeal in her eyes:

"Men will be here soon—men from the town. I overheard them. I wanted to let you know!" she hesitated; it had grown all at once difficult to put into words.

"Coming here? Why?"

"To arrest a man who is accused of murder."

If her eyes could have pierced the bolted door a few feet away! If she could have seen that listening face behind it, as her clear tones fell, grow instinct with recognition, amazement, and evil suspicion—a look that her last word swept into a sickly gray terror! If she could have heard the groan from the wretched man beyond!

"Whose murder?"

"Doctor Moreau's."

In all Harry Sanderson's life was to be never such a moment of revealment. He knew that she meant himself. The murderer of Doctor Moreau—Hugh's one-time crony and loose associate, who had shared in the plunder of the forged draft, and had then abandoned his cat's-paw to discovery! The man Hugh had promised to "pay off for it some time!" Had Moreau also made this his stamping-ground? A swift memory swept him of Hugh's hang-dog look, his nervous dread when he had begged in the chapel study for money with which to leave the country. It did not need the smothered gasp from behind the bolted door to point the way to the swift conclusion Harry's mind was racing to. A dull flush spread to his forehead.

Jessica waited with caught breath, searching his countenance. It was told now, but he must know that she had not credited it—that "for better, for worse," she

must believe in him now. "I knew, oh, I knew!" she cried. "You need not tell me!"

The hell of two passions that were struggling within him—a savage exultation and a submerging wave of pity for her utter ignorance, her blind faith, for the painful dénouement that was rushing upon her—died, and left him cold and still. "No," he said gravely, "I am not the man they want. It has all come back to me—the past that I had lost. Such a crime has no part in it."

At another time the abrupt news of this retrieval must have affected her strangely, for she had wondered much concerning the return of that memory that held alike their early love and his own tragedy and shame. Now, however, a greater contingency absorbed her. He must go, and without delay. Her lips were opened to speak when he closed the door behind him and stepped quickly down toward her. At all odds, he was thinking, she must not see the man in that inner room! If she remained he could not guess what shock might result.

"Jessica," he said, "you have tried to save me from danger to-night. I need a greater service of you now; it is to ask no questions, but to go at once. I can not explain why, but you must not stay here a moment."

"Oh," she cried bitterly, "you don't intend to leave! You choose to face it, and you want to spare me. If you really want to spare me, you will go! Why, you would have no chance where they have hated you so. Prendergast was killed robbing the sluice to-night, and he lied—lied—lied! He swore you did it, and they will believe it!"

He put back her beseeching hands. How could he explain? Only to get her away—to gain time—*to think*!

"Listen!" she went on wildly. "They will wait to carry him to the town. I can go and bring my horse here for you. There is time! You have only to send me word, and I will follow you to the end of the world! Only say you will go!"

He caught at the straw. The expedient might serve.

"Very well," he said; "bring him to the upper trail, and wait there for me."

She gave a sob of relief at his acquiescence. "I will hurry, hurry!" she cried, and was gone, swift as a swallow-flight, into the darkness.

As he reëntered the cabin, the calmness fell from Harry Sanderson as a mask drops, and the latent passion sprang in its place. He crossed the room and drew the bolt for the wretched man who, after one swift glance at his face, grovelled on his knees before him, sobered and shivering.

"For God's sake, Harry, you won't give me up?" Hugh cried. "You can't mean to do that! Why, we were in college together! I'd been drinking to-night, or I wouldn't have talked to you as I did. I'm sober enough now, Harry! You can have the claim. I'll give it to you and all you've got out of it. Only let me go before they come to take me!"

Harry drew his feet from the frantic hands that clasped them. "Did you kill Moreau?" he asked shortly.

"It was an accident," moaned Hugh. "I never intended to—I swear to Heaven I didn't! He hounded me, and he tried to bleed me. I only meant to frighten him off! Then—then—I was afraid, and I ran for it. That was when I came to you at Aniston and—we played." Hugh's breath came in gasps and drops of sweat stood on his forehead.

A weird, crowding clamor was sweeping through Harry's brain. When, at the sound of Jessica's voice, he had thrust Hugh into the inner room, it had been only to gain time, to push further back, if by but a moment, the shock which was inevitable. Then, in the twinkling of an eye, Fate had swept the board. Hugh's worthless life was forfeit. He would stand no longer between him and Jessica! The enginery of the law would be their savior.

Neither crime nor penalty was of his making. He owed Hugh nothing—the very money he had taken from the ground, save a bare living, had gone to pay his thievery. He could surrender him to the law, then take Jessica far away where the truth would come mercifully softened by distance and lightened by future happiness. It was not his to intervene, to cozen Justice, to compound a felony and defeat a righteous Providence! He owed mercy to Jessica. He owed none to this cringing, lying thing before him, who now reminded him of that chapel game that had ruined the Reverend Henry Sanderson!

"When we played!" he echoed. "How have you settled your debt—the 'debt of honor' you once counted so highly? How have you lived since then? Have you paid me those days of decent living you staked, and lost?"

Hugh looked past him with hollow, hunted gaze. There was no escape, no weapon to his hand, and those eyes were on him like unwavering sparks of iron.

"But I will!" he exclaimed desperately. "If you'll only help me out of this, I'll live straight to my dying day! You don't know how I've suffered, Harry, or you'd have some mercy on me now! I can never get away from it! That's why I was drunk to-day. Night

and day I see him—Moreau, as I saw him lying here that night on the hillside. He haunts me! You don't know what it means to be always afraid, to wake up in the night with the feel of handcuffs on your wrists, to know that such a thing is behind you, following you, following you, never letting you rest, never forgetting!" A choking sob burst from his lips. "Let me go, Harry," he pleaded; "for my father's sake!"

"Your father is dead," said Harry.

"Then for old-time's sake!" He tried to clasp Harry's knees. "They may be here at any minute! I must have been seen as I crossed the mountain! I thought it would never come out, or I wouldn't have come! I'll go far enough away. I'll go to South America, and you will never see me alive again, neither you nor Jessica! I knew her voice just now—I know she's here. I don't care how or why! You don't need to give me up to get her! I'll give her to you! For God's sake, Harry, listen! Jessica wouldn't want to see me hung! For *her* sake!"

Harry caught his breath sharply. The thrust had gone deep; it had sheared through the specious arguments he had been weaving. The commandment that an hour before had etched itself in letters of fire upon his eyelids hung again before him. He had coveted his neighbor's wife. This man, felon as he was—pitiful hound to whom the news of his father's death brought no flicker of sorrow or remorse, who now offered to barter Jessica for his own safety!—he himself, however unwittingly, had irreparably wronged. Between them stood the accusing wraith of one immortal hour, when the heart of love had beat against his own. If he delivered Hugh to the hangman, would it be for justice's sake?

The scales fell from his eyes. For him, loving Jessica, it could be only a dastard act. Yet if he aided the real Hugh to escape, he, the supposititious Hugh who had played his rôle, must continue it. He must second the villainy, and in so doing play the cheaply tragic part. He must pose as an accused murderer before the town whose good opinion he had longed to gain—before Jessica!—until Hugh had had time to win safe away! He might do even more. The real Hugh would stand small chance; even were the evidence not flawless, the old record would condemn him. But he himself had lightened that record. He had gained liking and sympathy; there might be a chance for him of acquittal.

If this might only be! The truth then need never be known and Hugh Stires, to all belief having been put once in jeopardy, need fear no more. Life would be

before him again, to pay the days of righteous living he had played for in the chapel game, to reverse the record of his selfish and remorseless career. If the trial went against him—Hugh would have had his chance, would be far away. He, Harry Sanderson, would not have betrayed him. A hundred people, if he chose to summon them, would establish his own identity. It would be cheating justice, making a mock of law, but he was in a position where human statute must yield to a higher rule of action. The law might punish, but he would have been true to his own soul. Jessica would understand. The truth held pain and shame for her, but he would have tried to save her from a greater. And he would have cancelled his debt to Hugh!

It was the Harry Sanderson of St. James parish, of the scrupulous conscience—whose college career as Satan Sanderson had come to be a fiery sore in his breast—who now spoke:

"Get up!" he said. "Have you any money?"

Hugh rose, trembling and ashen. "Hardly ten dollars," he answered.

Harry considered hastily. He was almost penniless; nearly all his share of the strike had gone to repay the forged draft. "I have no ready cash," he said, "but the night we played in the chapel, I left a thousand dollars in my study safe. I have not been there since." He took pencil and paper from his pocket and wrote down some figures hastily. "Here is the combination. You must try to get that money."

"Wait," he added, as Hugh's hand was on the latch. He must risk nothing; he could make assurance doubly sure. "A half-mile from the foot of the mountain, where the road comes in from Funeral Hollow, wait for me. I will bring a horse there for you."

Hugh crushed the paper into his pocket and opened the door. "I'll wait," he said. He darted out, slipped around the corner of the cabin, and stealthily disappeared.

Harry sat down upon the doorstep. The strain had been great; in the reaction, he was faint, and a mist was before his eyes. The die was cast. Hugh could easily escape; until he himself spoke, he would not even be hunted. He, Harry Sanderson, was the scapegoat, left to play his part.

How long he sat there he did not know. He sprang up at a muffled sound. He had still a work to do before they came—for Hugh! He saw in an instant, however, that it was Jessica, leading her horse by the bridle.

"I could not wait," she breathed. "You did not come, and I was afraid!"

Mounting, he leaned from the saddle and took both her hands in his— still he did not kiss her.

"Jessica, you believe I am innocent?" he asked anxiously.

"Yes—yes!"

"Will you believe what I am doing is for the best?"

"Always, always!" she whispered, her voice vibrating. "Only go!"

"Whatever happens?"

"Whatever happens!"

He released her hands and rode quickly up the grassy path.

As she stood looking after him, a dog's whine came from the cabin. She ran and released the spaniel and took him up in her arms.

As she did so a sparkle caught her eye. It came from the tiny gold cross lying where Hugh had flung it, near the lighted doorway. She picked it up, looked at it a moment abstractedly and thrust it into her pocket—scarce consciously, for her heart was keeping time to the silenced hoof-beat that was bearing the man she loved from danger.

Where the way opened into the gloomy cut of Funeral Hollow, Harry dismounted and went forward slowly

afoot, leading the horse, till a figure stepped from a clump of bushes to meet him with an exclamation of relief. Hugh had waited at the rendezvous in shivering apprehension and dismal suspicion of Harry's intentions, and had not approached till he had convinced himself that the other came alone. He wrung Harry's hand as he said:

"If I get out of this, I'll do better the rest of my life, I will, upon my soul, Harry!"

"You may not be able to get into the chapel," said Harry; "my rooms"—he felt his cheek burn as he spoke—"may be occupied. On the chance that you fail, take this." He took off the ruby ring, whose interlaced initials had once fortified him in his error of identity. "The stone is worth a good deal. It should be enough to take you anywhere."

Hugh nodded, slipped the ring on his finger, and rode quickly off. Then Harry turned and walked rapidly back toward the town.

CHAPTER XXXV FELDER TAKES A CASE

The sheriff stopped his automobile before the dingy telegraph office. The street had been ringing that evening with more exciting events than it had known in a year.

"He's off," he said disgustedly to the men who had curiously gathered. "He must have got wind of it somehow, and he had a horse ready. We traced the hoof-prints from the cabin as far as the Hollow. I'm going to use the wire."

"That's a lie!" rumbled an angry voice behind him, as Devlin strode into the crowd. "Hugh Stires gave himself up fifteen minutes ago at the jail."

"How do you know that?" demanded the sheriff, relieved but chagrined at his fool's-errand.

"Because I saw him do it," answered Devlin surlily. "I was there."

"Well, it saves trouble for me. That'll tickle you, Felder," the sheriff added satirically, turning toward the lawyer. "You're a sentimentalist, and he's been your special fancy. What do you think now, eh?"

"I'll tell you what *I* think," said Devlin, his big hands working. "I think it's a damned lie of Prendergast's!"

"Oh, ho!" exclaimed the sheriff amusedly. "You once danced to a different tune, Devlin!"

The blood was in the big, lowering face. "I did," he admitted. "I went up against him when the liquor was in me, and by the same token he wiped this street with me. He stood me fair and he whipped me, and I needed it, though I hated him well enough afterwards. An'—an'—"

He gulped painfully. No one spoke.

"It's many's the time since then I've wished the hand was shrivelled that heaved that rock at him in the road! The day when I saw my bit of a lass, holdin' to the horse's mane, ridin' to her death in the Hollow—an'—when he brought her back—" He stopped, struggling with himself, tears rolling down his cheeks.

"No murderer did that!" he burst out. "We gave him the back of the hand an' the sole of the foot, an' we kept to it, though he fought it down an' lived straight an' decent. He never did it! I don't care what they say! I'll see Prendergast in hell before I'll believe it, or any dirty paper he saved to swear a man's life away."

The listeners were silent. No one had ever heard such

a speech from the huge owner of the dance-hall. The sheriff lighted a cigar before he said:

"That's all right, Devlin. We all understand your prejudices, but I'm afraid they haven't much weight with legal minds, like Mr. Felder's here, for instance."

"Excuse me," said Felder. "I fear my prejudices are with Devlin. Good night," he added, moving up the street.

"Where are you bound?" asked the other casually.

"To the jail," answered the lawyer, "to see a client—I hope."

The sheriff emitted a low whistle. "*I* hope there'll be enough sane men left to get a jury!" he said.

CHAPTER XXXVI THE HAND AT THE DOOR

At the sound of steps in the jail corridor and the harsh grating of the key in the lock, Harry rose hastily from the iron cot whereon he had been sitting and took a step forward.

"Jessica!" he exclaimed.

She came toward him, her breath hurried, her cheek pale. Tom Felder's face was at her shoulder. "I have a little matter to attend to in the office," he said, nodding to Harry. "I shall wait for you there, Miss Holme."

She thanked him with a grateful look, and as he vanished, Harry took her hand and kissed it. He longed to take her in his arms.

"I heard of it only at noon," she began, her voice uncertain. "I was afraid they would not let me see you, so I went to Mr. Felder. They were saying on the street that he had offered to defend you."

"I had not been here an hour when he came," he said.

"I know you have no money," she went on; "I know

what you did with the gold you found. And I have begged him to let me pay for any other counsel he will name. I have not told him—what I am to you, but I have told him that I am far from poor, and that nothing counts beside your life. He says you have forbidden him to do this—forbidden him to allow any help from any one. Hugh, Hugh! Why do you do this? The money should be yours, not mine, for it was your father's! It *is* yours, for I am your wife!"

He kissed her hand again without answering.

"Haven't I a right now to be at your side? Mayn't I tell them?"

He shook his head. "Not yet, Jessica."

"I must obey you," she said with a wan smile, "yet I would share your shame as proudly as your glory! You are thinking me weak and despicable, perhaps, because I wanted you to go away. But women are not men, and I—I love you so, Hugh!"

"I think you are all that is brave and good," he protested.

"I want you to believe," she went on, "that I knew you had done no murder. If an angel from Heaven had come to declare it, I would not have believed it. I only want now to understand."

"What do you not understand?" he asked gently.

She half turned toward the door, as she said, in a lower key: "Last night I was overwrought. I had no time to reason, or even to be glad that you had recovered your memory. I thought only of your escaping somewhere—where you would be safe, and where I could follow. But after you had gone, many things came back to me that seemed strange—something curious in your manner. You had not seemed wholly surprised when I told you you were accused. Why did you shut the cabin door, and speak so low? Was there any one else there when I came?"

He averted his face, but he did not answer. She was treading on near ground.

"My horse came back this afternoon," she continued. "He had been ridden hard in the night and his flanks were cut cruelly with a whip. You did not use him, but some one did."

She waited a moment, still he made no reply.

"I want to ask you," she said abruptly, "do you know who killed Doctor Moreau?"

His blood chilled at the question. He looked down at her speechless. "You must let me speak," she said. "You won't answer that. Then you do know who really did it. Oh, I have thought so much since last night! For some reason you are shielding him. Was it the

man who was in the cabin—who rode my horse? If he is guilty, why do you help him off, and so make yourself partly guilty?"

He looked down at her and put a finger on her lips. "Do you remember what you told me last night—that you would believe what I did was for the best?"

"But I thought then you were going away! How can I believe it now? Why, they hang men who murder, and it is you who are accused! If you protect the real murderer, you will have to stand in his place. The whole town believes you are guilty—I see it in all their faces. They are sorry, many of them, for they don't hate you as they did, but they think you did it. Even Mr. Felder, though I have told him what I suspect, and though he is working now to defend you!"

"Jessica," he urged, "you must trust me and have faith in me. I know it is hard, but I can't explain to you! I can't tell you—yet—why I do as I am doing, but you must believe that I am right."

She was puzzled and confused. When she had put this and that together, guided by her intuition, the conclusion that he knew the guilty one had brought a huge relief. Now this fell into disarray. She felt beneath his manner a kind of appeal, a deprecation, almost a hidden pity for her—as though the danger were hers,

not his, and she the one caught in this catastrophe. She looked at him pale and distraught.

"You speak as if you were sorry for me," she said, "and not for yourself. Is it because you know you are not in real danger—that you know the truth must come out, only you can't tell it yourself, or tell me either? Is that it?"

A wave of feeling passed over Harry, of hopeless longing. Whichever way the issue turned there was anguish for her—for she loved him. If he were acquitted, she must learn that past love between them had been illicit, that present love was shame, and future love an impossibility. Convicted, there must be added to this the bitter knowledge that her husband in very truth was a murderer, doomed to lurk in hiding so long as he might live. Yet not to reassure her now was cruelty.

"It is not that, Jessica," he said gravely; "yet you must not fear for me—for my life. Try to believe me when I say that some time you will understand and know that I did only what I must."

"Will that be soon?" she asked.

"I think it may be soon," he answered.

Her face lighted. The puzzle and dread lifted. "Oh, then," she said—"oh, then, I shall not be afraid. I can not share your thoughts, nor your secret, and I must

rebel at that. You mustn't blame me—I wouldn't be a woman if I did not—but I love you more than all the world, and I shall believe that you know best. Hugh," she added softly, "do you know that—you haven't kissed me?"

Before her upturned, pleading eyes and trembling lips, the iron of his purpose bent to the man in him, and he took her into his arms.

CHAPTER XXXVII THE PENITENT THIEF

A frosty gloom was over the city of Aniston, moon and stars hidden by a cloudy sky, from which a light snow—the first of the season—was sifting down. The streets were asleep; only occasional belated pedestrians were to be seen in the chilly air. These saw a man, his face muffled from the snowflakes, pass hurriedly toward the fountained square, from whose steeple two o'clock was just striking. The wayfarer skirted the square, keeping in cover of the buildings as though avoiding chance observation, till he stood on the pavement of a Gothic chapel fronting the open space.

Here he paused and glanced furtively about him. He could see the entrance to the minister's study, at which he had so often knocked and the great rose-window of the audience-room where he had once gamed with Harry Sanderson. This was the building he must enter like a thief.

On the night of his flight from Smoky Mountain, Hugh had ridden hard till dawn, abandoning the horse

to find its way back as best it might. Hidden in a snug retreat, he had slept through the next day, to recommence his journeying at nightfall. He had thus been obliged to make haste slowly and had lost much valuable time. For two days after his arrival, he had hung about outside the town in a fever of impatience; for though he had readily ascertained that the premises were unoccupied, the first night he had been frightened away by the too zealous scrutiny of a policeman, and on the next he had been unable to force the door. That morning he had secured a skeleton-key, and now the weather was propitious for his purpose.

After a moment's reconnoitering, he scaled the frost-fretted iron palings and gained the shelter of the porch. He tried the key anxiously; to his relief it fitted. Another minute and he stood in the study, the door locked behind him, his veins beating with excitement.

He felt along the wall, drawing his hand back sharply as it encountered the electric switch. He struck a wax *fusée* and by its feeble ray gazed about him. The room looked as it had always looked, with Harry's books on the shelves, and his heavy walking-stick in the corner, and there against the wall stood the substantial iron safe that held his own ransom. Crouching down before it, he took from his pocket the paper upon which was

written the combination; ten to the right, five to the left, twice nineteen to the right—

The match scorched his fingers, and he lighted another and began to turn the knob. The lock bore both figures and letters in concentric rings, and he saw that the seven figures Harry had written formed a word. Hugh dropped the match with a smothered exclamation, for the word was Jessica! So Harry really had loved her in the old days! Had he profited by that wedding-day expulsion to make love to her himself? Yet on the night of the game with Harry in the chapel the house in the aspens had been closed and dark. How had she come to be in Smoky Mountain? His father was dead—so Harry had said. If so, the money had gone to her, no doubt. Well, at any rate, she had never been anything to him and he was no dog-in-the-manger. What he needed now was the thousand dollars, and here it was. He swung the massive door wide and took out the canvas bag. With this and the ruby ring—it must easily be worth as much again—he could put the round world between himself and capture.

He closed the safe, and with the bag of coin in his hand, groped his way to the door of the chapel. It was less dark there, for the snow was making a white night outside, and the stained glass cast a wan glimmer across

the aisles. He could almost see himself and Harry Sanderson sitting in the candle-light at the communion table inside the altar-rail, almost hear the musical chink of the gold! His hand wandered to his pocket, where lay the one wax wafer he had kept as a pocket-piece. At that altar he had sworn to pay a day of clean living for each of the counters he had lost. He had not kept that oath, and now vengeance was near to overtaking him. He shuddered. He had turned over a new leaf this time in earnest, and he would make up for the broken vow!

But meanwhile he greatly needed sleep, and to-night in the open that was out of the question. He could gain several good hours' rest where he was, and still get away before daybreak. He drew together the altar-cushions and lay down, the canvas bag beside him, but he was cold, and at length he rose and went into the vestry for a surplice. He wrapped this about him, and, lighting a cigarette, lay down again. He was very tired, but his limbs twitched from nervousness. He lighted one cigarette after another, but sleep was coy. He tried to woo it with nonsense rhymes, but the lines ran together. He tried the remedy of his restless, precocious childhood—the counting of innumerable sheep as they leaped the hurdle one by one; but now all of the sheep were black. There came before his eyes, uncalled, the portrait of his

dead mother, that had always hung at home in the wainscoted library. In her memory his father had built this very chapel. He wondered again whether she had looked like the picture.

A softer feeling came to him. She would be sorry if she could know his plight. Perhaps if she had lived his life might have been different. Slow tears stole down his cheeks—not now of affected sentimentalism, or of hysterical self-pity, but warmer drops from some deeper well that had not overflowed since he was a little boy. If he had the chance he would live from now on so that if she were alive she need not be ashamed! The promise he made himself at that moment was an honester one than all his selfish years had known, for it sprang not from dread, but from the better feeling that his maturity had trampled and denied. He felt a kind of peace— the first real peace he had known since his school-days—and with it drowsiness came at last. With the drops wet on his cheek, forgetfulness found him. In a few minutes he was sleeping heavily.

The last half-consumed cigarette dropped from his relaxing fingers to the cushion, where it made a smoldering nest of fire. A tiny tongue of flame caught the edge of a wall-hanging, ran up to the dry oaken rafters and speedily ignited them. In fifteen minutes the

interior of the chapel was a mass of flame, and Hugh woke gasping and bewildered.

With a cry of alarm he sprang to his feet, seized the bag of coin and ran to the door of the study. In his haste he stumbled against it, and the dead-lock snapped to. He was a prisoner now, for he had left the skeleton-key in the inside of the outer door. Clutching his treasure, he ran to the main entrance; it was fast. He tried the smaller windows; iron bars were set across them. He made shift to wrap the surplice about his mouth, against the stifling smoke and fiery vapors. The bag dropped from his hand and the gold rolled about the floor. He stooped and clutched a handful of the coins and crammed them into his pocket. Was he to die after all like this, caught like a rat in a trap? In his panic of terror he forgot all necessity of concealment; he longed for nothing so much as discovery by those whose cries he now heard filling the waking street. Many voices were swelling the clamor there. Bells were pealing a terror-tongued alarm, but those on the spot saw that the structure was doomed. Hugh screamed desperately, but the roar of the flames overhead and the angry crackling of the woodwork drowned all else. The roof timbers were snapping, the muffling surplice was scorching, a thousand luminous points about him

were bursting into fire in the sickening heat. He pounded with all his might upon the door panels, but in vain. Who outside could have imagined that a human being was pent within that fiery furnace?

Uttering a hoarse cry, with the strength of despair, Hugh wrenched a pew from the floor and made of it a ladder to reach the rose-window. Mounting this, he beat frantically with his fist upon the painted glass. The crystal shivered beneath the blows, and clinging to the iron supports, his beard burnt to the skin, he set his face to the aperture and drew a gulping breath of the sweet, cold air. In his agony, with that fiery hell opening beneath him, he could see the massed people watching from the safety that was so near.

"Look! Look!" The sudden cry went up, and a thrill of awe ran through the crowd. The glass Hugh had shattered had formed the face of the Penitent Thief in the window-design, and his outstretched arms fitted those of the figure. It was as though by some ghastly miracle the painted features had suddenly sprung into life, the haggard eyes opened in appeal. The watchers gasped in amazement.

The flame was upon him now. He was going to his last account—with no time to alter the record. But had not his sleeping vow been one of reformation? He tried

to shriek this to the deaf heavens, but all the spellbound watchers heard was the cry: "Lord, Lord, remember—" And this articulate prayer from the crucified malefactor filled them with a superstitious horror. In the crowd more than one covered his face with his hands.

All at once there came a shout of warning. The wall opened outward, tottered and fell.

Then it was that they saw the writhing figure, tangled in the twisted lead bars of the wrecked rose-window. Shielding their faces from the unendurable heat, they reached and bore it to safety, laying it on the crisp, snowy grass, and tearing off the singed and smoking ministerial robes.

Judge Conwell was one of these. In the flaring confusion he leaned over the figure—the gleam of the ruby ring on the finger caught his eye. He bent forward to look into the drawn and distorted face.

"Good God!" he said. "It's Harry Sanderson!"

CHAPTER XXXVIII A DAY FOR THE STATE

In communities such as Smoky Mountain the law moves with fateful rapidity. Harry had been formally arraigned the second morning after his self-surrender and had pleaded not guilty. The Grand Jury was in session—indeed, had about finished its labors—and there had been no reason for delay. All necessary witnesses for the state were on the ground, and Felder for his part had no others to summon. So that when Doctor Brent, one keen forenoon, swung himself off a Pullman at the station, returning from his ten days' absence, he found the town thrilling with the excitement of the first day of the trial. Before he left the station, he had learned of Prendergast's death and accusation and knew that Tom Felder had come to the prisoner's defense.

Doctor Brent had taken no stock in the young lawyer's view of Hugh Stires. The incident that they had witnessed on the mountain road—it had troubled him during his trip—had been to him only another chapter in the hackneyed tragedy of romantic womanhood

flattered by a rascal. He was inclined now to lay the championship as much to interest in Jessica as in the man who had won her love.

He walked thoughtfully to his friend's deserted office, and leaving his suit-case there, betook himself to the filled court-room, where Smoky Mountain had gathered to watch Felder's fight for the life and liberty of the man who for days past had been the center of interest. The court had opened two hours before and half the jury had been selected. He found a seat with some difficulty, and thereafter his attention was given first to the bench where the prisoner sat, and second to a chair close to the railing beside Mrs. Halloran's, where a girl's face glimmered palely under a light veil.

Toward this chair the hundreds of eyes in the room that morning had often turned. Since the day Mrs. Halloran had surprised Jessica at work upon the rock statue, she had kept her counsel, but as the physician had conjectured, the monument had been stumbled upon and had drawn curious visitors. Thus the name on the grave had become common property and the coincidence had been chattered of. That Jessica had chiselled the statue was not doubted—she had bought the tools in town, and old Paddy Wise, the blacksmith, had sharpened them for her. The story Prendergast had told in

the general store, too, had not been forgotten, and the aid she had given the fever-stricken man had acquired a new significance in face of the knowledge that she had more than once been admitted to the jail with Felder. No one in Smoky Mountain would have ventured to "pump" the lawyer, and the town had been too mindful of its manners to catechize her, but it had buzzed with theories. From the moment of the opening of the trial she had divided interest with the prisoner.

The first appearance of the latter, between two deputies, had caused a murmur of surprise. In the weeks of wholesome toil and mountain air, the sallow, haggard look that Harry had brought to the town had gradually faded; his step had grown more elastic, his cheek ruddier, his eye a clearer blue. The scar on his temple had become less noticeable. Day by day, he had been growing back to the old look. The beard and mustache now were gone; the face they saw was smooth-shaven, calm, alien and absorbed. He had bowed slightly to the judge, shaken hands gravely with Felder and sat down with a quick, flashing smile at the quivering face behind the veil. He had seemed of all there the one who had least personal concern in the deliberations that were forward. Yet beneath that mask of calmness Harry's every nerve was stretched, every sense restive.

In the interviews he had had with his client, Felder had been puzzled and nonplussed. To tell the truth, when he had first come to his defense it had been not with a conviction of his innocence, but with a belief in the present altered character that made the law's penalty seem excessive and supererogatory; in fine, that whatever he might have deserved when he did it—assuming that he did it—he did not deserve hanging now. But the man's manner had made him lean more and more upon an assumption of actual innocence. In the end, while discarding Jessica's reasoning, he had accepted her conclusion. The man was certainly guiltless. Since this time, he had felt his position keenly. It had been one thing to do the very best possible for a presumptively guilty man—to get him off against the evidence if he could; it was a vastly different thing to defend one whom he believed actually guiltless against damning circumstance.

With the filling of the jury-box the court adjourned for an hour and Doctor Brent saw the two women's figures disappear with Felder into a side room, while the prisoner was taken in charge by the deputies. The doctor lunched hastily at the Mountain Valley House, irritated out of his usual urbanity by the chatter of the crowded dining-room, realizing then how busy gossip

had been with Jessica's name. He walked back to the court-room moodily smoking.

The afternoon session commenced with a concise opening by the district attorney; Felder's reply was as brief, and the real business of the day began with the witnesses for the state.

Circumstantially speaking, the evidence was flawless. Doctor Moreau, while little known and less liked, had figured in the town as a promoter and an inventor of "slick" stock schemes. He had come there with Hugh Stires, from Sacramento, where they had had a business partnership—of short duration. There had been bad blood between them there, as the latter had once admitted. The prisoner had preëmpted the claim on Smoky Mountain in an abortive "boom" which Moreau had engineered, and over whose proceeds the pair, it was believed, had fallen out. He had then, to use the attorney's phrase, "swapped the devil for the witch," and had taken up with Prendergast, who by the manner of his taking off had finally justified a jail record in another state. Soon after this break Hugh Stires had vanished. On the day following his last appearance in the town, the body of Moreau had been found on the Little Paymaster Claim, shot by a cowardly bullet through the back—a fact which precluded the possibility

that the deed had been done in self-defense. There was evidence that he had died a painful and lingering death. Suspicion had naturally pointed to the vanished man, and this suspicion had grown until, after some months' absence, he had returned, alleging that he had lost his memory of the past, to resume his life in the cabin on the mountain and his partnership with the thief Prendergast. The two had finally quarrelled and Prendergast had taken up his abode in the town. Subsequent to this, the latter had been heard to make dark insinuations, unnoted at the time but since grown significant, hinting at criminal knowledge of the prisoner. The close of this chapter had been Prendergast's dismal end in the gulch, when he had produced the scrap of paper which was the crux of the case. He declared he had found Moreau dying; that the latter had traced with his own hand the accusation which fastened the crime upon Hugh Stires. Specimens of Moreau's handwriting were not lacking and seemed to prove beyond question its authenticity.

Such were the links of the coil which wound, with each witness, closer and closer—none knew better how closely than Harry Sanderson himself. As witness succeeded witness, his heart sank. Jessica's burden was not to be lightened; Hugh must remain a Cain, a

dweller in the dark places of the earth. In the larger part, his own sacrifice was to fail!

In his cross-examination Felder had fought gamely to lighten the weight of the evidence: The prisoner's old associations with Moreau had been amicable, else they would not have come to Smoky Mountain together; if he had been disliked and avoided, the circumstance was referable rather to his companionships than to his own actions; whatever the pervasive contempt, there had been nothing criminal on the books against him. The lawyer's questions touched the baleful whisper that had become allegation and indictment, a prejudged conviction of guilt. They made it clear that the current belief had been the fruit of antipathy and bias; that it had been no question of evidence; so far as that went, he, Felder, might have done the deed, or Prendergast, or any one there. But Smoky Mountain would have said, as it did say, "It was Hugh Stires!" He compelled the jury to recognize that but one bit of actual evidence had been offered—there had been no eye-witness, no telltale incident. All rested upon a single scrap of paper, a fragment of handwriting in no way difficult of imitation, and this in turn upon the allegation of a thief, struck down in an act of crime, whose word in an ordinary case of fact would not be worth a farthing.

No motive had been alleged for the killing of Moreau by the prisoner, but Prendergast had had motive enough in his accusation. It had been open knowledge that he hated Hugh Stires, and his own character made it evident that he would not have scrupled to fasten a murder upon him.

But as Felder studied the twelve grave faces in the jury-box, who in the last analysis were all that counted, he shared his client's hopelessness. Judgment and experience told him how futile were all theories in the face of that inarticulate but damning witness that Prendergast had left behind him. So the afternoon dragged through, a day for the State.

Sunset came early at that season. Dark fell and the electric bulbs made their mimic day, but no one left the room. The outcome seemed a foregone conclusion. The jurymen no longer gazed at the prisoner, and when they looked at one another, it was with grim understanding. As the last witness for the State stepped down and the prosecutor rested, the judge glanced at the clock.

"There is a bare half-hour," he said tentatively. "Perhaps the defense would prefer not to open testimony till to-morrow."

Felder had risen. He saw his opportunity—to bring out sharply a contrasting point in the prisoner's favor, the one circumstance, considered apart, pointing toward innocence rather than guilt—to leave this for the jury to take with them, to off-set by its effect the weight of the evidence that had been given.

"I will proceed, if your Honor pleases," he said, and amid a rustle of surprise and interest called Jessica to the stand.

As she went forward to the witness chair, she put back the shielding veil, and her face, pale as bramble-bloom under her red-bronze hair, made an appealing picture. A cluster of white carnations was pinned to her coat and as she passed Harry she bent and laid one in his hand. The slight act, not lost upon the spectators, called forth a sibilant flutter of sympathy. For it wore no touch of designed effect; its impulse was as pure and unmistakable as its meaning.

Harry had started uncontrollably as she rose, for he had had no inkling of the lawyer's intention, and a flush darkened his cheek at the cool touch of the flower. But this faded to a settled pallor, as under Felder's grave questioning she told in a voice as clear as a child's, yet with a woman's emotion struggling through it, the story of her disregarded warning. While she spoke pain and shame travelled through his every vein, for—though technically she had not brought herself into the

perplexing purview of the law—she was laying bare the secret of her own heart, which now he would have covered at any cost.

"That is all, your Honor," said Felder, when Jessica had finished her story.

"Do you wish to cross-examine?" asked the judge perfunctorily.

The prosecutor looked at her an instant. He saw the faintness in her eyes, the twitching of the gloved hand on the rail. "By no means," he said courteously, and turned to his papers.

At the same moment, as Jessica stepped into the open aisle, the ironic chance which so often relieves the strain of the tragic by a breath of the banal, treated the spellbound audience to a novel sensation. Every electric light suddenly went out, and darkness swooped upon the town and the court-room. A second's carelessness at the power-house a half-mile away—the dropping of a bit of waste into a cog-wheel—and the larger mechanism that governed the issues of life and death was thrown into instant confusion. Hubbub arose—people stood up in their places.

The judge's gavel pounded viciously and his stentorian voice bellowed for order.

"Keep your seats, everybody!" he commanded. "Mr. Clerk, get some candles. This court is not yet adjourned!"

To Jessica the sudden blankness came with a nervous shock. Since that first meeting in the jail she had pinned her faith on the reassurance that had been given her. She had fought down doubt and questioning and leaned hard upon her trust. But in her overwrought condition, as the end drew near with no solution of the enigma, this faith sometimes faltered. The mystery was so impenetrable, the peril so imminent! To-day, in the court-room, her subtle sense had told her that, belief and conviction aside, a pronounced feeling of sympathy existed for the man she loved. She had not needed Mrs. Halloran's comforting assurances on this score, for the atmosphere was surcharged with it. She had felt it when she laid the carnation in his hand, and even more unmistakably while she had given her testimony. She had realized the value of that one unvarnished fact, introduced so effectively—that he had had time to get away, and instead had chosen to surrender himself.

Yet even as she thrilled to the responsive current, Jessica had not been deceived. She felt the pitiful impotence of mere sympathy against the apparent weight of evidence that had frightened her. Surely,

surely, if he was to save himself, the truth must come out speedily! But the end of it all was in sight and he had not spoken. To-day as she watched his face, the thought had come to her that perhaps his reassurance had been given only to comfort her and spare her anguish. The thought had come again and again to torture her; only by a great effort had she been able to give her testimony. As the pall of darkness fell upon the court-room, it brought a sense of premonition, as though the incident prefigured the gloomy end. She turned sick, and stumbled down the aisle, feeling that she must reach the outer air.

A pushing handful opened the way to the corridor, and in a moment more she was in the starlit out-of-doors, fighting down her faintness, with the babble of talk behind her and the cool breeze on her cheek.

CHAPTER XXXIX THE UNSUMMONED WITNESS

In the room Jessica had left, the turmoil was simmering down; here and there a match was struck and showed a circle of brightness. The glimmer of one of them lit the countenance of a man who had brushed her sleeve as he entered. It was Hallelujah Jones. The evangelist had prolonged his stay at Smoky Mountain, for the town, thrilling to its drama of crime and judgment, had seemed a fruitful vineyard. He had no local interest in the trial of Hugh Stires, and had not attended its session; but he had been passing the place when the lights went out and in curiosity had crowded into the confusion, where now he looked about him with eager interest.

A candle-flame fluttered now, like a golden butterfly, on the judge's desk, another on the table inside the bar. More grew along the walls until the room was bathed in tremulous yellow light. It touched the profile of the prisoner, turned now, for his look had followed Jessica and was fixed questioningly on her empty seat. In the

unseeing darkness Harry had held the white carnation to his lips before he drew its stem through his lapel.

The street preacher's jaw dropped in blank astonishment, for what he saw before him brought irresistibly back another scene that, months before, had bit into his mind. The judge's high desk turned instantly to a chapel altar, and the table back of the polished railing to a communion table. The minister that had looked across it in the candle-light had worn a white carnation in his buttonhole. His face—

Hallelujah Jones started forward with an exclamation. A thousand times his zealot imagination had pictured the recreant clergyman he had unmasked as an outcast, plunging toward the lake of brimstone. Here it was at last in his hand, the end of the story! The worst of criminals, skulking beneath an alias! He sprang up the aisle.

"Wait! wait!" he cried. "I have evidence to give!" He pointed excitedly toward Harry. "This man is not what you think! He is not—"

Forensic thunder loosed itself from the wrathful judge's desk, and crashed across the stupefied room. His gavel thumped upon the wood. "How dare you," he vociferated, "break in upon the deliberations of this court! I fine you twenty dollars for contempt!"

Felder had leaped to his feet, every sense on the *qui vive*. Like a drowning man he grasped at the straw. What could this man know? He took a bill from his pocket and clapped it down on the clerk's desk.

"I beg to purge him of contempt," he said, "and call him as a witness."

The district attorney broke in:

"Your Honor, I think I am within my rights in protesting against this unheard-of proceeding. The man is a vagrant of unknown character. His very action proclaims him mentally unbalanced. Beyond all question he can know nothing of this case."

"I have not my learned opponent's gift of clairvoyance," retorted Felder tartly. "I repeat that I call this man as a witness."

The judge pulled his whiskers and looked at the evangelist in severe annoyance. "Take the stand," he said gruffly.

Hallelujah Jones snatched the Bible from the clerk's hands and kissed it. Knowledge was burning his tongue. The jury were leaning forward in their seats.

"Have you ever seen the prisoner before?" asked Felder.

"Yes."

"When?"

"When he was a minister of the gospel."

Felder stared. The judge frowned. The jury looked at one another and a laugh ran round the hushed room.

The merriment kindled the evangelist's distempered passion. Sudden anger flamed in him. He leaned forward and shook his hand vehemently at the table where Harry sat, his face as colorless as the flower he wore.

"That man's name," he blazed, "is not Hugh Stires! It is a cloak he has chosen to cover his shame! He is the Reverend Henry Sanderson of Aniston!"

CHAPTER XL FATE'S WAY

Harry's pulses had leaped with excitement when the street preacher's first exclamation startled the court-room; now they were beating as though they must burst. He was not to finish the losing struggle. The decision was to be taken from his hands. Fate had interfered. This bigot who had once been the means of his undoing, was to be the *deus ex machina*. Through the stir about him he heard the crisp voice of the district attorney:

"I ask your Honor's permission, before this extraordinary witness is examined further," he said caustically, "to read an item printed here which has a bearing upon the testimony." He held in his hand a newspaper which, earlier in the afternoon, with cynical disregard of Felder's tactics, he had been casually perusing.

"I object, of course," returned Felder grimly.

"Objection overruled!" snapped the irritated judge. "Read it, sir."

Holding the newspaper to a candle, the lawyer read

in an even voice, prefacing his reading with the journal's name and date:

"This city, which was aroused in the night by the burning of St. James Chapel, will be greatly shocked to learn that its rector, the Reverend Henry Sanderson, who has been for some months on a prolonged vacation, was in the building at the time, and now lies at the city hospital, suffering from injuries from which it is rumored there is grave doubt of his recovery."

In the titter that rippled the court-room Harry felt his heart bound and swell. Under the succinct statement he clearly discerned the fact. He saw the pitfall into which Hugh had fallen—the trap into which he himself had sent him on that fatal errand with the ruby ring on his finger. "Grave doubt of his recovery!"—a surge of relief swept over him to his finger-tips. Dead men can not be brought to bar—so Jessica would escape shame. With Hugh passed beyond human justice, he could declare himself. The bishop had guarded his secret, and saved the parish from an unwelcome scandal. He could explain—could tell him that illness and unbalance lay beneath that chapel game! He could take up his career! He would be free to go back—to be himself again—to be Jessica's—if Hugh died! The reading voice drummed in his ears:

"The facts have not as yet been ascertained, but it seems clear that the popular young minister returned to town unexpectedly last night, and was asleep in his study when the fire started. His presence in the building was unguessed until too late, and it was by little short of a miracle that he was brought out alive.

"As we go to press we learn that Mr. Sanderson's condition is much more hopeful than was at first reported."

Harry's heart contracted as if a giant hand had clutched it. His elation fell like a rotten tree girdled at the roots. If Hugh *did not* die! He chilled as though in a spray of liquid air. Hugh's escape—the chance his conscience had given him, was cut off. He had not betrayed him when the way was open; how could he do so now when flight was barred? If to deliver him then to the hangman would have been cowardice, how much more cowardly now, when it was to save himself, and when the other was helpless? And the law demanded its victim!

As a drowning man sees flit before him the panorama of his life, so in this clarifying instant these lurid pictures of the tangle of his past flashed across Harry's mental vision.

The judge reached for the newspaper the lawyer held, ran his eye over it, and brought his gavel down with an angry snort.

"Take him away," he said. "His testimony is ordered stricken from the records. The fine is remitted, Mr. Felder—we can't make you responsible for lunatics. Bailiff, see that this man has no further chance to disturb these proceedings. The court stands adjourned."

CHAPTER XLI FELDER WALKS WITH DOCTOR BRENT

Felder had been among the last to leave the court-room. He was discomfited and angry. He had meant to make a telling point for the defense, and the unbalanced imagination of a strolling, bigot gospeller had undone him. His own precipitate and ill-considered action had uncovered an idiotic mare's-nest, to taint his appeal with bathos and open his cause with a farcical anti-climax. He glumly gathered his scattered papers, put with them the leaf of the newspaper from which the district attorney had read, and despatched the lot to his office by a messenger.

At the door of the court-house Doctor Brent slipped an arm through his.

"Too bad, Tom," he said sympathizingly. "I don't think you quite deserved it."

Felder paced a moment without speaking. "I need evidence," he said then, "—anything that may help. I made a mistake. You heard all the testimony?"

The other nodded.

"What did you think of it?"

"What could any one think? I give all credit to your motive, Tom, but it's a pity you're mixed up in it."

"Why?"

"Because, if there's anything in human evidence, he's a thoroughly worthless reprobate. He lay for Moreau and murdered him in cold blood, and he ought to swing."

"The casual view," said the lawyer gloomily. "Just what I should have said myself—if this had happened a month ago."

His friend looked at him with an amused expression. "I begin to think he must be a remarkable man!" he said. "Is it possible he has really convinced you that he isn't guilty?"

Felder turned upon the doctor squarely. "Yes," he returned bluntly. "He has. Whatever I may have believed when I took this case, I have come to the conclusion—against all my professional instincts, mind you—that he never killed Moreau. I believe he's as innocent as either you or I!"

The physician looked puzzled. "You believe Moreau's hand didn't write that accusation?"

"I don't know."

"Do you think he lied?"

"I don't know what to think. But I am convinced Hugh Stires isn't lying. There's a mystery in the thing that I can't get hold of." He caught the physician's half-smile. "Oh, I know what you think," he said resentfully. "You think it is Miss Holme. I assure you I am defending Hugh Stires for his own sake!"

"She played you a close second to-day," observed the doctor shrewdly. "That carnation—I never saw a thing better done."

Felder drew his arm away. "Miss Holme," he said almost stiffly, "is as far from acting—"

"My dear fellow!" exclaimed the other. "Don't snap me up. She's a gentlewoman, and everything that is lovely. If she were the reason, I should honor you for it. I'm very deeply sorry for her. For my part, I'm sure I wish you might get him off. She loves him, and doesn't care who sees it, and if he were as bad as the worst, a woman like that could make a man of him. But I know juries. In towns like this they take themselves pathetically in earnest. On the evidence so far, they'll convict fast enough."

"I know it," said the lawyer despondently. "And yet he's innocent. I'd stake my life on it. It's worthless as evidence and I shan't introduce it, but he has as good as admitted to her that he knows who did it."

"Come, come! Putting his neck into the noose for mere Quixotic feeling? And who, pray, in this Godforsaken town, should he be sacrificing himself for?" the doctor asked satirically.

"That's the rub," said the lawyer. "Nobody. Yet I hang by my proposition."

"Well, he'll hang by something less tenuous, I'm afraid. But it won't be your fault. The crazy evangelist was only an incident. He merely served to jolt us back to the normal. By the way, did you hear him splutter after he got out?"

"No."

"You remember the story he told the other night of the minister who was caught gambling on his own communion table? Well, Hugh Stires is not only the Reverend Henry Something-or-other, but he is that man, too! The crack-brained old idiot would have told the tale all over again, only the crowd hustled him.

"There he is now," he said suddenly, as a light sprang up and voices broke out on the opposite corner. "The gang is standing by. I see your friend Barney McGinn," he added, with a grim enjoyment. "I doubt if there are many converts to-night."

Even as he spoke, there came a shout of laughter and warning. The spectators scattered in all directions, and
a stream of water from a well-directed hose deluged the itinerant and his music-box.

Ten minutes later the street preacher, drenched and furious, was trundling his melodeon toward Funeral Hollow, on his way to the coast.

CHAPTER XLII THE RECKONING

As Harry stood again in the obscure half-darkness of his cell, it came to him that the present had a far-reaching significance—that it was but the handiwork and resultant of forces in his own past. He himself had brewed the bitter wormwood he must drink. Jessica's quivering arraignment on that lurid wedding-day in the white house in the aspens—it had been engraven ever since on his buried memory!—rang in his mind:

You were strong and he was weak. You led and he followed. You were "Satan Sanderson," Abbot of the Saints, the set in which he learned gambling. You helped to make him what he has become!

They had made variant choice, and that choice had left Harry Sanderson in training for the gaiters of a bishop, and Hugh Stires treading the paths of dalliance and the gambler. But he himself had set Hugh's feet on the red path that had pointed him to the shameful terminus. He had gambled for Hugh's future, forgetting that his past remained, a thing that must be

covered. He had won Hugh's counters, but his own right to be himself he had staked and lost long before that game on the communion table under the painted crucifixion.

The words he had once said to Hugh recurred to him with a kind of awe: "Put myself in your place? I wish to God I could!"

Fate—or was it God?—had taken him at his word. He had been hurled like a stone from a catapult into Hugh's place, to bear his knavery, to suffer his dishonor, and to redeem the baleful reputation he had made. He had been his brother's keeper and had failed in the trust; now the circle of retribution, noiseless and inexorable as the wheeling of that vast scorpion cluster in the sky, evened the score and brought him again to the test! And, in the supreme strait, was he, a poor poltroon, to step aside, to cry "enough," to yield ignobly? Even if to put aside the temptation might bring him face to face with the final shameful penalty?

This, then, was the meaning of the strange sequence of events through which he had been passing since the hour when he had awakened in the box-car! Living, he was not to betray Hugh; the Great Purpose behind all meant that he should go forward on the path he had chosen to the end!

A step outside the cell, the turning of the key. The door opened, and Jessica, pale and trembling, stood on the threshold.

"I can not help it," she said, as she came toward him, "though you told me not to come. I have trusted all the while, and waited, and—and prayed. But to-day I was afraid."

She paused, locking her hands before her, looking at him in an agony of entreaty. When she had fled from the court-room to the open air, she had walked straight away toward the mountain, struggling in the cool wind and motion against the feeling of physical sickness and anguish. But she had only partly regained her self-possession. Returning, the thinning groups about the dim-lit door had made it clear that the session was over. In her painful confusion of mind she had acted on a peremptory impulse that drove her to the jail, where her face had quickly gained her entrance.

"Surely, surely," she went on, "the man you are protecting has had time enough! Hasn't he? Won't you tell them the truth now?"

He knew not how to meet the piteous reproach and terror of that look. She had not heard the street preacher's declaration, he knew, but even if she had, it would have been to her only an echo of the old mooted

likeness. He had given her comfort once—but this was no more to be. No matter what it meant to him, or to her!

"Jessica," he said steadily, "when you came to me here that first day, and I told you not to fear for me, I did not mean to deceive you. I thought then that it would all come right. But something has happened since then— something that makes a difference. I can not tell who was the murderer of Moreau. I can not tell you or any one else, either now or at any time."

She gazed at him startled. She had a sudden conception of some element hitherto unguessed in his make-up, something inveterate and adamant. Could it be that he did not intend to tell at all? The very idea was monstrous! Yet that clearly was his meaning. She looked at him with flashing eyes.

"You mean you will not?" she exclaimed bitterly. "You are bent on sacrificing yourself, then! You are going to take this risk because you think it brave and noble, because somehow it fits your man's gospel! Can't you see how wicked and selfish it is? You are thinking only of him, and of yourself, not of me!"

"Jessica, Jessica!" he protested with a groan. But in the self-torture of her questionings she paid no heed.

"Don't you think I suffer? Haven't I borne enough in the months since I married you, for you to want to

save me this? Do you owe me nothing, me whom you so wronged, whose—"

She stopped suddenly at the look on his face of mortal pain, for she had struck harder than she knew. It pierced through the fierce resentment to her deepest heart, and all her love and pity gushed back upon her in a torrent. She threw herself on her knees by the bare cot, crying passionately:

"Oh, forgive me! Forget what I said! I did not mean it. I have forgiven you a thousand times over. I never ceased to love you. I love you now, more than all the world."

"It is true," he said, hoarse misery in his tone. "I have wronged you. If I could coin my blood drop by drop, to pay for the past, I could not set that right. If giving my life over and over again would save you pain, I would give it gladly. But what you ask now is the one thing I can not do. It would make me a pitiful coward. I did not kill Moreau. That is all I can say to you or to those who try me."

"Your life!" she said with dry lips. "It will mean that. That counts so fearfully much to me—more than my own life a hundred times. Yet there is something that counts more than all that to you!"

His face was that of a man who holds his hand in

the fire. "Jessica," he said, "it is like this with me. When you found me here—the day I saw you on the balcony—I was a man whose soul had lost its compass and its bearings. My conscience was asleep. You woke it, and it is fiercely alive now. And now with my memory has come back a debt of my past that I never paid. Whatever the outcome, for my soul's sake I must settle it now and wipe it from the score for ever. Nothing counts— nothing can count—more than you! But I must sail by the needle; I must be truthful to the best that is in me."

She rose slowly to her feet with a despairing gesture.

"'*He saved others*,'" she quoted in a hard voice, "'*himself he could not save!*' I once heard a minister preach from that text at home; it was your friend, the Reverend Henry Sanderson. I thought it a very spiritual sermon then—that was before I knew what his companionship had been to you!"

In the exclamation was the old bitterness that had had its spring in that far-away evening at the white house in the aspens, when Harry Sanderson had lifted the curtain from his college career. In spite of David Stires' predilection, since that day she had distrusted and disliked, at moments actively hated him. His mannerisms had seemed a pose and his pretensions hypocrisy.

On her wedding-day, when she lashed him with the blame of Hugh's ruin, this had become an ingrained prejudice, impregnable because rooted deeper than reason, in the heritage of her sex, the eternal proclivity, which saw Harry Sanderson, his motley covered with the sober domino of the Church, standing self-righteously in surplice and stole, while Hugh slid downward to disgrace.

"If there were any justice in the universe," she added, "it should be he immolating himself now, not you!"

His face was not toward her and she could not see it go deadly white. The sudden shift she had given the conversation had startled him. He turned to the tiny barred window that looked out across the court-yard square—where such a little time since he had found his lost self.

"I think," he said, "that in my place, he would do the same."

"You always admired him," she went on, the hard ring of misery in her tone. "You admire him yet. Oh, men like him have such strange and wicked power! Satan Sanderson!—it was a fit name. What right has he to be rector of St. James, while you—"

He put out a hand in flinching protest. "Jessica! Don't!" he begged.

"Why should I not say it?" she retorted, with quivering lips. "But for him you would never be here! He ruined your life and mine, and I hate and despise him for a selfish hypocrite!"

That was what he himself had seemed to her in those old days! The edge of a flush touched his forehead as he said slowly, almost appealingly:

"He was not a hypocrite, Jessica. Whatever he was it was not that. At college he did what he did too openly. That was his failing—not caring what others thought. He despised weakness in others; he thought it none of his affair. So others were influenced. But after he came to see things differently, from another standpoint—when he went into the ministry—he would have given the world to undo it."

"That may have been the Harry Sanderson you knew," she said stonily. "The one I knew drove an imported motor-car and had a dozen fads that people were always imitating. You are still loyal to the old college worship. As men go, you count him still your friend!"

"As men go," he echoed grimly, "the very closest!"

"Men's likings are strange," she said. "Because he never had temptations like yours, and has never done what the law calls wrong, you think he is as noble as

you—noble enough to shield a murderer to his own danger."

"Ah, no, Jessica," he interposed gently. "I only said that in my place, he would do the same."

"But *you* are shielding a murderer," she insisted fiercely. "You will not admit it, but I know! There can be no justice or right in that! If Harry

Sanderson is all you think him—if he stood here now and knew the whole—he would say it was wicked. Not brave and noble but wicked and cruel!"

He shook his head, and the sad shadow of a bitter smile touched his lips. "He would not say so," he said.

A dry sob answered him. He turned and leaned his elbows on the narrow window-sill, every nerve aching, but powerless to comfort. He heard her step—the door closed sharply.

Then he faced into the empty cell, sat down on the cot and threw out his arms with a hopeless cry:

"Jessica, Jessica!"

CHAPTER XLIII THE LITTLE GOLD CROSS

Jessica left the jail with despair in her heart. The hope on which she had fed these past days had failed her. What was there left for her to do? Like a swift wind she went up the street to Felder's office.

A block beyond the court-house a crowd was enjoying the watery discomfiture of Hallelujah Jones, and shrinking from recognition even in the darkness—for the arc lights were still black—she crossed the roadway and ran on to the unpretentious building where the lawyer had his sanctum. She groped her way up the unlighted stair and tapped on the door. There was no answer. She pushed it open and entered the empty outer room, where a study lamp burned on the desk.

A pile of legal looking papers had been set beside it and with them lay a torn page of a newspaper whose familiar caption gave her a stab of pain. Perhaps the news of the trial had found its way across the ranges, to where the names of Stires and Moreau had been known. Perhaps every one at Aniston already knew of

it, was reading about it, pitying her! She picked it up and scanned it hastily. There was no hint of the trial, but her eye caught the news which had played its rôle in the court-room, and she read it to the end.

Even in her own trouble she read it with a shiver. Yet, awful as the fate which Harry Sanderson had so narrowly missed, it was not to be compared with that which awaited Hugh, for, awful as it was, it held no shame!

In a gust of feeling she slipped to her knees by the one sofa the room contained and prayed passionately. As she drew out her handkerchief to stanch the tears that came, something fell with a musical tinkle at her feet. It was the little cross she had found in front of the hillside cabin, that had lain forgotten in her pocket during the past anxious days. She picked it up now and held it tightly in her hand, as if the tangible symbol brought her closer to the Infinite Sympathy to which she turned in her misery. As she pressed it, the ring at the top turned and the cross parted in halves. Words were engraved on the inside of the arms—a date and the name *Henry Sanderson.*

The recurrence of the name jarred and surprised her. Hugh had dropped it—an old keepsake of the friend who had been his *beau idéal*, his exemplar, and whose

ancient influence was still dominant. He had clung loyally to the memento, blind in his constant liking, to the wrong that friend had done him. She looked at the date—it was May 28th. She shuddered, for that was the month and day on which Doctor Moreau had been killed—the point had been clearly established to-day by the prosecution. To the original owner of that cross, perhaps, the date that had come into Hugh's life with such a sinister meaning, was a glad anniversary!

Suddenly she caught her hand to her cheek. A weird idea had rushed through her brain. The religious symbol had stood for Harry Sanderson and the chance coincidence of date had irresistibly pointed to the murder. To her excited senses the juxtaposition held a bizarre, uncanny suggestion. This cross—the very emblem of vicarious sacrifice!—suppose Harry Sanderson had never given it to Hugh! Suppose he had lost it on the hillside himself!

She snatched up the paper again: "Who has been for some months on a prolonged vacation"—the phrase stared sardonically at her. That might carry far back—she said it under her breath, fearfully—beyond the murder of Doctor Moreau! Her face burned, and her breath came sharp and fast. Why, when she brought her warning to the cabin, had Hugh been so anxious to get her

away, unless to prevent her sight of the man who was there—to whom he had taken her horse? Who was there in Smoky Mountain whom he would protect at hazard of his own life? Yet in this crisis, even, her appeal to his love had been fruitless. He had called Harry Sanderson his closest friend, had said that in his place Harry would do the same. She remembered his cry: "What you ask is the one thing I can not do. It would make me a pitiful coward!" She had asked only that he tell the truth. To protect a vulgar murderer was not courageous. But what if they were bound by ties of old friendship and college *camaraderie*? Men had their standards.

Jessica's veins were all afire. A rector-murderer? A double career? Was it beyond possibility? At the sanatorium she had re-read *The Mystery of Edwin Drood*; now she thought of John Jasper, the choir-master, stealing away from the cathedral to the London opium den to plan the murder of his nephew. The mad thought gripped her imagination. Harry Sanderson had been wild and lawless in his university days, a gamester, a skeptic— the Abbot of the Saints! To her his pretensions had never seemed more than a graceful sham, the generalities of religion he spread for the delectation of fashionable St. James only "as sounding brass and a

tinkling cymbal." He had been a hard drinker in those days. What if the old desire had run on beneath the fair exterior, denied and repressed till it had burst control—till he had fled from those who knew him, to Hugh, in whose loyalty he trusted, to give it rein in a debauch? Say that this had happened, and that in the midst of it Moreau, whom he had known in Aniston, had come upon him. Anticipating recognition, to cover his own shame and save his career, in drunken frenzy perhaps, he might have fired the shot on the hillside—that Moreau, taken unawares, had thought was Hugh's!

It came to her like an impinging ray of light—the old curious likeness that had sometimes been made a jest of at the white house in the aspens. Moreau and Prendergast had believed it to be Hugh! So had the town, for the body had been found on his ground! But on the night when the real murderer came again to the cabin—perhaps it was his coming that had brought back the lost memory!—Hugh had known the truth. In the light of this supposition his strained manner then, his present determination not to speak, all stood plain.

What had he meant by a debt of his past that he had never paid? He could owe no debt to Harry Sanderson. If he owed any debt, it was to his dead father, a thousand times more than the draft he had repaid. Could he be

thinking in his remorse that his father had cast him off—counting himself nothing, remembering only that Harry Sanderson had been David Stires' favorite, and St. James, which must be smirched by the odium of its rector, the apple of his eye?

Jessica had snatched at a straw, because it was the only buoyant thing afloat in the dragging tide; now with a blind fatuousness she hugged it tighter to her bosom. The joints of her reasoning seemed to dovetail with fateful accuracy. She was swayed by instinct, and apparent fallacies were glozed by old mistrust and terror of the outcome which was driving her to any desperate expedient. Beside Hugh's salvation the whole universe counted as nothing. She was in the grip of that fierce passion of love's defense which feeds the romance of the world. One purpose possessed her: to confront Harry Sanderson. What matter though she missed the remainder of the trial? She could do nothing—her hands were tied. If the truth lay at Aniston she would find it. She thought no further than this. Once in Harry Sanderson's presence, what she should say or do she scarcely imagined. The horrifying question filled her thought to the exclusion of all that must follow its answer. It was surety and self-conviction she craved—only to read in his eyes the truth about the murder of Moreau.

She suddenly began to tremble. Would the doctors let her see him? What excuse could she give? If he was the man who had been in Hugh's cabin that night, he had heard her speak, had known she was there. He must not know beforehand of her coming, lest he have suspicion of her errand. Bishop Ludlow—he could gain her access to him. Injured, dying perhaps, maybe he did not guess that Hugh was in jeopardy for his crime. Guilty and dying, if he knew this, he would surely tell the truth. But if he died before she could reach him? The paper was some days old; he might be dead already. She took heart, however, from the statement of his improved condition.

She sprang to her feet and looked at her chatelaine watch. The east-bound express was overdue. There was no time to lose—minutes might count. She examined her purse—she had money enough with her.

Five minutes later she was at the station, a scribbled note was on its way to Mrs. Halloran, and before a swinging red lantern, the long incoming train was shuddering to a stop.

CHAPTER XLIV THE IMPOSTOR

In the long hospital the air was cool and filtered, drab figures passed with soft footfalls and voices were measured and hushed. But no sense of coolness or repose had come to the man whose racked body had been tenderly borne there in the snowy dawn which saw the blackened ruins of Aniston's most perfect edifice.

Because of him tongues clacked on the street corner and bulletins were posted in newspaper windows; carriages of tasteful equipment halted at the hospital porte-cochère, messages flew back and forth, and the telephone in the outer office whirred busily at unseasonable hours; but from the clean screened room where he lay, all this was shut out. Only the surgeons came and went, deftly refreshing the bandages which swathed one side of his face, where the disfiguring flame had smitten—the other side was untouched, save for a line across the brow, seemingly a thin, red mark of excoriation.

Hugh had sunk into unconsciousness with the awestruck exclamation ringing in his ears: "Good God!

It's Harry Sanderson!" He had drifted back to conscious knowledge with the same words racing in his brain. They implied that, so far as capture went, the old, curious resemblance would stand his friend till he betrayed himself, or till the existence of the real Harry Sanderson at Smoky Mountain did so for him. The delusion must hold till he could have himself moved to some place where his secret would be safer—till he could get away!

This thought grew swiftly paramount; it overlapped the rigid agony of his burns that made the bed on which he lay a fiery furnace; it gave method to his every word and look. He took up the difficult part, and after the superficial anguish dulled, complained no more and successfully counterfeited cheerfulness and betterment. He said nothing of the curiously recurrent and sickening stab of pain, searching and deep-seated, that took his breath and left each time an increasing giddiness. Whatever inner hurt this might betoken, he must hide it, the sooner to leave the hospital, where each hour brought nearer the inevitable disclosure.

He thanked fortune now for the chapel game; few enough in Aniston would care to see the unfrocked, disgraced rector of St. James! He did not know that the secret was Bishop Ludlow's own, until the hour when he opened his eyes, after a fitful sleep, upon the latter's face.

The bishop was the first visitor and it was his first visit, for he had been in a distant city at the time of the fire. Waiting the waking, he had been mystified at the change a few months had wrought in the countenance of the man whose disappearance had cost him so many sleepless hours. The months of indulgence and rich living—on the money he had won from Harry—had taken away Hugh's slightness, and his fuller cheeks were now of the contour of Harry's own. But the bishop distinguished new lines in the face on the pillow, an expression unfamiliar and puzzling; the firmness and strength were gone, and in their place was a haunting something that gave him a flitting suggestion of the discarded that he could not shake off.

Waking, the unexpected sight of the bishop startled Hugh; to the good man's pain he had turned his face away.

"My dear boy," the bishop had said, "they tell me you are stronger and better. I thank God for it!"

He spoke gently and with deep feeling. How could he tell to what extent he himself, in mistaken severity, had been responsible for that unaccustomed look? When Hugh did not answer, the bishop misconstrued the

silence. He leaned over the bed; the big cool hand touched the fevered one on the white coverlid, where the ruby ring glowed, a coal in snow.

"Harry," he said, "you have suffered—you are suffering now. But think of me only as your friend. I ask no questions. We are going to begin again where we left off."

The words and tone had shown Hugh the situation and given him his cue. He could put himself fairly in Harry's place, and with the instinct of the actor he did so now, meeting the other's friendliness with a hesitant eagerness.

"I would like to do that," he said, "—to begin again. But the chapel is gone."

"Never mind that," said the bishop cheerfully. "You are only to get well. We are going to rebuild soon, and we want your judgment on the plans. Aniston is hanging on your condition, Harry," he went on. "There's a small cartload of visiting-cards down-stairs for you. But I imagine you haven't begun to receive yet, eh?"

"I—I've seen nobody." Hugh spoke hurriedly and hoarsely. "Tell the doctor to let no one come—no one but you. I—I'm not up to it!"

"Why, of course not," said the bishop quickly. "You need quiet, and the people can wait."

The bishop chatted a while of the parish, Hugh replying only when he must, and went away heartened. Before he left Hugh saw his way to hasten his own going. On the next visit the seed was dropped in the bishop's mind so cleverly that he thought the idea his own. That day he said to the surgeon in charge:

"He is gaining so rapidly, I have been wondering if he couldn't be taken away where the climate will benefit him. Will he be able to travel soon?"

"I think so," answered the surgeon. "We suspected internal injury at first, but I imagine the worst he has to fear is the disfigurement. Mountain or sea air would do him good," he added reflectively; "what he will need is tonic and building up."

The bishop had revolved this in his mind. He knew a place on the coast, tucked away in the cypresses, which would be admirable for convalescence. He could arrange a special car and he himself could make the journey with him. He proposed this to the surgeon and with his approval put his plan in motion. In two days more Hugh found his going fully settled.

The idea admirably fitted his necessity. The spot the bishop had selected was quiet and retired, and more, was near the port at which he could most readily take ship for South America. Only one reflection made him

shiver: the route lay through the town of Smoky Mountain. Yet who would dream of looking for a fugitive from the law in the secluded car that carried a sick man? The risk would be small enough, and it was the one way open!

On the last afternoon before the departure, Hugh asked for the clothes he had worn when he was brought to the hospital, found the gold-pieces he had snatched in the burning chapel and tied them in a handkerchief about his neck. They would suffice to buy his sea-passage. The one red counter he had kept—it was from henceforth to be a reminder of the good resolutions he had made so long ago—he slipped into a pocket of the clothes he was to wear away, a suit of loose, comfortable tweed.

Waiting restlessly for the hour of his going, Hugh asked for the newspapers. Since the first he had had them read to him each day, listening fearfully for the hue and cry. But to-day the surgeon put his request aside.

"After you are there," he said, "if Bishop Ludlow will let you. Not now. You are almost out of my clutches, and I must tyrannize while I can."

A quick look passed from him to his assistant as he spoke, for the newspapers that afternoon had worn startling head-lines. The sordid affairs of a mining town across the ranges had little interest for Aniston, but the names of Stires and Moreau on the clicking wire had waked it, thus late, to the sensation. The professional caution of the tinker of human bodies wished, however, that no excitement should be added to the unavoidable fatigue of his patient's departure.

This fatigue was near to spelling defeat, after all, for the exertion brought again the dreadful, stabbing pain, and this time it carried Hugh into a region where feeling ceased, consciousness passed, and from which he struggled back finally to find the surgeon bending anxiously over him.

"I don't like that sinking spell," the latter confided to his assistant an hour later as they stood looking through the window after the receding carriage. "It was too pronounced. Yet he has complained of no pain. He will be in good hands at any rate." He tapped the glass musingly with his forefinger. "It's curious," he said after a pause; "I always liked Sanderson—in the pulpit. Somehow he doesn't appeal to me at close range."

The special car which the bishop had ready had been made a pleasant interior; fern-boxes were in the corners, a caged canary swung from a bracket, and a softly cushioned couch had been prepared for the sick man. A

moment before the start, as it was being coupled to the rear of the resting train, while the bishop chatted with the conductor, a flustered messenger boy handed him a telegram. It read:

I arrive Aniston to-morrow five. Confidential. Must see you. Urgent. Jessica.

The bishop read it in some perplexity. It was the first word he had received from her since her marriage, but, aware of Hugh's forgery and disgrace, he had not wondered at this. Since the news of David Stires' death, he had looked for her return, for she was the old man's heir and mistress now of the white house in the aspens. But he realized that it would need all her courage to come back to this town whence she had fled with her trouble—to lay bare an unsuspected and shameful secret, to meet old friends, and answer questions that must be asked. The newspapers to-day pictured a still worse shame for her, in the position of the man who, in name still, was her husband—who had trod so swiftly the downward path from thievery to the worst of crimes. Could Jessica's coming have to do with that? He must see her, yet his departure could not now be delayed. He consulted with the conductor and the latter pored over his tablets.

As a result, his answering message flashed along the wires to Jessica's far-away train:

Sanderson injured. Taking him to coast train forty-eight due Twin Peaks two to-morrow afternoon.

And thus the fateful moment approached when the great appeal should be made.

CHAPTER XLV AN APPEAL TO CÆSAR

The evidence of the first day's trial of the case of the People against Hugh Stires was the all-engrossing topic that night in Smoky Mountain. In the "Amen Corner" of the Mountain Valley House it held sway. Among the sedate group there gathered, there seemed but one belief: that the accused man was guilty—but one feeling: that of regret. Gravity lay so heavily upon the atmosphere there that when Mrs. Halloran momentarily entered the discussion to declare fiercely that "if Hugh Stires was a murderer, then they were all thieves and she a cannibal" she aroused no smile. Barney McGinn perhaps aptly expressed the consensus of opinion when he said: "I allow we all know he's guilty, but nobody believes it."

Late as Smoky Mountain sat up that night, however, it was on hand next morning, rank and file, when the court convened.

All the previous evening, save for a short visit to the cell of his client, Felder had remained shut in his office, thinking of the morrow. In his talk with Harry he had

not concealed his deep anxiety, but to his questions there was no new answer, and he had returned from the interview more nonplussed than ever. He had wondered that Jessica, on this last night, did not come to his office, but had been rather relieved than otherwise that she did not. He had gone to bed heavy with discouragement and had waked in the morning with foreboding.

As he shook hands with the prisoner in the packed court-room, Felder felt a keen admiration that his sense of painful impotence could not overlay. He read in the composed face the same prescience that possessed him, but it held no fear or shadow of turning. He was facing the scaffold; facing it—if the woman he loved was right in her conclusions—in obedience to a set idea of self-martyrdom and with indomitable spirit. It was inconceivable that a sane man would do this for a sneaking assassin. It was either aberration or a relentless purpose so extraordinary that it lay far removed from the ordinary courses of reasoning. Felder's own conviction had no bolstering of fact, no logical premise; indeed, as he had admitted to Doctor Brent, it was thoroughly unprofessional. Even to cite the circumstances on which Jessica based her belief that Hugh knew the real murderer would weaken his case. The suggestion would seem a mere bungling expedient to inject the tantalizing

fillip of mystery and unbelievable Quixotic motive, and, lacking evidence to support it, would touch the whole fabric with the taint of the meretricious. The sense of painful responsibility and hopelessness oppressed him, for, so far as real evidence went, he had entered on this second day of the struggle without a tangible theory of defense.

As he turned from greeting his client, Felder noted with surprise that Jessica was not in her place. Not that he needed her further testimony, for he had drawn from her the day before all he intended to utilize, but her absence disturbed him, and instinctively he turned and looked across the sea of faces toward the door.

Harry's glance followed his, and a deeper pain beleaguered it as his eyes returned to the empty chair. He saw Mrs. Halloran whisper eagerly with the lawyer, who turned away with a puzzled look. In his bitterness the thought came to him that the testimony had sapped her conviction of his innocence—that his refusal to answer her entreaties had been the last straw to the load under which it had gone down—that she believed him indeed the murderer of Moreau. To seem the cringing criminal, the pitiful liar and actor in her eyes! The thought stung him. Her faith had meant so much!

The ominous feeling weighed heavily on Felder when he rose to continue the testimony for the prisoner, so rudely disturbed the evening before. In such a community pettifogging was of no avail. Throwing expert dust in jurors' eyes would be worse than useless. In his opening words he made no attempt to conceal the weakness of the defense, evidentially considered. Stripped of all husk, his was to be an appeal to Cæsar.

Through a cloud of witnesses, concisely, consistently—yet with a winning tactfulness that disarmed the objections of the prosecution—he began to lead them through the series of events that had followed the arrival of the self-forgotten man. Out of the mouths of their own neighbors—Devlin, Barney McGinn, Mrs. Halloran, who came down weeping—they were made to see, as in a cyclorama, the struggle for rehabilitation against hatred and suspicion, the courage that had dared for a child's life, the honesty of purpose that showed in self-surrender. The prisoner, he said, had recovered his memory before the accusation and asserted his absolute innocence. Those who believed him guilty of the murder of Doctor Moreau must believe him also a vulgar liar and *poseur*. He left the inference clear: If the prisoner had fired that cowardly shot, he knew it now; if he lied now he had lied all along, and the later life he had lived at Smoky Mountain—eloquent of fair-dealing, straightforwardness of purpose, kindliness and courage—had been but hypocrisy, the bootless artifice of a shallow buffoon.

It was an appeal sustained and moving, addressed to folk who, untrammelled by a complex and variform convention, felt simply and deeply the simplest and deepest passions of human kind. Often, as the morning grew, Felder's glance turned toward the empty chair near-by, and more than once, though his active thought never wavered from the serious business in hand, his subconscious mind wondered. Mrs. Halloran had told him of the note from Jessica—it had said only that she would return at the earliest possible moment. The wonder in Felder's mind was general throughout the court-room, for none who had listened to Jessica's testimony—and the whole town had heard it—could doubt the strength of her love. The eyes that saw the empty chair were full of pity. Only the knot of serious faces in the jury-box was seldom turned that way.

The session was prolonged past the noon hour, and when Felder rested his case it seemed that all that was possible had been said. He had done his utmost. He had drawn from the people of Smoky Mountain a dramatic story, and had filled in its outlines with color, force and feeling. And yet, as he closed, the lawyer felt a sick sense of failure.

Court adjourned for an hour, and in the interim Felder remained in a little room in the building, whither Doctor Brent was to send him sandwiches and coffee from the hotel.

"You made a fine effort, Tom," the latter said, as they stood for a moment in the emptying court-room. "You're doing wonders with no case, and the town ought to send you to Congress on the strength of it! I declare, some of your evidence made me feel as mean as a dog about the rascal, though I knew all the time he was as guilty as the devil."

The lawyer shook his head. "I don't blame you, Brent," he said, "for you don't know him as I do. I have seen much of him lately, been often with him, watched him under stress—for he doesn't deceive himself, he has no thought of acquittal! We none of us knew Hugh Stires. We put him down for a shallow, vulgar blackleg, without redeeming qualities. But the man we are trying is a gentleman, a refined and cultivated man of taste and feeling. I have learned his true character during these days."

"Well," said the other, "if you believe in him, so much the better. You'll make the better speech for it. Tell me one thing—where was Miss Holme?"

"I don't know."

The doctor raised his eyebrows. "Good-by," he said. "I'll send over the coffee and sandwiches," he added as he turned away.

"She thinks he is guilty!" he said to himself as he walked up the street. "She thinks he is guilty, too!"

CHAPTER XLVI FACE TO FACE

To stand face to face with Harry Sanderson—that had been Jessica's sole thought. The news that the bishop, with the man she suspected, was speeding toward her—to pass the very town wherein Hugh stood for his life—seemed a prearrangement of eternal justice. When the telegram reached her, she had already gone by Twin Peaks. To proceed would be to pass the coming train. At a farther station, however, she was able to take a night train back, arriving again at Twin Peaks in the gray dawn of the next morning. At the dingy station hotel there she undressed and lay down, but her nerves were quivering and she could not close her eyes. Toward noon she dressed and forced herself to breakfast, realizing the need of strength. She spent the rest of the time of waiting walking up and down in the crisp air, which steadied her nerves and gave her a measure of control.

When the train for which she waited came in, the curtained car at its end, she did not wait for the bishop to

find her on the platform, but stepped aboard and made her way slowly back. It started again as she threaded the last Pullman, to find the bishop on its rear platform peering out anxiously at the receding station.

He took both her hands and drew her into the empty drawing-room. He was startled at her pallor. "I know," he said pityingly. "I have heard."

She winced. "Does Aniston know?"

"Yes," he answered. "Yesterday's newspapers told it."

She put her hand on his arm. "Can you guess why I was coming home?" she asked. "It was to tell Harry Sanderson! I know of the fire," she went on quickly, "and of his injury. I can guess you want to spare him strain or excitement, but I must tell him!"

"It is a matter of physical strength, Jessica," he said. "He has been a sick man. Forgive my saying it, child, but—what good could it do?"

"Believe, oh, you must believe," she pleaded, "that I do not ask this lightly, that I have a purpose that makes it necessary. It means so much— more than my life to me! Why, I have waited here at Twin Peaks all through the night, till now, when this very day and hour they are trying him there at Smoky Mountain! You must let me tell him!"

He reflected a moment. He thought he guessed what

was in her mind. If there was any one who had ever had an influence over Hugh for good, it was Harry Sanderson. He himself, he thought, had none. Perhaps, remembering their old comradeship, she was longing now to have this influence exerted, to bring Hugh to a better mind—thinking of his eternal welfare, of his making his peace with his Maker. Beneath his prosy churchmanship and somewhat elaborate piety, the bishop had a spirituality almost medieval in its simplicity. Perhaps this was God's way. His eyes lighted.

"Very well," he said. "Come," and led the way into the car.

Jessica followed, her hands clenched tightly. She saw the couch, the profile on its cushions turned toward the window where forest and stream slipped past—a face curiously like Hugh's! Yet it was different, lacking the other's strength, even its refinement. And this man had molded Hugh! These vague thoughts lost themselves instantly in the momentous surmise that filled her imagination. The bishop put out his hand and touched the relaxed arm.

The trepidation that darted into the bandaged face as it turned upon the girlish figure, the frosty fear that blanched the haggard countenance, spoke Hugh's surprise and dread. It was she, and she knew the real

Harry Sanderson was in Smoky Mountain. Had she heard of the chapel fire, guessed the imposture, and come to denounce him, the guilty husband she had such reason to hate? The twitching limbs stiffened. "Jessica!" he said in a hoarse whisper.

For an instant a fierce sense of triumph flamed through her every nerve. But a cold doubt chilled it. Her suspicion might be the veriest chimera. It seemed suddenly too wild for belief. She sat down abruptly and for a fleeting moment hid her face. The bishop touched the bowed, brown head.

"Harry," he said, "Jessica is in great trouble. She has come with sad news. Hugh, her husband, your old college mate, is in a terrible position. He is accused of murder. I kept the newspapers from you to-day because they told of it."

She had caught the meaning of the pity in his tone—for her, not for Hugh! "Ah," she cried passionately, lifting her head, "but they did not tell it all! Did they tell you that he is unjustly, wickedly accused by an enemy? That, though they may convict him, he is innocent—innocent?"

The bishop looked at her in surprise. In spite of all the past—the shameful, conscienceless past and her own wrong—she loved and believed in her husband!

Hugh's hand lifted, wavered an instant before his brow. Did she say he was innocent? "I don't—understand," he said hoarsely.

Jessica's wide eyes fastened on his as though to search his secret soul. "I will tell it all," she said, "then you will understand." The bishop drew a chair close, but her gaze did not waver from the face on the cushions—the face which she must read!

As she told the broken tale the car was still, save for the labored, irregular breathing of the prostrate man, and the muffled roar that penetrated the walls, a multitudinous, elfin din. Once the swinging canary broke forth into liquid warbling, as though in all the world were no throe of body or dolor of mind. In that telling Jessica's mind traversed wastes of alternate certainty and doubt, as she hung upon the look of the man who listened—a look that merged slowly into a fearful understanding. Hugh understood now!

Jessica had believed him to be her husband, and she believed so still. And Harry did not intend to tell. He was safe ... safe! In the reaction from his fear, Hugh felt sick and faint.

The bishop had been listening in some anxiety, both for her and for his charge. There was a strained intensity in her manner now that betokened almost

unbalance—so it seemed to him. The side-lights he had had of Hugh's career led him to believe him incapable of such a self-sacrifice as her tale recited. A strange power there was in woman's love!

"You see," she ended, "that is why I know he is innocent. *You* can not"—her eyes held Hugh's—"*you* can not doubt it, can you?"

Hugh's tongue wet his parched lips. A tremor ran through him. He did not answer.

Jessica started to her feet. Self-possession was falling from her; she was fighting to seize the vital knowledge that evaded her. She held out her hand—in the palm lay a small emblem of gold.

"By this cross," she cried with desperate earnestness, "I ask you for the truth. It is his life or death—Hugh's life or death! He did not kill Doctor Moreau. *Who did?*"

Hugh had shrunk back on the couch, his face ghastly. "I know nothing—nothing!" he stammered. "Do not ask me!"

The bishop had risen in alarm; he thought her hysterical. "Jessica! Jessica!" he exclaimed. He threw his arm about her and led her from the couch. "You don't know what you are saying. You are beside yourself." He forced her into the drawing-room and made her sit

down. She was tense and quivering. The cross fell from her hand and he stooped and picked it up.

"Try to calm yourself," he said, "to think of other things for a few moments. This little cross—I wonder how you come to have it? I gave it to Sanderson last May to commemorate his ordination." He twisted it open. "See, here is the date, May twenty-eighth—that was the day I gave it to him."

She gave a quick gasp and the last vestige of color faded from her cheek. She looked at him in a stricken way. "*Last* May!" she said faintly. Harry Sanderson had been in Aniston, then, on the day Doctor Moreau had been murdered. Her house of cards fell. She had been mistaken! She leaned her head back against the cushion and closed her eyes.

Presently she felt a cold glass touch her lips. "Here is some water," the bishop's voice said. "You are better, are you not? Poor child! You have been through a terrible strain. I would give the world to help you if I could!"

He left her, and she sat dully trying to think. The regular jar of the trucks had set itself to a rhythm—no hope, no hope, no hope! She knew now that there was none. When the bishop reëntered she did not turn her head. He sat beside her a while and she was aware

again of his voice, speaking soothingly. At moments thereafter he was there, at others she knew that she was alone, but she was unconscious of the flight of time. She knew only that the day was fading. On the chilly whirling landscape she saw only a crowded room, a jury-box, a judge's bench, and Hugh before it, listening to the sentence that would take him from her for ever. The bright sunlight was mercilessly, satanically cruel, and God a sneering monster turning a crank.

Into her conscious view grew distant snowy ranges, hills unrolling at their feet, a straggling town, a staring white court-house and a grim low building beside it. She rose stumblingly, the train quivering to the brakes, as the bishop entered.

"This is Smoky Mountain," she said with numb lips. "That is the building where he is being tried. I am going there now."

The bishop opened the door. "We stop here twenty minutes," he said. "I will walk a little way with you."

CHAPTER XLVII BETWEEN THE MILLSTONES

Hugh's haggard face peered after them through a rift in a window curtain. What could she have suspected? Not the truth! And only that could betray him. Presently the bishop would return, the train would start again, and this spot of terror would be behind him. What had he to do with Harry Sanderson?

He bethought himself suddenly of the door—if some one should come in upon him! With a qualm of fear he stood up, staggered to it and turned the key in the lock. There was not the wonted buzz about the station; the place was silent, save for the throb of the halted engine, and the shadow of the train on the frosty platform quivered like a criminal. A block away he saw the court-house—knots of people were standing about its door, waiting for what? A fit of trembling seized him.

All his years Hugh had been a moral coward. Life to him had been sweet for the grosser, material pleasures it held. He had cared for nobody, had held nothing sacred. When his sins had found him out, he had not repented; he had only cursed the accident of discovery. The sincerest feeling of regret he had known had been in the chapel when he had thought of his dead mother. Since one dismal night on Smoky Mountain, dread, dogging and relentless, had been his hateful bedfellow. He had now only to keep silence, let Harry Sanderson pay the penalty, and he need dread no more. Hugh Stires, to the persuasion of the law, would be dead. As soon as might be he could disappear—as the rector of St. James had disappeared before. He might change his name and live at ease in some other quarter of the world, his alarm laid for ever.

But a worse thing would haunt him, to scare his sleep. He would be doubly blood-guilty!

In the awful moment while he clung to the iron bars of the collapsing rose-window, with the flames clutching at him, Hugh had looked into hell, and shivered before the judgment: *The wages of sin is death.* In that fiery ordeal the cheapness and swagger, the ostentation and self-esteem had burned away, and his soul had stood naked as a winter wood. Dying had not then been the Austere Terror. What came after—that had appalled him. Yet Harry Sanderson was not afraid of the hereafter; he chose death calmly, knowing that he, Hugh, was unfit to die!

He thought of the little gold cross Jessica had held before him. The last time he had seen it was during that memorable game when Harry had set it on the table. In his pocket was a battered red disk—a reminder of the days that Harry had won, which had never been rendered. He thought of the stabbing agony that had come and come again, to strike each time more deeply. The death that he had cheated in the chapel might be near him now. But whenever death should come, what should he say when he stood before his Judge, with such a fearful double burden on his soul? He was horribly afraid!

Suppose he waited. Harry might be convicted, sentenced, but he could save him at the last moment. When he was safe on his way to South America, he could write the bishop—beg him to go to Smoky Mountain and convince himself. But how soon would that be? It would be long, long—and justice was swift. And what if death should take him unawares beforehand? It would be too late then, too late for ever and ever!

Suppose he told the truth now and saved Harry. He had never done a brave deed for the sake of truth or righteousness, or for the love of any human being, but he could do one now. For the one red counter that had been a symbol of a day of evil living, he could render a deed that would make requital for those unpaid days!

He would not have played the coward's part. It would repair the wrong he had done Jessica. He would have made expiation. Forgiveness and pity, not reproaches and shame, would follow him. And it would balance, perhaps, the one dreadful count that stood against him. He thought of the scaffold and shivered. Yet there was a more terrible thought: *It is a fearful thing to fall into the hands of the living God!*

He made his way again to the door and unlocked it. It was only to cross that space, to speak, and then the grim brick building—and the penalty.

With a hoarse cry he slammed the door to and frantically locked it. The edge of the searching pain was upon him again. He stumbled back to the couch and fell across it face down, dragging the cushions in frantic haste over his head, to shut out the sick throbbing of the steam, that seemed shuddering at the fate his cowering soul dared not face.

The groups outside of the court-house made way deferentially for Jessica, but she was unconscious of it. Some one asked a question on the steps, and she heard the answer: "The State has just finished, and the judge is charging."

The narrow hall was filled, and though all who saw gave her instant place, the space beyond the inner door was crowded beyond the possibility of passage. She could see the judge's bench, with its sedate gray-bearded figure, the jury-box at the left, the moving restless faces about it, set like a living mosaic. Only the table where the lawyers and the prisoner sat she could not see, or the empty chair where she had sat yesterday. What had Hugh thought, she wondered dully, when he had not seen her there that day? Had he thought that her trust had failed?

She became aware suddenly that the figure at the high bench was speaking, had been speaking all along. She could not think clearly, and her brain struggled with the incisive matter-of-fact sentences.

"With the prisoner's later career in Smoky Mountain they had nothing to do, nor had the law. The question it asked—the only question it asked— was, did he kill Moreau? They might be loath to believe the same man capable of such contradictory acts—the courageous saving of a child from death, for example, and the shooting down of a fellow-mortal in cold blood—but it had been truly said that such contrasts were not impossible, nay, were even matters of common observation. Prejudice and bias aside, and sympathy and liking aside, they constituted a tribunal of justice. This the State had a

right to demand, and this they, the jury, had made solemn oath to give."

The words had no meaning for her ears. "What did he say?" she whispered to herself piteously.

In her abyss of torture she felt the tense expectancy stirring audibly in the room like a still breeze in forest leaves—saw the averted faces of the jury as they rose to file out. She caught but a glimpse of the prisoner, as the sheriff touched his arm and led the way quickly to the door through which he had been brought.

It opened and closed upon them, and the tension of the packed room broke all at once in a great respiration of relief and a buzz of conversation.

A voice spoke beside her. It was Doctor Brent. "Come with me," he said. "Felder asked me to watch for you. We can wait in the judge's room."

CHAPTER XLVIII THE VERDICT

Meanwhile in the narrow cell Harry was alone with his bitterness. His judicial sense, keenly alive, from the very first had appreciated the woeful weakness, evidentially speaking, of his position. He had no illusions on this score. A little while—after such deliberation as was decent and seemly—and he would be a condemned criminal, waiting in the shadow of the hempen noose. In such localities justice was swift. There would be scant time between verdict and penalty—not enough, doubtless, for the problem to solve itself. For the only solution possible was Hugh's dying in the hospital at Aniston. So long as the other lived, he must play out the rôle.

And if Hugh did die, but died too late? What a satire on truth and justice! The same error which put the rope about his own neck would fold the real Hugh in the odor of sanctity. He would lie in the little jail yard in a felon's grave, and Hugh in the cemetery on the hill, beneath a marble monument erected by St.

James Parish to the Reverend Henry Sanderson. He was in an *impasse*. In the dock, or in the cell with the death-watch sitting at its door, it was all one. He had elected the path, and if it led to the bleak edge of life, to the barren abyss of shame, he must tread it.

His own life—he had come in his thinking to a point where that mattered least of all. Harry Sanderson, the vanished rector of St. James, mattered. And Jessica! On the cot lay a slender blue-bound book—Tennyson's *Becket*. She had sent it to him, in a hamper of her favorites, some days before. He picked it up and held it in his hand, touching the limp leather gently. It was as soft as her cheek, and there was about the leaves a hint of that intangible perfume that his mind always associated with her—

Far more than his life, more than the name and fame of the Reverend Henry Sanderson, she mattered! Could he write it for her eye, the whole truth, so that sometime—afterward—the bishop might know, and the blot be erased from his career? Impossible! With Hugh buried in Aniston and he in Smoky Mountain, who was there but would smile at such a tale? She might shout it to

the world, and it would answer with derision. And what comfort would the truth be to her?

Could he say to her: "Your husband lies dead under my tombstone, not innocent, but unregenerate and vile. I, who you think am your husband, am not and never was. You have come to my call—but I am nothing to you.

You are the wife of the guilty murderer of Moreau!" Could he leave this behind him, and, passing from her life for ever, turn the memory of their love into an irremediable bitterness? No—no! Better never to tell her! Better to let her live her life, holding her faith and dream, treasuring her belief in his regeneration and innocence!

He thought of the closing chapter in his life at Aniston, when in that hour of his despair he had prayed by his study desk. The words he had then said aloud recurred to him: "If I am delivered, it must be by some way of Thine Own that I can not conceive, for I can not help myself." He was powerless to help himself still. He had given over his life into the keeping of a Power in which his better manhood had trusted. If it exacted the final tribute for those ribald years of Satan Sanderson, the price would be paid!

A step came in the corridor—a voice spoke his name. The summons had come. As he laid the blue book back

on the cot, its closing words—the dying utterance of the martyred Becket—flashed through his mind, the personal cry of his own soul:

"Into Thy hands, O Lord—into Thy hands!"

Before the opening door the hum of voices in the court-room sank to stillness itself. The jury had taken their places; their looks were sober and downcast. The judge was in his seat, his hand combing his beard. Harry faced him calmly. The door of a side room was partly open and a girl's white face looked in, but he did not see.

"Gentlemen of the jury, have you arrived at a verdict?"

"We have."

There was a confusion in the hall—abrupt voices and the sound of feet. The crowd stirred and the judge frowningly lifted his gavel.

"What say you, guilty or not guilty?"

The foreman did not answer. He was leaning forward, looking over the heads of the crowd. The judge stood up. People turned, and the room was suddenly a-rustle with surprised movement. The crowd at the back of the room parted, and up the center aisle, toward the judge's desk, staggered a figure—a man whose face,

ghastly and convulsed, was partly swathed in bandages. At the door of the judge's room a girl stood transfixed and staring.

The crowd gasped. They saw the familiar profile, a replica of the prisoner's—the mark that slanted across the brow—the eyes preternaturally bright and fevered.

A pale-faced, breathless man in clerical dress pushed forward through the press, as the figure stopped ... thrust out his hands blindly.

"Not—guilty, your Honor!" he said.

A cry came from the prisoner at the bar. He leaped toward him as he fell and caught him in his arms.

CHAPTER XLIX THE CRIMSON DISK

The group in the judge's room was hushed in awestruck silence. The door was shut, but through the panels, from the court-room, came the murmur of many wondering voices. By the sofa on which lay the man who had made expiation stood the bishop and Harry Sanderson. Jessica knelt beside it, and the judge and those who stood with him in the background knew that the curtain was falling upon a strange and tangled drama of life and death.

After the one long, sobbing cry of realization, throughout the excitement and confusion, Jessica had been strangely calm. She read the swift certainty in Doctor Brent's face, and she felt a painful thankfulness. The last appeal would not be to man's justice, but to God's mercy! The memories of the old blind days and the knowledge that this man—not the one to whom she had given her love at Smoky Mountain, at whom she dared not look—had then been her lover, rolled about her in a stinging mist. But as she knelt by the sofa the hand that chafed the nerveless one was firm, and she wiped the cold lips deftly and tenderly.

Hugh's eyes were filming. That harrowing struggle of soul, that convulsive effort of the injured body, had demanded its price. The direful agony and its weakness had seized him—his stiffening fingers were slipping from the ledge of life, and he knew it.

He heard the bishop's earnest voice speaking from the void: "*Greater love hath no man than this, that a man lay down his life for his friends!*" The words roused his fading senses, called them back to the outpost of feeling.

"Not because I—loved," he said. "It—was because—I—was afraid!"

False as his habit of life had been, in that moment only the bare truth remained. With a last effort the dying man thrust his hand into his pocket, drew out a small, battered, red disk, and laid it in the other's hand. He smiled.

"Satan—" he whispered, as Harry bent over him, and the flicker of light fell in his eyes, "do you—think it will—count—when I cash in?"

But Harry's answer Hugh did not hear. He had passed out of the sound of mortal speech for ever.

CHAPTER L WHEN DREAMS COME TRUE

There came a day when the brown ravines of Smoky Mountain laughed in genial sunshine, when the tangled thickets, and the foliaged reaches, painted with the cardinal and bishop's-purple of late autumn, flushed and stirred to the touch of their golden lover, and the silver water gushing through the flumes sang to a quicker melody. There was no wind; everywhere, save for the breathing life of the forest, was dreamy beauty and waiting peace.

In the soft stillness Harry stood on the doorstep of the hillside cabin—for the last time. Below him in the gulch the light glanced and sparkled from the running flume, and beyond glimmered the long street of the town where the dead past of Satan Sanderson had been buried for ever and the old remorseful pain of conscience had found its surcease. In that last lack-luster year before the rector of the old St. James had been snuffed out in the wild motor-ride, he had come to doubt the ultimate Prescience and Purpose. How small and futile now

seemed those doubts in face of the new conception he had apprehended, in the tacit acceptance of a watchful Will and Plan not his own.

Here had been the theater of his pain and his temptation. Sitting on that very spot, with the wise stars overhead, he had drawn from Old Despair's violin the strain that had brought him Jessica, her hand in his, her head upon his breast! In the far distance, a tender haze softening their outline, stood the violet silhouette of the enduring ranges, and far beyond them lay Aniston, where waited his newer life, his newer, better work—and the hope that was the April of his dreams.

Since that tragic day in the court-room he had seen Jessica once only—in the hour when the bishop's solemn "dust to dust" had been spoken above the man who had been her husband. One thought had comforted him—the town of Smoky Mountain had never known, need never know, the secret of her wifehood. And Aniston was far away. About the coming of Hugh injured and dying to his rescue, would be thrown a glamour of knight-errantry that would bespeak charity of judgment. When Jessica went back to the white house in the aspens she would meet only tenderness and sympathy. And that was well.

He shut the door of his cabin and, whistling to his

dog, climbed the steep path, where the wrinkled creeper flung its new splash of scarlet, and along the trail to the Knob, under the needled song of the redwoods. There in the dappled shade stood Jessica's rock-statue, and now it looked upon two mounds. The Prodigal had returned at last, father and son rested side by side, and that, too, was well.

He went slowly through the brown hollows to the winding mountain road, crossed it, and entered the denser forest. He wanted to see once more the dear spot where he and Jessica had met—that deep, sweet day before the rude awakening. He walked on in a reverie; his thoughts were very far away.

He stopped suddenly—there before him was the little knoll where she had stood waiting, on the threshold of his Palace of Enchantment, that one roseate morning. And she was there to-day—not standing with parted lips and eager eyes under the twittering trees, but lying face down on the moss, her red bronze hair shaming the gold of the fallen leaves.

There was a gesture in the outstretched arms that caught at his heart. He stepped forward, and at the sound she looked up startled.

He saw the creeping color that mounted to her brow,

the proud yet passionate hunger of her eyes. He dropped on his knees and took her hands and kissed them:

"My dear love that is!" he whispered. "My dearer wife that is to be!"